Queen of Incense

The Journey of Bilqis of Saba

Signe Kopps

Rainhorse Press
Portland, Oregon

Queen of Incense

First Edition

For permissions and information, please contact
Signe Kopps at signekopps.com/contact

Editing by Joanna Rose
Cover art by Amalia Chitulescu
Author photo by William Howell

Published by Rainhorse Press
631 NE Broadway # 542.
Portland, OR 97232

Paperback ISBN 978-0-9991290-2-9
Ebook ISBN 978-0-9991290-3-6

To Douglas Rees, my Ilumqah,
thank you for lighting this long journey,
and to my father,
Richard L Kopps (1923- 2017),
fly high, daddy.

Also by Signe Kopps

Anthra's Moon

~ Prologue ~

The moon of Ilumqah rose full and bright on the night I left Myrb. Hailed by the temple priests, our radiant god of the night had returned to shine his face upon us and light our journey across the dark sands.

I pulled open the back curtain of my riding tent and breathed in cold air that tasted of dust kicked up by camels. Myrb was behind me now, a black shape on the moonlit sands. Watch fires burning on the top of the city walls were gold sparks floating in the night. Two fires marked the iron-strapped gates at the front and back entrances to the city. A third fire burned above the massive side gate leading into the camel pens. The three gates were locked for the night. Travelers and caravans arriving after dark would make camp outside the gates until they were pushed open again at sunrise.

The gates were closed to me, too. Three years ago I had been welcomed into the city as the wife of Darmalay, chieftain of Myrb. I was young and in love with my new husband. I had willingly left my village and my family to live with Darmalay in his great house in Myrb, the biggest city in all of southern Arabia, in the land known as Saba.

I was leaving my home again. My husband had asked me to travel across the vast desert to take a great treasure to King Solomon in Jerusalem. He had softened his request by assuring me I would travel in comfort during the long journey. At the end, he said, the great Solomon would welcome me as a queen.

I shook my head. The real reason for sending me away, I thought, was to let Darmalay enjoy his new wife in peace.

I looked back at my city on the sand. I wondered if I would ever see it again.

~ One ~

Every woman smiled at me. Wives of visiting chieftains, Darmalay's old aunts and their companions, slaves sweeping the halls; every woman greeted me with a smile. "A son, Bilqis," they said. "You will bear a son."

Men congratulated Darmalay with a kiss on his cheek. My husband accepted their good wishes with pleasure. We had been married a year before I became pregnant, and I knew he worried that I would not give him a child.

I met Darmalay for the first time when my father and I brought a small caravan of wine and honey to the marketplace in Myrb. Darmalay drank a cup of our wine and praised it. He asked my father why his daughter accompanied him on the caravan. Father patted my shoulder. "My son is a baby in his mother's arms. Bilqis is my right hand until my boy is old enough to ride with me."

Darmalay appeared again a month later when my father and I brought another caravan to Myrb. He talked to my father while I unpacked jars of honey for a merchant to sell in his stall. Darmalay offered to help me. My father stood to one side while I handed clay jars to Darmalay. Our fingers touched. We looked at each other until my father cleared his throat. Darmalay handed the last of the jars to the merchant, bowed his head to me and left. My father asked another merchant about Darmalay. I heard the man say he was the chieftain of the city. I thought about Darmalay during the day and fell asleep at night thinking about meeting him again. He was tall and handsome, more comely than any man or boy in my village. He laughed easily and his smile was kind.

I saw Darmalay again a few days later. He walked down the row of stalls, looking straight at me. He greeted my father with a kiss on both cheeks. He said he had looked for us every day at the marketplace. Then he said to my father that he wanted me for his wife. My father hesitated. I knew what worried him. As Darmalay's wife, I would be well taken care of, but he was not of our village. If I married Darmalay, I would leave our family and live far from home.

My father finally said I would decide. Darmalay took my hand. "Heart of my heart," he said. "Come to me, I will shelter you always."

My heart felt as if it were leaping in my chest. Barely able to speak, I said yes, I would be honored to be his wife.

Darmalay gave my father a pregnant camel as payment for taking me from my family. My father hugged me and whispered that my mother would visit me when I gave birth to my first child. He mounted his camel and rode from the marketplace, holding the leads to my small camel, the camel that carried the goods we sold in the marketplace, and the new camel from Darmalay.

Darmalay's mother, Hazza, glazed at me when my husband brought me into the house. My son is chieftain of Myrb, she said. He should have wed the daughter of a chieftain, not the daughter of a poor trader. Darmalay kissed her cheek and said, please me, mother, by receiving my wife. Hazza stepped back from her son. She waved her hand as though flicking a fly, said welcome, my daughter, and left the room without kissing me to show her approval.

The next morning she entered my room after my husband had left my bed. "Camel girl," she said, clapping her hands as if I were her slave. "Get up. I will show you my house. "

I dressed quickly and followed Hazza who moved quickly down a hall, up a stairway to the next floor, and up another few steps into a round room at the top of the house. The walls of the room were pierced with small windows; the floor was covered with brightly colored wool cushions. This was the men's room, she said. Here Darmalay would sit with his guests at sunset, enjoying the evening breeze that blew through the windows.

Hazza hurried back down the steps to the floor below, the men's floor. Three curtained doorways flanked the stairs. Darmalay's room was to the right. I heard water splashing behind the curtain and started to open it to see if my husband was inside. Hazza grabbed my hand, saying her son wished to be alone while he bathed.

She pushed aside the curtain to one of the opposite rooms. "For my son's guests," she said. A black and red patterned rug covered the floor. Cushions for seating and a rolled sleeping mat were placed against a wall under a small window glowing with sunlight.

We walked back down the stairs to the long hall on the second floor where the women slept. Eight curtains lined the hall. "My room," Hazza said and pointed to the curtained doorway by the stairs. Darmalay's old widowed aunts lived with their companions in two connecting rooms in the middle of the hall.

My room was at the far end. A small room for my new companion, Tylos, was next to mine. Tylos was an older woman who Darmalay had chosen to accompany me whenever I left the house. I had not met her yet. Her brother was to bring her to me soon. On the other side of the hall, three smaller rooms were reserved for the wives of Darmalay's guests.

Hazza gestured at me to follow and led the way down the stairs to the first floor. We walked through a curtain into the kitchen, a long room with one side opened to a sunny courtyard. A shelf along one side of the kitchen was heaped with clay pots and stone pestles and mortars to grind grain. Two cooks stood at a table in the middle of the room, mixing bread dough and cutting up meat. The women looked up as we entered the room. They nodded at Hazza and glanced at me, but did not stop talking or working.

In the courtyard, a young girl fed a lump of dried camel dung into the fire at the bottom of a tall clay oven. Another girl brought over a paddle with a round of dough on it. She slid the dough from the paddle onto an iron plate set inside the oven.

Hazza pointed to a wooden door on one side of the courtyard. Beyond it was a garden, she said, where the women of the house and the wives of Darmalay's guests could sit at night and enjoy the cool evening air. I asked Hazza if she sat in the garden. She shook her head. "I do not have time to be lazy." I followed her back into the kitchen. She stopped behind the bread cook who was adding a pinch of salt to a bowl of flour. "Not so much," Hazza said. "My son does not like his bread too salty."

We left the kitchen and entered a large room. This was the feast room, said Hazza, where Darmalay ate his meals and entertained his guests. "We will hold your wedding feast here," she said.

Two long rugs, seating for Darmalay's guests, ran down the center of the room. A large window faced north, away from the hot glare of the sun. Overhead, a large flower was carved in the middle of the high stone ceiling. Hazza smiled when I tilted my head back to look at the flower, the smile of a woman proud of her house.

A doorway on the far side of the room led to the council room. Hazza said her son and his counselors met in room every morning to hear grievances from men and women of Myrb.

Hazza stopped talking and looked at me. I wondered what she wanted me to say. I said the house was beautiful and it was so large that I feared I would get lost. She nodded, satisfied with my words. "Stay here," she said. "My son will come soon for his morning meal."

After she left, I looked around the big room. I spoke the truth to Hazza; it would take time for me to become comfortable in the great house. In my village, I lived in a house with three rooms. My father and brother slept in one room, my mother, sisters, and I slept in another. We ate together in a small room in the middle.

I looked at the flower in the high ceiling. My father would have returned to our village by now. My mother would cry when she heard I had married a man not of our village and rush to visit her friends to tell them that her youngest daughter was the wife of the chieftain of Myrb. I wished I could hear her say I had brought honor to our family, but she lived far from Myrb. I would not see her again until she visited me after I gave birth to my first child.

I accompanied Hazza every morning on her walk through the house. She would walk through my curtain after Darmalay left, clapping her hands, saying lazy girl, get up. I followed her with my eyes heavy with sleep, into every room. I thought they looked clean enough, but Hazza found fault everywhere. She pointed at spider webs hidden in the darkest part of the ceiling and said the sleeping mats were not rolled tightly enough. She bustled around the house all morning, ending up in the kitchen to oversee the preparation of our midday meal. I was allowed to leave her then and join my husband in the feast room. Though we had parted that morning, we spent the few minutes before Hazza joined us, kissing and whispering that we missed each other.

A month or so after I came to the great house, Darmalay told Hazza that he wanted me to sit on the morning council with him. Hazza was shocked at his words and could not speak for a moment. When she recovered her breath, she scolded her son. "Your wife must concern herself with women's work. Bilqis should not meddle in the business of men."

Darmalay replied that he talked about council matters with me at night and thought my advice was sound. He said it was his wish. His mother could say nothing more. Darmalay was her son and the head of the house; she could not refuse his request. I turned my head so Hazza would not see my smile. I was honored that my husband wanted me to join his council. Judging disputes our people brought to the council seemed more interesting to me than watching the cooks to make sure they didn't oversalt the bread.

Hazza was not alone in opposing my presence on the council. Darmalay's counselors, four men he trusted and called brother, were surprised the first time Darmalay entered the big room with me at his side. They objected to Darmalay's announcement that I was to join them. A woman does not judge men, they said.

Darmalay insisted I stay. "Bilqis is young, but she speaks wisely. Many women come before us seeking justice, a woman on the council will help them feel easier in recounting their troubles."

The men stroked their beards, looked at each other, and reluctantly nodded their acceptance. Darmalay trusted his counselors and listened to their advice, but he was chieftain of Myrb; in the end, his word was law.

Darmalay placed me on his right at the council table. Damri Samar, my husband's closest friend, sat at Darmalay's left. Samar did not try to conceal his dislike that a woman sat on the council. He interrupted me the first time I asked a question of a man bringing a claim before the council and talked over my words. I didn't know how to respond to Samar's insulting behavior. I looked to my husband for guidance, but Darmalay did not tell Samar to stop. I sat quietly at the table until the council was over.

That night in my room, I asked my husband to order Samar to show respect to me. Darmalay refused my plea. "Do not let his words anger you," he said. "You must learn to be calm and listen for the truth when our people come before you. Do not be persuaded by a woman's tears or frightened by a man's strong words."

I remembered Darmalay's advice the next morning. Toward the end of the meeting, I spoke for a woman who brought claim against a builder for a wall in her home that had collapsed. Samar turned to the counselor seated next to him and said something to make the man laugh. I took a deep breath and continued to speak. My efforts gained the approval of the other men on the council. They gestured at Samar and the counselor to be quiet. "Let Bilqis speak," they said. "We would hear her opinion."

I stayed on the council for a year before I finally became pregnant. Samar had learned to hold his tongue when I spoke, but he did not hide his smile on the day I left the council. I was heavy with my unborn child and could not sit easily for hours listening to the complaints our people dragged into the room.

"Your wife will be more comfortable with her companion," he said as I walked out of the council room. "That is where she belongs."

My husband did not silence him. I was a woman nearing childbirth; my thoughts should be with my baby.

~ Two ~

I soon regretted leaving the council. Hazza had died the winter after I became pregnant. During one of our morning meals she complained that her head ached and the sunlight hurt her eyes. I offered my arm when she stood to leave us. She shook off my hand, saying she was not a feeble old woman. She rested in her darkened room that day, allowing one of Darmalay's old aunts to attend her. I talked to the woman when she opened the curtain to accept a jar of cool water from a slave. The old aunt said Hazza's headache was worse and her neck was so stiff that she could not turn her head.

During our evening meal, Darmalay said he could not remember his mother being sick. He laughed, saying she would be up again in the morning to inspect the house and make sure the slaves had swept every room thoroughly while she was sick.

The wailing of slaves woke us the next morning. Darmalay rushed from my room to his mother's. He returned before I had finished dressing and stood in the doorway with his eyes closed, holding on to the curtain like a man who has drunk too much wine.

I cried out, "Oh, no, oh, no," and wiped my dry eyes on my sleeve.

Hazza was buried in the hillside graves of Darmalay's family. Darmalay laid her, shrouded in bleached linen, on a stone ledge. At her feet, he placed a silver and ivory box that held her wedding jewelry for Hazza to wear in the next world. I stood quietly while Darmalay wept and slaves rolled a boulder in front of her grave. Afterwards, we returned to the house to feast her memory. "A good cook," said the chieftains who had eaten at Hazza's table. I said, "Hazza of Myrb was a great teacher," and nothing more.

After her burial, I thought I should take over her daily inspection of the house. I started with the kitchen. The cooks nodded at me while they continued to prepare our food. I watched them for a moment, found I had nothing to say and left. As I walked through the tidied guest rooms, I realized that the house was running smoothly even after Hazza's death. The rooms were cleaned and the halls swept. The housekeeper, a woman no taller than Hazza, approached me once and asked if I wanted to make any changes. I rarely saw her again after I told her I was pleased with her work.

The head cook continued to ask my approval. She sent a slave at midday to ask what meat I wished for the evening meal and if I desired it boiled or roasted, but that was all I said about our food. I could have asked for other dishes, but we were well fed and I was not like Hazza, I didn't care about giving orders.

Without Hazza to scold me, I spent the cool of the morning alone in the women's garden outside the kitchen. Two gardeners, an old man and his young son, tended big pots of red, orange, purple, and yellow flowers. They worked without speaking as they plucked dead flowers off the stems and wiped heavy dew from the fleshy green leaves. I sat on a bench by a water fountain in the middle of the courtyard, enjoying the sweet scent of the flowers. The fountain was made of white stone and carved in the shape of a tall flower with its petals open to the sun. Water bubbled from the top of the flower and slid down the stem like glass ropes and dripped from the tips of the stone petals into a water basin at the foot of the fountain. The splash of water in the basin sounded like voices heard from far away.

I had little else to do. Darmalay had forbidden my daily walk to the market with Tylos, fearing people in the busy marketplace would jostle me and harm the child in my belly. Nor could I attend the monthly ceremony to celebrate the return of Ilumqah. The temple was more crowded than the market, Darmalay said; I would be safer at home.

Tylos thought I would welcome the company of other women and suggested I visit Darmalay's old aunts. We sat on cushions in one of their rooms, drinking cooled wine while the old women asked about my baby. They laughed and called him a young lion when I said his kicking kept me awake at night. They felt my belly with their wrinkled hands, said I wasn't big enough and urged me to eat more meat and drink cups of goat milk, sheep milk, and watered wine. After the third visit, I returned to my room, wearied from the attention. I told Tylos I didn't want another woman touching me or talking about the baby until he was born.

Tylos then brought in her handloom to teach me to weave. I quickly grew bored with passing the shuttle of camel wool back and forth through the threads to make a bit of woven cloth. Tylos next brought in her spindle. I would learn to spin wool, she said. Holding a spindle while it spun around, twisting a handful of camel hair into thread was more tedious than weaving. I told her I was content to sit by the window in my room and watch merchants and their slaves on the road below taking goods to the caravans waiting in the camel pens.

Myrb was the gathering place for caravans carrying goods from villages around the city. Merchants were eager to add their wares to the caravans; wine, honey, salt, and gold jewelry sold well in the northern markets. Most precious of all was frankincense, the dried sap from trees that grew only in the south. Frankincense was prized in temples all over Arabia. When burned, it produced a sweet-smelling smoke that carried prayers from the mouths of the priests upward to the ears of the gods.

Merchants visiting the great house spoke of the markets they would stop at during their journey to the north. The greatest market of all, they said, was in Jerusalem. They described a street of stalls for spices, one for silks, another for precious stones. Upon their return, merchants brought Darmalay gifts from Jerusalem: jars of pear wine, baskets of black pepper seeds, and once for me, a fan of green peacock feathers.

I stayed in my room during the day, but at night, Darmalay wanted me by his side when he feasted his many guests. He wished everyone to see that he soon would be a father. I obeyed my husband and sat next to him on a cushion in the feast room, my belly heavy in my lap as I received good wishes from Darmalay's visitors and their wives.

Woman guests asked to sit with me during the feast. They reclined on cushions with cups of wine in their hands and talked about childbirth, their eyes shining with remembered pain as they told me about the birth of their children.

"I bled so much with my last child, I almost died." I leaned away from the woman's breath of cheese and onions. Her words made me want to run out of the room and the sound of her voice made my baby kick and kick inside my belly.

"The birth wife said I was near death." She lay back against the cushions and drank a cupful of wine. "But I bore a son and we both lived."

"I tore from belly to ass," said a cook. She sliced the air in front of me with her kitchen knife. "Belly to ass. I shit and pissed out of the same hole." She dropped a handful of dried meat into a pot of steaming water. "You do not forget the pain, Bilqis, but you won't care when you hold your baby."

I feared the day of my baby's birth. I was tired of the heavy weight I carried but the stories I heard frightened me. Tylos tried to offer words of comfort. "The baby will slip from you as if he was made of butter."

I didn't believe her. Other women had talked only of the terrible pain I would suffer.

My pains started late one night and by morning light I could not sit quietly. I walked around my room, leaning against Tylos, moaning from the stabbing pain. It felt as though a hand inside my belly was pinching me hard.

"This hurts," I groaned. "I don't want to have a baby."

"Too late, my girl," said Tylos. "Be brave, this is your battle."

She looked at the doorway as two women parted the curtain and hurried into the room. "Ah, here are the birth wives."

The younger birth wife was as tall as Darmalay. The older woman was shorter, with white hair braided down her back. Both wore bags of herbs tied around their waists. The tall wife carried a clay basin of water, the older woman held a stack of white birthing cloths.

Both women paused inside the room and smiled at me, as I held on to Tylos with my mouth open and my hair hanging over my face. "You look ready, Bilqis," said the older woman. "Let us feel the baby."

They helped me kneel on my sleeping mat and put their hands between my legs, pressing against my belly. "Your baby is coming," they said. "It's time for you to bear down."

Pain rolled through me as I grunted and pushed. The room grew hotter; sweat dripped from my face, soaking the mat. The birth wives said push, Bilqis, push. I screamed as I bore down again and again until I thought my back would break.

Between pushes I rested on my side, utterly relieved that the pain had lessened. The older wife wiped my face with cool water. Tylos knelt and fanned my face with her hand, asking me if I wanted a sip of barley water or a cup of sweet wine.

I moaned as my belly tightened again. Tylos flapped her hand faster, hitting my cheek. I yelled at her to stop. The tall wife asked Tylos to fetch another basin of water from the kitchen. Tylos said she would send a slave; she didn't want to leave me. "Bilqis will be pleased if you bring water," said the wife.

The room was quieter after Tylos left; the only sounds were my groans and the soothing voices of the wives saying the birth was close. Tylos returned as the wives were telling me to push one last time. I held my breath and bore down hard until my eyes felt as though they were going to burst from my head. I didn't stop pushing until the baby slid out of me in a hot gush of blood and water.

I collapsed on the mat. Tylos patted my leg, saying you have a boy, a boy. I looked at the end of the mat, at my newborn son in the hands of the birth wives. His head and shoulders were streaked with my blood. His lips were pale blue, not rosy like the lips of other newborns, and something dark and ugly was wrapped around his neck. The birth wives did not speak as they moved their hands together, slipping their fingers under the birth cord to loosen it, pressing the tips of their fingers into his stomach. He breathed once, then cried like an angry little bird. My eyes filled with tears at the sound.

"Praise to Ilumqah," said the tall wife. She placed her big hand on the baby's head, covering his dark wet hair. "Your son comes early, but he lives."

The older woman lightly squeezed my belly to force out the afterbirth, while the tall wife cut the cord and washed the blood off the baby. He cried when she trickled water through his hair and quieted when she wrapped a length of cloth around him, binding his arms and legs close to his body.

"Keep him wrapped like this." She placed him in my arms and knelt with the other wife to wipe blood off the mat.

"Is he healthy?" The sleeping baby was heavy as a small sack of flour. I felt my hand become gentle as I caressed his soft, warm head.

The older woman sat back on her heels. "I've seen many babies born with the cord wrapped around their necks. Some live. Your son is alive and he cried. Watch his breath. Push his stomach as we did if his chest does not rise."

The women bundled the bloody cloths, bowed to me and left the room. Tylos laid fresh linen on my mat and brought over the basin of water she had left to warm in the sun. She wiped inside my legs, gently touching my sore flesh as I lay back, holding my sleeping boy. I smelled his neck and hair, breathing in the scent of lavender from his bath water. By now, Darmalay knew of his birth and would be running through the house toward my room, telling everyone he met, family, guests, and slaves that he had a son.

Tylos handed a clean tunic to me and took the baby from my arms. I smoothed the garment over my strangely flat, aching belly.

"He should suck." Tylos kissed the air in front of his face to wake him. She handed him back to me. "We shouldn't let him sleep too long."

Darmalay was smiling when he entered the room. "I have a son," he said. He spoke softly when he saw the baby sleeping in my arms.

I smiled at my husband. "He's small because he came early. He was eager to meet his father."

Tylos left the room, leaving us alone. Darmalay and I sat together, watching our baby's small chest rise and fall. I touched my son's soft cheek to make him turn to my breast. He did not wake, and he breathed so quietly that we did not see the moment when the sun moved away from the windows and his breath stopped in the darkened room.

We buried our son on the hillside, next to Darmalay's father in the family graves. My heart felt like it was breaking into sharp pieces as I watched my husband place the tiny, linen wrapped body into the black opening. As Darmalay rolled a small boulder over the hole to close the grave, I fell to my knees, screaming and scratching my face and arms until they were bloody, because my baby was cold and alone in the dark.

Tylos helped me to my room. For three days I would not leave my sleeping mat. I turned my back against sunlight and opened my eyes at night to look at the blackness between the stars.

"Get up." On the fourth day, Tylos stood before me in the morning sun and yanked the blanket off my body. "You are the wife of Darmalay of Myrb." She grabbed my hands and pulled me to sitting. "Get up and live in this house again."

My bones felt like they were made of wax. All I wanted to do was lie down on my mat and sleep, but she sat behind me, unraveled my braids and pulled a comb through my hair.

"Ouch, Tylos, you're hurting me."

"So you can speak." Tylos smelled of the cinnamon oil she rubbed on her skin to kill pests. She shook out a length of gold thread and wove it through my hair. "You have many years to live, my girl. Invite your husband back to your room tonight and you'll soon hold another baby in your arms."

Her voice sounded like a dog barking, but Tylos was saying what every woman would say, "You will bear other children."

I dressed in a clean tunic and joined Darmalay for the morning meal. He was pleased to see me and gave me choice bits of meat from his plate. The smell of roasted goat meat made me feel sick. I placed a shred of meat in my mouth and chewed it slowly until the meal was over.

Darmalay and I stood together after our meal. I couldn't think of anything to say. We didn't speak of our dead child; he was buried and gone from our lives. Darmalay finally said he was late and walked toward the door to the council room.

The next day Darmalay sent Tylos to bring me to the feast room. "Your husband wishes to give you a gift," she said. "Smile and show him you are grateful for his attention."

Inside the room waited Ma'zur of Myrb, a dealer in gold and precious stones. He was a familiar sight in the streets of our city, his arms filled with leather bundles as he hurried to the houses of rich women. Ma'zur stood near a small table that shimmered in sunlight. Darmalay took my hand and led me to the table and the wealth of gold that was mine to choose.

Gold necklaces hung with chunks of amber, turquoise, and dark blue lapis were laid next to braided gold bracelets woven with amethyst and jade beads. At the end of the table stood a headdress of red carnelian flowers twined around a circlet of beaten gold.

Darmalay rocked back on his heels and pointed to the table, "Choose whatever you wish, my Bilqis. Or take all, it is yours."

Ma'zur rubbed his hands and smiled at my husband's words. Darmalay touched a bracelet of silver stars. "This is beautiful, or this." He held up a gold necklace strung with crimson beads. "Choose this, my love, it will help you forget."

The necklace hung between us; the beads lost their fire, gold turned to iron. Darmalay stepped forward so Ma'zur would not see my tears and signaled Tylos to lead me away. She pulled me from the room. Her hands were cold as claws of a bird.

Samar sat at my husband's right hand a month later when I returned to the council. The men in the room stopped talking as I stepped through the curtain and looked at me as though I were an unexpected guest. My husband gained his smile, took my arm and walked me from the room.

"I will join you later, Bilqis," he said. We stopped in the hall outside the curtain. "You are newly grieved. The men on the council are uneasy with your tears."

Oh, that made me angry, I walked fast down the halls and no one dared smile at me or ask what meat to serve at our evening meal.

Darmalay came to my room at midday after my anger had softened. We ate together, and lay down on my sleeping mat. I kissed his mouth, brushing my tongue across his lips until he groaned and rolled on top of me. Tears slid from my eyes when he cried out.

He rolled off and we lay side by side, breathing hard, until he pulled me into his arms. I rubbed my face against his chest so he would not see my tears and breathed his smell of sweat and incense and the mint leaves we chewed after our meal.

"Will you hear of the morning council?" he asked. I nodded and he held me closer. "Two men came before me, each claiming ownership of the stream that separates their lands."

"What advice did you give them?"

"Samar spoke for the council. He said each man would bring two witnesses to prove his claim to the streambed. One man yelled he would bring ten witnesses. The other said,

'Bring your witnesses; they are thieves like you. I'll bring my father. He'll say he bought the streambed from your father many years ago.' They left the room with their hands on their daggers. I fear they'll fight for ownership of the water."

I laid my hand on his chest. "Samar's advice did not cool their anger," I said. "Call the men back and tell them to divide the streambed. Each man will get half of the water that flows down the river."

I felt his laughter under my hand. "You are as wise as King Solomon, my love," he said.

"But not wise enough to join your council again?"

"Bilqis." He covered my hand with his. "You'll have another child soon. Care for the house and our children and leave the quarrels of our people to me."

I followed the wisdom of the birth wives and drank bitter herbs in the light of Ilumqah's moon, hoping our god of the night would bless my womb with his fertile light. But my belly did not swell again and I heard the word "barren," whispered by the wives of chieftains when they left my room.

That word frightened me. I was not yet with child. How long would my husband wait for me to give him a son?

~ Three ~

Amida appeared four months ago, on the night we celebrated the reappearance of Ilumqah. The feast room was noisy with men and their wives, sitting on cushions laid around low tables. As was custom in Myrb, on the night of the full moon Darmalay invited chieftains from nearby villages and their guests, to feast with him

I dressed carefully in a tunic of white silk embroidered along the hem with gold and silver beads that sparkled when I moved. Darmalay smiled at me when I entered the room and helped me to the cushion to his right. My husband did not comment on my beautiful dress, but left me to walk around the room, welcoming every man with a kiss on the cheek and smiling at their wives, who looked down in respect. I sat quietly, waiting for him to return. Damri Samar approached and took his seat at Darmalay's left. We nodded at each other across Darmalay's empty cushion but did not speak.

Amida and her father were the last to enter the room. I saw an old man walking in front of a plump girl younger than me, who wore a girdle of white shells, the sign of a maiden. Her dark hair fell unbound to her waist. She smiled when Darmalay greeted her, the smile of a child being offered a sweet. But she was not a child. Her hips were full and pulled at the sides of her tunic. "Birthing hips," my mother would have called them. This girl would grunt out fat babies.

They sat together, the old man between them. The girl picked a handful of dates from the platter in front of her. Darmalay grabbed a wineskin from a slave and filled the old man's cup again and again, until the old man fell back against the cushions and closed his eyes. Amida licked date sugar from her fingers, gazing at my husband. He smiled and reached for her, rolling her sleeping father on his side in his desire to get closer to the girl.

Hot anger ran through my body, seizing my breath as I watched my husband lean over the girl. I wanted to scream at Darmalay to stay away from her. I wanted to throw a jar of wine across the room at his head.

He whispered into her ear, pushing her hair from her cheek. I turned my back to him and talked to a woman sitting next to me. When the food was served, I said I had to speak to the cook and slipped out of the room. My head ached, my eyes burned with tears I did not shed until I pushed through the curtains of my room.

Tylos had gone to bed. I sat on the cold window ledge, looking across the sleeping city as I waited for my husband to come to me. But the watch fires burned down to smoke and the night sky paled to blue, and still he did not come.

The next morning while Tylos swept my room, she said the girl, Amida, and her father were Darmalay's guests in the house. I asked her if Darmalay had asked about me, if he feared I was unwell after I left the feast early the night before. My heart felt sore when she shook her head. After Tylos left, I paced the room, worried because my husband had not asked me to join him in welcoming the girl and her father.

I heard voices outside my window. The road below was swarming with men hurrying toward the camel pens. Bare-chested slaves leaned into leather straps, pulling wagons filled with baskets of crushed salt and golden incense, bundles of fine-spun wool, and clay jars of olive oil and sweet Myrb wine. Merchants in black and white robes walked behind the wagons, slapping their hands against the wooden wheels, yelling at their slaves to pull faster toward the caravans loading for the markets in the north. Women returning from the city wells walked along the edge of the road, out of the way of the wagons. They balanced jars of water on their shoulders with one hand and gestured to their friends with the other. The women talked as if they had not met for many days, while I stood above them, alone in my window.

I watched as the road emptied under the midday heat, until Tylos opened the curtain and walked into my room. She stood before me with her hands clasped at her waist, biting her bottom lip and looking at the corners she had swept that morning. There was nothing to fill her hands, yet she looked at the floor for dust, at the ceiling for spider webs and I wondered why she did not meet my eyes.

Finally, she looked at me. "Darmalay has taken a new wife, Bilqis." Her amber eyes were gold in the sunlight. She bit her lip again, waiting for me to speak.

The air felt pushed from my body. "When?" I asked.

"After the midday meal. Darmalay told me to bring a jar of wine and three silver cups. He poured wine for the old man and called him father and poured a cup of wine for the girl and called her wife. He told me to leave the room. He knew I would tell you he had taken a new wife."

"He cannot tell me this himself?" My voice sounded old and broken. I could not breathe enough air.

"He knew it would grieve you," said Tylos. "She'll give him a child, Bilqis. Your husband has waited a long time and he wants a son."

"I will give him a son."

"My girl, your belly has not quickened for many months." Tylos placed her hand on my arm. "The slaves say the new wife talks of gold bracelets and ivory combs for her hair. She is not clever like you. Your husband will come back for your counsel."

"Counsel!" I pulled away from her hand. My heart felt weighted with rocks. "Old men give him counsel. I will give him a son and I will not be pushed aside by that little cow."

"Darmalay is a young man, Bilqis, and he may take another wife after Amida. He may take many wives."

"Do not say her name, it stinks up my room." I glared at my companion, hating her words. "My father did not take another wife. He waited a long time for my mother to give him a son."

Tylos dropped her hand. "My husband took a second wife when I did not give him a child in the first year. His new wife said there was not room in his bed for two women and sent me back to my brother's house."

She looked past me at the sky outside my window. "My brother did not want me, but he had to take me in. All I brought was an armful of old robes and a bracelet of green beads my mother gave to me before she died. My husband's new wife, that slut of a dog, kept my good robes and my box of jewelry. She said they belonged to the house. My husband did not protect me. He hid behind her robes and said, 'I do not listen to the quarrels of women. Take only what you brought.'"

Tylos rubbed her bare wrist. "She did not find my bracelet. I kept it under my mat at night to help me dream of my mother. My brother's wife asked for the bracelet as a present for her youngest daughter. I slid it off my hand so fast I scratched my wrist. I hoped my brother's wife would love me if I gave her the bracelet. She took it and that was the last time she spoke kindly to me. I cleaned her house and cared for her children until they were grown, but she would not love me no matter how hard I worked."

"And then you came to me," I said.

"Yes, blessed was the day my brother brought me to this house to be companion for you." She smiled. "I found you in the garden. You were sitting behind a pot of flowers, hiding from Darmalay's mother."

"Hazza was angry because Darmalay told her he wanted me to sit in council with him. She said I was a stupid village girl who did not speak well enough to talk to men."

"Hazza was unhappy because you took her place with Darmalay," said Tylos. "He listened to her before he married and then he listened to you."

My throat tightened. "And now he has a new wife to take my place."

"Oh, child," said Tylos, patting my arm. We turned to look out of the window, our shoulders soft against each other. I leaned against her with tears in my eyes, blurring the road below my window. My husband had taken a new wife. He didn't want me in his bed or on his council. I felt old and pushed aside.

A small herd of goats walked down the road, their hooves clicking on the packed dirt. Behind the goats walked a boy, whistling and flicking a long stick over his animals to keep them from turning into an open courtyard.

Tylos spoke again when the boy's whistle had faded and the road was quiet. "You're fortunate, Bilqis. Darmalay trusts you. He will continue to seek your advice."

I didn't want to hear that I was fortunate. I wanted my husband to say I was his sweet love, the jewel of his heart. But

Darmalay had married again, and I had to learn to live in the same house with his second wife.

The next morning I decided to show my husband that I would be kind to his new wife and sent Tylos to Amida's room, Hazza's old room to invite her to visit me. Amida settled into my cushions, stretched her arms and yawned. "This feels good," she said. "Oh, I have not rested since Darmalay took me to wife."

She picked up a piece of bread from a platter of dates and fresh figs and chewed it while her eyes moved around my room, looking at the gold-worked hangings covering my walls, the carved ivory boxes that held my wedding jewelry, and two painted wooden chests, one for the linen tunics I wore every day and the other containing the embroidered robes and silk tunics I wore to feasts.

"Your room is hot in the morning." She dropped the chewed bread on the platter and pushed up from the rug. Like a baby camel stuck in mud, I thought. "Darmalay waits for me," she said. "I must go to my husband."

Tylos sighed when I kicked the platter across the floor after Amida left. "Do not let her anger you, Bilqis," she said. "Amida knows Darmalay trusts your counsel above all women and he will not put you aside for her."

Trust: another bitter word.

Darmalay came to my room the day after Amida's visit. Tylos dressed me in a tunic of blue-glazed silk and braided gold and turquoise beads in my hair. She held up a bronze hand mirror after she was finished. I glanced at it and looked away. My skin looked dry, the color of river clay, my mouth turned down like an old woman's.

I heard Darmalay whistling as he walked down the hall to my room. Tylos put away the mirror and left the room. A moment later, Darmalay pushed aside the curtain. He stood tall in the doorway, smiling as he held a basket out to me. "Amida sends a gift to you, Bilqis, she wishes to please the first wife."

"Your new wife is generous." Amida's basket was tightly woven and filled with dates. I pointed toward the cushions, inviting my husband to sit with me.

Oh, he was happy with his new wife. He yawned and could not stop smiling and laughed at everything I said. I did not say anything clever; I asked if he was well and if he needed anything and thought of Hazza running to the tall water jar to dip a cup for her son that was cooler than the water I poured for him.

"Ah, Bilqis," he said. "I have missed talking with you."

My lips trembled as I poured a cup of wine. I wanted to beg him to turn Amida out of the house and give me time, another year, to become pregnant again.

He took the wine, selected a date from Amida's basket and held the date to me. "Beloved wife," he said. "I wish to talk with you. There is something I desire from you."

I chewed the date, wondering what he would ask. Did he want me to give up my larger room for his new wife?

He continued, "I am gathering a treasure of gold and incense to send to King Solomon in Jerusalem. Damri Samar will ride with the caravan and present the gold to Solomon in my name. He will ask the king to make a treaty with us that will protect our caravans from bandits when they approach his lands."

He set his cup on the rug and looked at me. "I wish you to travel to Jerusalem with Damri Samar."

"You wish me to leave our house?" I spit the date pit into my hand. "My husband, I welcomed your new wife. This house has room enough for both of us."

He poured wine into my cup and handed it to me. "I do not send you from the house, Bilqis. I ask you to take my greetings to King Solomon. I would go to Jerusalem to meet with the king, but I cannot leave; I'm needed here. Every day our city grows more crowded with strangers bringing their goods to add to the caravans until I have to push back the walls to make room."

I knew of his troubles. Darmalay and the council had talked of opening a wall to the south of the city for additional camel pens and land for new houses.

"Why do you ask me to meet King Solomon?" I said. "Why not send another counselor to travel with Samar?"

Darmalay hesitated. "I must offer more than the gold and incense that any rich merchant would give. I would have my gifts presented to the king by a beautiful queen from Arabia."

I almost smiled when he called me beautiful and then remembered my husband wanted to send me away. "Queen, when did I become a queen?" I said.

"I am the chieftain of Myrb. Chieftains of other big cities are called kings and their wives are queens. Samar says King Solomon will not look at Bilqis, wife of the chieftain of Myrb, but he will give welcome to Queen Bilqis of Saba."

"So I am to entice another man?" I stared at my husband, not sure what he was asking of me.

"Beloved." Darmalay held his hand across the rug to me. "Listen to me. Samar will talk to Solomon and arrange the treaty. I send you because you are clever as well as beautiful, and I have heard that Solomon wishes to talk with anyone, man or woman, whose words make him think."

"Samar is clever, let him talk with King Solomon."

"Samar is skillful in making a treaty, but he is impatient with the idle talk the king is said to enjoy." I pulled my hand away, irritated that he called my talk idle. "You will enjoy the journey, Bilqis. You traveled with your father when you were a girl and you told me you loved riding in the desert with him."

"That was years ago," I said.

Darmalay held his hand up to stop me from interrupting him. "This journey will be long, but you will be well guarded and your tent will have every comfort. Take Tylos and all the slaves you wish to accompany you to Jerusalem."

Darmalay picked up his wine, watching me over the edge of his cup. I looked down and smoothed the blue silk in my lap. I knew my husband wanted me to leave our home so he could enjoy his new wife and I knew what would happen if I stayed. I would live in the shadows, pitied and ignored as the childless first wife, or I would become like Hazza and loudly demand Darmalay's attention.

My hand slowed as I thought about his offer. If I joined the caravan, I would travel in honor, chosen by my husband, chieftain of the great city of Myrb, to meet the famous King Solomon. The silk warmed under my hand and my heart beat faster as I thought of riding at the head of an enormous caravan carrying a golden treasure toward glittering Jerusalem. At the end of the journey, I would be welcomed as a queen by a powerful king.

Stay home and be pitied or travel to Jerusalem as a queen. My decision seemed easy.

"I will go to Jerusalem, my husband. I will take your greetings to King Solomon."

Darmalay put his cup down and smiled, his teeth white against his dark beard. He gazed at my eyes and my mouth, as though he was remembering me before I left. I tightened my lips. I wanted to cry because my husband had not looked at me with pleasure for a long time.

~ Four ~

I left Myrb on a night the priests had declared most favorable, when Ilumqah rose in his glory to pour his cool light upon us. The full moon would measure our time in the desert, said the head priest. Two more times during our journey would he rise. On the second rising, our caravan would be close to Jerusalem and the end of our travels.

The city gates were locked after our leavetaking. Inside the city, people who had gathered to call good journey to friends on the caravan had returned to feasting the appearance of Ilumqah or else hurried homeward to their warm beds.

Darmalay had come alone to the pens to wish me farewell. "Amida wanted to come," he said, "but she is tired from the child she carries."

"I welcome her good wishes," I said to please my husband. I didn't want his new wife pushing between us, complaining she was cold or the smell of the camels made her sick or the torchlight hurt her eyes.

"You will be safe on this journey, my Bilqis." Darmalay wrapped his outer robe around me and pulled me close. "Samar vowed his life for yours. He will protect you."

I sank into my husband's warmth and said nothing. Damri Samar was not friendly to me, but he was loyal to my husband and I believed he would protect me until we reached Jerusalem.

I covered my mouth with the edge of my headcloth against the dust as camel men around us pulled their beasts to standing. Torchlight flared over the riding camels being led toward the open gates. Tall riding tents perched high on their backs jerked back and forth with every step. Under the tents, thick wool blankets padded the backs of the camels against the weight of the tent. The edges of the blankets were fringed with long strands of knotted wool. Silver bells sewn on the end of the fringe swung in and out, adding their noise to the voices of men and women calling goodbye, goodbye, and the skinny caravan dogs that barked and chased each other around the long-legged animals.

"Here is your tent," said Darmalay. A young boy stopped before us and pulled my camel to her knees. The animal was a big brown female. I held Darmalay's hand, put my foot on the animal's knee and stepped up and through the front curtain of my riding tent. The camel rose to her feet, throwing me back against the cushions. She stood quietly while the tent settled on her back.

The tent was small inside, a wide basket lined with silk cushions. The tall frame was draped with panels of blue-dyed wool, the cloth dark and heavy enough to give me shade during the heat of the day. Curtains of coarse-woven linen hung along the sides of the tent, dimming the torchlight. A folded sheepskin and a small red bag were laid on a cushion at my feet, next to a leather bag of food and a goat bladder filled with water.

I stretched my legs. The cushioned basket was comfortable, though the soft cushions would flatten during our long journey to Jerusalem. We would stop at village markets along the way. I would buy new cushions if I needed them.

"Bilqis, Bilqis." Darmalay's face was shining in the torchlight as I looked out of my tent. He looked excited as a boy riding into his first battle. "I envy your journey. I wish I were meeting the great King Solomon."

I laughed too, for the first time in many months. "I will greet him in your name, my husband."

The camel boy pulled my animal forward. I leaned out of my tent and waved at my tall husband as I was carried out of the pens and through the caravan gates.

The air outside the city walls felt colder than the torch-lit air in the pens. Moonlit sand stretched far into the desert, ending in a black wall beyond Ilumqah's gaze. My excitement faded as I looked at the empty blackness before me. I had not been outside the city walls and in the open desert since I married Darmalay over three years ago.

The boy pulled my beast into a long line of men and animals walking across the sand, away from Myrb. We entered the middle of the caravan, joining a group of camels biting at other camels when they walked too close.

Darmalay had drawn the caravan in the sand before I left. "You will ride here." He pointed his stick at the middle of the long line. "This is the safest place. Pack animals with my gifts to King Solomon walk behind you." He drew a big circle around the herd of camels that carried bags of gold, incense, and precious stones to King Solomon. "Camels bearing food and water and the ground tents walk along the outside. The star guides ride at the front." He touched the head of the line with his stick. "They will lead the caravan to Jerusalem."

My camel moved, startling me from my thoughts. The back curtain to the riding tent in front of me was pulled open and my companion, Tylos, looked out. Silver hair showed around the edge of her black headcloth. "Ah, Bilqis, there you are." Her eyebrows were as dark as her head covering. "I'm cold." She rubbed her arms. "My bones are cold."

"Wrap up in your sheepskin and close your curtains," I said. "You'll soon warm."

"You sound cheerful. Your tent must be more comfortable than mine."

"My cushions are no softer than yours. Where is Damri Samar? Darmalay said he is to travel close to me."

"I saw him ride toward the front of the caravan." Tylos scratched her arms "Fleas! Our first night on caravan and I have fleas in my tent."

"Oh, you always find something to complain about. Close your curtain and try to sleep."

"I will." She yawned as she closed her curtain. "I'm going to sleep, there is nothing to see."

Around me, camels walked with their heads up, smelling the night air. Moonlight shone white on their long necks. Along the outside of the caravan rode the guards, talking with each other in voices so low I could not hear their words. A man rode beside me: Farium, leader of the guards that Darmalay had hired to protect me and the gold and precious stones we carried to King Solomon of Jerusalem. Farium looked back and forth, from the open desert on one side of the caravan to the shadowed folds in the mountains on the other side. Lines across his forehead were cut deeper in moonlight.

A camel man walking behind me patted his beast, his hand dark against her neck. "Beautiful one, step softly," he sang. Camel bells rang in the cold air, as clear as a knife tapped against a silver cup.

I looked back over the heads of my camels to the riding tents of the merchants and the women they brought to share their journey. Men and women were shaking out blankets and sheepskins and closing their curtains against the night. A woman snapped her curtains closed when the man riding next to her stretched out his hand to her, leaning so far over the side of his camel that I feared he would fall out of his tent.

I closed the back curtain to my tent and settled into the cushions. I pulled the sheepskin up to my neck. Darmalay would be with Amida by now. He would hold her the way he had held me when I was pregnant, lying behind me with one hand on my belly, his laughter quick breaths against my neck when he felt our child move. "You carry a strong boy who loves his mother," he laughed. "Feel how he tries to kick my hand from you."

Would Darmalay miss me while I was gone? I pushed the sheepskin from my shoulders and looked at shadows gathered at the top of my tent. He would miss talking with me about the complaints our people brought into the council room: quarrels over water rights, lost goats, and rock boundaries that moved in the night, but he had a new wife in his bed, a new wife to listen to his words.

My tent swayed as each step of my camel carried me farther away from Myrb. I pulled the sheepskin over my shoulders, closed my eyes, and listened to the low voices of the guards and the camel bells ringing in the night.

~ Five ~

My father used to say the smell of fresh bread would make a sick man dance and a dead man sing. He was right this morning, the aroma of baking bread pulled me out of sleep before I opened my eyes. I opened my red traveling bag and took out a scented wooden comb Tylos had packed. I combed the knots from my hair, wrapped a robe around my shoulders and followed the warm scent through the tent curtain.

The desert spread before me, golden in sunlight. Smoke from cookfires blew past my camp, carrying the sharp smell of burning camel dung. The sand was cool under my bare feet. The warmth of the rising sun against my face felt like a blessing.

The camel boy, Farium's son, Khe, walked toward my herd, chewing a piece of bread. A female slave named Timora sat before my cookfire, mixing dough in a wooden bowl with quick sweeps of her hand. Tylos had chosen Timora to attend us on the journey. I had not noticed her in the great house; she was another female slave carrying platters of food at the feasts, but Tylos liked her because she worked hard and did not smile at the sons of visiting chieftains. "She will not bring trouble to your tent, Bilqis," she said. "Timora is a good cook, we'll be well fed."

Tylos was not happy that I took one slave only to attend me on the journey. "You travel as a queen," she said. "You must have many attendants."

"More slaves are more mouths to feed," I replied. "The camel boys will lead our camels and put up our tent. Timora will fetch water and cook our meals and keep our tent clean. You and I will manage what little else needs to be done."

Tylos wanted more slaves to assure that every moment we were on the caravan would be comfortable. She did not want to leave the great house or Myrb. She said the journey to Jerusalem would be hard on her old bones, but she could not spend the five months I was gone in sweeping my empty room. And if she were idle, Darmalay might give her to Amida as a servant or send her back to her brother's house until I returned.

I entered my riding tent after our morning meal and rode with the caravan until the late afternoon, when we stopped for the night. I kept my curtain open in the morning, watching the desert slide past. At midday, Tylos and I rode side by side, talking as we ate our meal of dates and cheese. At night, Khe helped Timora raise our sleeping tent and the supply tent where Timora slept. He fetched water and gathered camel dung for the cookfire. Khe was about twelve years, almost a man. I watched him out on the sand with his father, searching the ground for animal tracks. Farium was an experienced guide and was training his son to become a caravan guide.

As he had for the past three days of our journey, Damri Samar had raised his long black and red striped tent close to the black stone that marked the boundary between his camp and mine. Every merchant had brought boundary stones to separate his camp from his neighbor's. The sand around the many tents was dotted with black stones.

On the other side of Samar's camp stood a black tent with white stripes woven along the side. Behind the black tent I could see a woman's round tent, white with one black stripe.

The favored spot next to Damri Samar had remained empty since we left Myrb. I wondered who had been bold enough when we stopped last night to claim close friendship with the leader of the caravan, and raise his tent next to Samar's.

A man stepped through the curtain of the black tent, his fat belly leading the way to his cookfire. Ma'zur, the jeweler from Myrb, who had unrolled his bundles of jewelry for me after my baby died. Ma'zur's trade in jewelry had made him prosperous. His tent was larger than Samar's and rugs for many guests were laid around his cookfire.

Ma'zur shouted to Samar as the counselor stepped from his tent. Samar held up his hand in greeting. Samar looked taller this morning as he walked toward Ma'zur's camp. In the great house, he walked with his head bent forward, his hands in fists at his side, hurrying through the house toward the council room as if afraid another man would take his seat next to Darmalay. As he had taken mine when I left the council.

Samar had not yet joined my cookfire for a guest meal. Tylos scolded me on the first morning after we left Myrb. "Damri Samar is leader of this caravan, Bilqis. Invite him to your fire."

"He did not want me in the council room," I said. "I will not share my fire with him until I wish it."

I waited until we stopped for the night and sent Tylos to Samar's tent to invite him to join us for our evening meal. He refused my invitation, saying he would not intrude upon us so late at night. Tylos returned to his tent the next morning to ask him eat with us when we stopped for our midday meal. He refused again. He was busy with matters of the caravan, he said.

This was the Samar of the council; careful to show respect when I sat at my husband's right hand, but quick to ignore me after I left the council.

Tylos walked around the side of the tent. "Ah, Bilqis, I called you before sunrise but you would not wake."

I yawned and stretched, breathing in the warm, smoky air, "Well, I'm awake now and I'm hungry."

"Where are your sandals? " said Tylos. "You look like a goat girl with your bare feet."

"I like feeling cold sand in the morning and there is no one to see me."

Tylos grumbled about poisonous snakes and scorpions hiding in the sand while we walked to the cookfire. We sat on rugs Timora had laid out. Bowls of butter and honey were placed in the sand between our two rugs. Timora pulled a round of cooked bread from the hot iron plate, tore it in half, leaned over and handed a piece to me and a piece to Tylos. The bread was soft and warm in my hand. I folded it around a lump of butter and swirled the bread through honey.

Oh, the first meal was the best food of the day; the sheep butter was salty and rich, the dark honey slowly melted in my mouth until I could taste the flowers that scented it. Smoke from cookfires drifted through the camps. Caravan dogs gnawed bones tossed by the cooks. Beyond my tent, Khe and Farium walked through my herd of camels, tightening straps around the bundles of gifts for King Solomon, while the beasts chewed their fodder.

Tylos rubbed her shoulders. "I am not sleeping well. The sand is hard."

I smiled and handed her another piece of bread; Tylos's snores filled the tent as soon as I blew out the candle.

We heard laughter from a women's tent on the other side of our camp. "We are too quiet," said Tylos. "We have been on caravan for three days. It is time for you to feast the women of Myrb." She pointed to Timora. "She hears slaves at the well say their mistresses call you proud because you do not invite them to your fire or let them ride with you during the day." Timora nodded but did not look up from patting another handful of dough on the cookplate.

"I don't want to share my riding tent," I said. "It's too small for two women to ride together without crowding each other. And they speak only of their children and their houses. I do not want to talk about the home I left."

"You do not have to ride with them, Bilqis, but you should offer hospitality and invite them to your fire."

"I will, I will," I said.

"There is someone else who wishes to talk with you," said Tylos. "Damri Samar asked to visit our cookfire when we stop at midday."

"What does he want? Is he no longer welcome in the other camps?"

"Receive him as a friend, Bilqis, let your battle be over."

"It will never be over. He took my place next to Darmalay after I left the council and he will do the same when we reach Jerusalem. He'll push me aside to get to the king. He wants his name alone on the treaty with King Solomon."

Tylos looked at me in surprise. "Damri Samar doesn't act alone. Your husband sent you to stand with Samar and greet the king in Darmalay's name."

"King Solomon will look for a queen from Arabia. He won't see me, covered with dust and smelling of camels."

"You will not greet him covered with dust," Tylos said. "Timora packed enough sweet oil to bathe every woman in Jerusalem. You will be dressed in silk and jewels. King Solomon will meet Queen Bilqis, wife of Darmalay of Saba."

"Jewels alone won't make me a queen."

Tylos glanced at me as she wiped her fingers in the sand. "What troubles you, my girl? You're clever and King Solomon is said to enjoy the conversation of women. Speak your mind and he will not leave your side."

I hesitated. I had talked to many men who came before me when I sat on the council, but I didn't know how to speak to a king who was famous for his wisdom. Would King Solomon give me audience? Or would I be sent to the women's rooms, rejected if he did not find me beautiful or clever enough.

Tylos waited for my reply. "I've heard that King Solomon likes puzzles," I said. "I'll think of hard questions to ask him to gain his attention."

"You would challenge the king?"

"He would be insulted if my questions were easy. A king known for his wisdom would appreciate difficult questions." I didn't know what those questions were yet, but I had many long days to think of them while we traveled through the desert.

Samar walked toward my fire at midday, followed by a slave carrying a jar of wine. "Accept my gift, Bilqis," said the counselor. "I bring wine from Myrb to remind us of the home we left."

"Be welcome at my fire, Damri Samar. You honor me with your visit." The greeting did not come easily from me, but in truth, I was eager to talk to Samar about the journey before us.

We sat in the shade of a thorn bush, drinking cooled wine and eating barley soup and bread spiced with cinnamon. Tylos sat under the awning in front of our tent, drinking her soup.

Samar patted his stomach as he reached for a date. "Ah, I have not eaten so well since we left Myrb."

"Are the slaves of the merchants bad cooks?" I said.

"No, but their masters tell them to please me and they pour butter over every dish until it drips into the sand. I like your girl's cooking; her food awakens my appetite but does not make me regret eating."

He leaned back against his cushions. "It feels good to rest," he said. His beard was longer and soft looking, not the shaved edge he wore in council.

"You are busy with the caravan?" I asked.

"Yes, but there is not much yet to worry me, though Farium says there is one problem that will grow stronger the farther we travel from our homes."

"What problem does he see? Theft? Disputes over camels?"

"No, the trouble is with wives on the caravan who leave their tents at night and seek the beds of other men."

The words leapt from my mouth. "And what of the men who lure these women, or men who enter a woman's tent uninvited, are they not at fault?"

Samar looked at me as if I were speaking in a foreign tongue. "Men will always look at women who are not virtuous."

"Virtue is honor and men desire honor, so they share the blame when women come to them from their husband's beds."

Samar rolled a date pit between his fingers. "Your tongue is as quick as it was in the council room, Bilqis."

"Yet you said a woman does not belong on the council."

"A quick tongue does not always bring a wise answer."

"Are you saying my advice was not wise?" Darmalay, I thought, had been pleased with my counsel.

"Your advice was clever but you did not respect the men who came before you. They had daughters your age. You talked to them as if they were foolish boys."

"I did not intend to humiliate the men who came before us." I remembered Darmalay warning me to slow down when I spoke. He said the men needed time to hear the wisdom in my words. I tried to be more deliberate with my speech, but the room was filled with people bringing their complaints to the council. I could not waste time; I wanted to hear each man's problem, advise him, and look to the next man approaching the table.

"Perhaps you did not intend to dishonor them," said Samar, "but they remembered your manner toward them more than your words."

He dropped the date pit into the sand. The air between us seemed filled with unsaid words. I waited for him to speak as he watched black kites hang in the air over the camps, searching for bits of bones left by the dogs.

"There is another problem," he said. "You are too much alone with your companion. The wives of the merchants wait for you to invite them to your fire. You are the wife of our chieftain, Bilqis; the women will look to you for guidance during the journey. You must ask them to feast with you."

I was growing tired of his advice. I said, "What other problems does Farium see?"

Samar frowned, not fooled by my desire to change our talk. "Look behind you," he said. Dark clouds hung low above the mountains behind us. Rain was falling in the highlands and rushing down the rocky mountains toward the desert sand.

The dry riverbeds, wadis, soon would fill with water. The fast moving water, a sayl, would sweep away camels, trees, rocks, anything it could catch in its race through the desert. The banks of the wadis were not safe; the water could turn, devouring huts, goats, and people who lived close to the wadi. Sayls would flow for a day or many days, and no one dared cross the wadis until the water slowed and sank beneath the sand.

Samar brushed breadcrumbs from his tunic. "We have rested long enough. There is a large wadi in front of us that we must cross. We'll ride all night to reach it before the water comes."

He stood and looked down at me. "Remember my words, Bilqis, you'll need the friendship of the other women on this journey. Invite them to your fire or they will feel slighted and close their tents to you."

He strode from my fire. I watched him leave, feeling as though I was back in the great house under Samar's command instead of Darmalay's.

~ Six ~

Cold morning wind blew through our riding tents, fluttering curtains throughout the caravan. We waited on the bank of the wadi, watching a line of guards ride up the center of the dry riverbed. One guard stopped at the bend in the river, the other guards rode up the wadi. Khe explained they were making a line with each man in sight of the next to pass the signal that the water was coming.

We were uneasy waiting on the side of the riverbed. Camel men patted the necks of their animals, while caravan dogs wove through the long legs of their beasts. Merchants and their wives complained to their neighbors, impatient to cross while the sand was dry.

Samar rode up next to me. "Hold tight to your basket," he said. "We're running the camels as soon as we see the signal."

The guard at the bend pointed up the wadi with a quick gesture, as if he were throwing a dagger. From one moment to the next, my animal was pulled from standing to plunging down the sandy bank. Around me, camels bellowed as they were yanked forward, men shouted, women shrieked, and dogs barked as the great mass of camels poured down the side of the wadi. Khe and the other handlers ran across the riverbed, pulling tent and pack animals at the ends of their long leads. Guards rode alongside, yelling at the men to run faster, faster.

I grabbed the side of my basket and was jerked back and forth so hard I feared I would be thrown from my tent. Bushes growing in the center of the riverbed flashed by in a smear of green. I looked at the far side of the wadi, "I'm almost there," I said out loud to keep from thinking about the wall of water rushing down the riverbed. "I'll reach it before the water comes."

A roaring sound filled my ears. It was louder than a herd of mating camels. The wind blew harder. My hair unraveled and flew around my head like a rush of birds. A cushion bounced out of my tent. I reached for it, leaning over the edge of my riding basket and my camel stumbled on a rock. I lost my balance and fell out of my tent. I grabbed the side of the basket as I fell and hung on with one hand. My whole body banged against the side of my camel as she ran. Every pounding footstep made my hand slip more and more. I was terrified I would plunge to the ground and be crushed under the hooves of hundreds of camels running behind me.

I screamed at Khe to help me, but he could not hear me above the thundering noise of the camels racing across the hard sand. My face smacked into the riding blanket. I bit at the stiff wool like a dog snatching at a bone. I would hang on with my teeth if I had to.

At that moment, a hand grabbed me and hauled me up, away from my camel and onto the back of another beast. I panted as I clung to the arm around me, unable to catch my breath in the dusty air. The arm tightened, holding me close as the camel under us ran faster across the sand. As we neared the far side of the wadi, I heard Samar's voice in my ear, asking if I was hurt. I shook my head.

Khe ran my camel up the bank of the wadi. Samar's camel followed mine. Khe looked up to see me on Samar's camel. At his command, Khe pulled the camel to kneeling. He held up his hand as Samar loosened his grip on me. I slid from his arm, grabbing Khe's hand as I reached the ground.

"I fell from my tent," I said to the boy. "Damri Samar caught me as I fell."

We backed away from the edge of the wadi as the huge herd of camels climbed out of the riverbed. Tents on the back of riding camels rocked from side to side. On the pack camels, flapping ropes showed where bundles of goods had fallen off during the wild run across the wadi. Men and women stepped from their beasts onto the sand and stood in the brightening sunlight, watching the last of the camels run across the riverbed. Two pack camels behind the rest had stopped in the middle of the wadi, fighting to free themselves from their leads that had become entangled as they ran across the wadi.

"Look!" A woman sitting in her riding tent pointed to the mouth of the river as muddy yellow water churned around rocks at the bend.

"Hold this," said Khe. He threw the leads to me and pushed through people standing in front of us. "Move, move," he yelled. I saw men and women step aside and then his small body was running across the wadi.

Samar followed, riding past Khe until he reached the fighting camels. He shoved his big camel between them, grabbed up the tangled leads, pulled out his dagger and cut them apart. Samar tossed the lines down to Khe. The boy caught one, pulled down the camel and jumped onto her back. He kicked her into a run through the rushing water. The other camel followed close behind.

The last camel in the wadi, a small female burdened with heavy bags, dragged a young boy hanging on her leads, through the yellow water. An uprooted tree swirled past, hitting the front legs of the camel and knocking her over. She screamed, a harsh cry as she fell onto the slave, smashing him under the water.

"Oh, no!" yelled an old man. He held his arms out to his beast, as she and the boy struggling to free himself were swept downstream. "My silks, my silks," he screamed. He fell to his knees on the edge of the bank and tore at his grey beard. His wife ran to her husband, knelt beside him and put her hands over her face.

Men looked solemn at the sight of the camel and the boy being whirled away in the fast moving water. They turned to their own beasts. Their women followed, brushing sand from their tunics and straightening their headcloths.

Samar rode through the crowd. He stopped in the middle and waved his dagger until it flashed in the light of the rising sun. "Hear me, hear me," he shouted. He pointed to the flowing water. "We camp here today. Fill your bags. We'll move again before sunrise."

Tylos and Timora pushed through the crowd toward me. One of Timora's braids had loosened; her dark hair blew over her shoulder in the morning breeze. Khe followed, smiling as he led Tylos's camel toward us, a boy enjoying the adventure of outrunning a sayl.

"Did we lose anything?" I asked.

No," Khe said. "Your treasure is safe." He pointed to an area of sand between two large rocks where Farium walked among my herd of pack camels, patting their necks as he tugged straps around the bags tied to their sides.

"My father told me to tie the packs twice last night. He has crossed many sayls; he knew the camels would run."

"Farium is wise," I said.

The boy walked in front of me toward the rocks. I staggered in the deep sand and he turned, holding out his thin brown arm. "Lean on me," he said.

Khe set another bucket of water next to the shallow bathing basin he had carried into my tent. "We have enough," Tylos said. "Come back later to empty the bath."

Three leather buckets stood beside the basin. Two were filled with cool water from the wadi; the third bucket was filled with water Timora had heated over the cookfire.

Tylos peeled waxed linen from a small stone jar and poured a stream of golden oil into the bucket of hot water until the air in the tent was rich with the scent of jasmine.

I untied the shoulder knots of my tunic and slid it from my body. I sat down in the basin while Tylos mixed cool water into the bucket of hot water. She poured a bowl of the warm, scented water over my head. She knelt beside me, rubbing the oiled water through my hair.

"Timora will wash our clothes," she said. "I saved clean tunics to wear today."

I washed dirt from my face and arms as Tylos walked toward bags piled at the back of the tent. She pulled out two garments, dropped them next to our cushions and walked back to the basin with two drying cloths. "You are plump again, Bilqis," she said, holding one of the cloths to me. "You no longer look hungry."

"Timora is a good cook."

"You did not eat enough in our house." Tylos did not say what we both knew; I had not enjoyed food since Amida joined our house. Now I lay all day in my riding tent, dreaming of the meals Timora would prepare after we made camp: roasted goat rubbed with garlic and handfuls of dried rosemary, bread with herbed butter, honeyed nuts, and figs stuffed with soft cheese. I would be well-fleshed when we reached Jerusalem.

I stepped out of the basin and dried my arms and legs while Tylos pulled off her tunic. Her body was thin and looked as strong as braided leather. Her breasts were small, the dark nipples pointed down. She combed her fingers through her hair until it covered her shoulders, a thin silver veil. She stepped into the bath, holding the sides of the basin and lowered her body into the water. "Ah," she said. "This feels good."

I knelt beside her and poured a bowl of warm water over her hair. The silver turned darker, old silver.

"Your hair is beautiful." I rubbed water down the slippery lengths of her hair.

"I am an old woman with old hair."

"How many years do you have, Tylos?"

"I have forty years," she said. "My mother died at thirty years."

"You'll live long to tell about this journey," I said. She wiped her face and arms while I picked up the clean tunics, laid one next to the basin, and pulled the other garment over my head. I walked to the rug and sat down with a sigh. My body was clean and soft with sweet oil. I felt at peace.

"I could sit here forever, Tylos. Tell Samar we will stay here until he returns from Jerusalem."

"Damri Samar would drag you to Jerusalem himself." Tylos hung the drying cloth over the side of the basin. "Without you, he is just another rich merchant seeking to meet King Solomon."

"He's not a merchant and the king would respect his bravery if he knew of his battles," I said.

"You sound as if Samar is a friend and not your enemy." Tylos sat next to me and pulled a wide-toothed comb through her wet hair, leaving tracks in the silver.

"Samar saved me today. He caught me when I fell from my camel as we were crossing the wadi." I squeezed the ends of my hair, wiping the oiled water on my face and neck as I remembered Samar's arm around me. "I would not make an enemy of my husband's friend."

"You are wise to think of him as your friend," Tylos said.

Light filled the opening as the curtain was pushed aside and Timora stepped into the tent. The curtain fell closed behind her. "Do you wish for more water?" she asked.

"No," I said. "We're finished and there is water enough for your bath."

"Timora will wash in the supply tent after we eat," said Tylos.

"It is wiser for her to bathe here," I said.

"No one will watch her inside her tent."

"The supply tent is small, Tylos, and I have seen men entering the tents of female slaves. She will bathe with us."

Tylos did not reply, but pushed off her cushions and walked to the back of the tent. She untied a bag on top of the pile and dug inside the bag with both hands.

The girl stood in front of the curtain, looking down at the rug. "Timora," I said. "You may bathe."

She untied her tunic, holding it up with one arm, and began to unravel her braids. She kept her eyes on the ground as she walked toward the basin.

"Be quick, girl, we're hungry," Tylos said and turned back to her bag.

Timora dropped her tunic and stepped into the bath. Her face and arms were dark; the skin under her tunic was smooth gold. Her full breasts were tipped with wide brown circles and her belly was small and rounded, the body of a girl who had not given birth. She wore a gold chain around her neck. Three tiny gold bees hung in the middle of the chain.

She squatted and I emptied a bowl of warm water over her head. Tylos threw down a drying cloth and a clean tunic next to the basin and walked back to the rug. While Timora bathed, I followed Tylos through the steamy, scented air. She lay down on her cushions with her back to me.

I knew she was angry that I allowed a slave to bathe with us. In the great house, Timora lived in a small room behind the kitchen with other female slaves, but we were far from home and I would not have her bathe alone in the supply tent that any man, merchant or guard, might enter.

Timora dried her arms and legs and stepped from the basin. She pulled the clean tunic over her head and knelt to gather the bath cloths and our clothing with a graceful movement that reminded me of a dancer at a feast. She stood and started to leave the tent.

"Stay, Timora." I patted the rug next to me. "Take your ease with us."

She glanced at Tylos and sat a little distance from me, combing her fingers through her hair. Her face was small, like a child's. Her eyes slanted up.

"When did you join Darmalay's house?" I said.

"I was six years when Hazza bought me."

"Why were you sold? Was your family captured?"

Timora looked down at her lap and began to fold one of the damp cloths. "No, my mother died when my brother was born. I had an older sister and my father could not keep another girl, so he took me to the market. He stood with me until I was sold. He did not want a cruel master to buy me."

"Hazza was not cruel to you?" I said.

Timora looked at me. "She was kind. She bought me because I did not cry when she squeezed my arms to feel if I was strong."

"That sounds like Hazza," I said. "She used to feel my arms, too, and tell me to work harder instead of watching the caravans."

I remembered Hazza's fingers pinching my arm as she pulled me from the courtyard garden and into the kitchen. During our meals, she spoke of me as if I were not in the room. "Your lazy wife must learn to cook the dishes you love, my son." She complained about me as she poured cooled wine into Darmalay's cup or picked out a choice piece of meat from the platter for him. She talked until she had to stop to suck in a breath as if it were the last air she would taste.

Darmalay had laughed. "As you had to learn when you came to this house, my mother."

I smiled at his words. Hazza had glared at me, her lips drawn tight as a sewn bag. Before she could speak, a slave walked through the open doorway, carrying a silver platter.

"Beloved mother," said Darmalay. "What have you prepared for me today?"

Hazza unfolded her lips to smile at Darmalay. "Lamb with pepper. Choose first, my son, your wife and I will wait until you have eaten all you wish. We are happy to take what you leave."

Tylos sat up when Timora said Hazza was kind. "Hazza yelled at her slaves," she said. "We heard her from our rooms."

"She was small and she thought no one would listen to her if she was quiet," Timora said. "But she did not beat me or the other slaves."

Tylos pointed to the necklace around the girl's neck. "Your necklace is pretty, was it a gift from a man?"

The bees were beautifully made with wings of pierced gold. "I have not been with a man." Timora touched one of the bees. "Hazza said we did not have to go with a man unless we wished it. She gave the necklace to me when I was ten years. She said I worked as hard as a bee."

Timora stood with our soiled clothing and bath cloths. "I will wash these and send Khe to empty the basin."

"You are welcome in my tent, Timora," I said.

The girl smiled, the first smile she had given me. It was a small white circle in her dark face. She pushed open the curtain and left the tent.

"Hazza was kinder to a slave than she was to me," I said.

"Timora was a child, Bilqis, you were a woman who took her son from her."

"Hazza never gave me a gift."

"She gave you her son."

"She gave him unwillingly."

"What mother willingly gives her son to another woman?" Tylos sat behind me on the rug. "Let me braid gold in your hair. You will look like the wife of a great chieftain."

Ilumqah was a belly of light in the dark sky when we finished eating our evening meal. "I wonder if Amida has moved into my room." I pushed my hands through warm sand near the fire. "I wonder if she sleeps with Darmalay in my bed."

"Does Amida think of you?" Tylos poked a stick into a lump of burning dung. Sparks flew up, lighting the amber in her eyes. "Rest easy, my girl, Darmalay will not allow her to take over your room. He will honor your rights as first wife."

"First wife, I hate those words." I pushed my hands deeper until I felt cold sand. Tylos had woven my hair into many braids that fell over my shoulders. Gold discs that she tied at the ends of the braids glittered in the firelight. "The first wife has nothing," I said. "She turns into an old woman sitting in the corner, watching her husband drool over his young new wives."

"Bilqis, Darmalay sent you to meet a great king. He trusts you more than his new wife, more than any other woman in Myrb or all of Saba."

I listened to her words and did not say what I was thinking. My husband had sent me to entice the king. I felt like a rare bird kept in a cage with its wings clipped, displayed for its beauty.

Samar stepped over my boundary stone and walked into the light of the cookfire. Gold discs slid over my shoulders as I sat up, brushing sand from my arms.

"You look like a great lady tonight, Bilqis." He held his hands over the fire. "King Solomon gave the title of great lady to his mother."

"I will not be called great lady." I was Darmalay's wife, not his mother.

"Will you be called queen?" he asked.

"When we reach Jerusalem. My husband said you wished me to have that honor."

"A queen from Arabia is a great gift."

"I think you wish to present me covered with gold dust when you say I am a gift."

Firelight gleamed on his teeth when he laughed. "You are a jewel, Bilqis, even when you walk barefoot."

Tylos raised her eyebrows at me in the silence. She dropped her stick, nodded to Samar and walked toward our tent.

"I owe you my life, Damri Samar," I said.

"I vowed to protect you. I would not let you come to harm."

"You were brave to cut the camels loose during the sayl."

"I was not brave, bravery is in battle."

I gritted my teeth. I wanted to praise him and be done with it. "Birth wives say women are brave in childbirth," I said. "They say bearing children is our battle."

Samar picked up Tylos's stick. Lines gathered in his face when he bent over to stir the fire.

"That is true," he said. "I watched my first wife give birth. My mother tried to pull me away but I would not leave. Our boy was too big; he killed his mother when he was born."

Samar threw the glowing stick into the darkness beyond the fire. "My mother and my aunts looked for another wife. I said yes to the first woman they brought before me. She bore three sons and died. Now I have many wives and many sons."

People in other camps walked from cookfires to their lighted tents, their long shadows slanting across the sand.

"We leave before sunrise." Samar pointed to the mountains in front of the caravan, crooked black shapes against the starry sky. "The guards want to travel through the mountain pass before the sun is high."

"Do you think of your first wife, Samar?"

"No," he said. "That was long ago. She is gone from my dreams."

~ Seven ~

Sand-colored cliffs swept up one side of the mountain path that was wide enough for several camels to walk side by side. The ridge above us was brushed with golden light from the rising sun; clumps of grass fluttered in the wind along the edge of the cliff. The far side of the path opened to a valley below.

"Hold." The guard riding beside me held up his hand.

"Why do we stop?" I asked.

"A camel dropped its packs," he said. "We wait until they are tied again." White hairs wagged at the end of his chin. One of his eyes was sunken and closed from an old wound. He pointed to the path before us. "There's a girl in the rocks."

I leaned out of my tent to see a girl of about ten years standing between two rocks, with her back to the valley. She held the ears of a young goat with one hand. Short braids hung in a row around her head.

She moved her eyes from the guard pointing at her, to me. Her family must be herding goats below the pass, I thought. I smiled and she waved at me, a little wave, keeping her fingers close to her chest.

My tent rocked as the camel began to move again. The girl picked up a handful of sand and threw it into the air above her head. The little goat blinked at sand falling into his eyes.

The old guard laughed, a wheezing sound, like air squeezed from a sheep's bladder. "She makes the sign for friend," he said. "Does she think we fear her?"

Laughter passed among the guards. I leaned over the edge of my tent and watched as she threw another handful of sand in the air.

"What has happened?" a man asked from the tent in front of me. "Are we being attacked?" cried a woman. The girl bit her lips as curtains opened in the passing tents, but she bent over again to fill her hands and stood under the falling sand, looking at me.

"Ask her what she wants," I said.

The guard clicked his tongue and his camel began to walk faster. "Old man," I said, "I am Bilqis, wife of Darmalay of Saba. Go back and ask her what she needs." I scratched a line of fleabites on my wrists. I was in no mood to be ignored.

The guard blinked his one eye fast, as though I had yelled harshly at him, turned his camel and rode back to the girl. She pointed to the valley and then at the rocks around her. The old man spoke and she shrugged her shoulders. He rode back to me, shaking his head.

"What did she say?" I asked.

"She's alone. Her father and mother were taken by the sayl yesterday. She ran from the water and slept in the rocks."

"She slept alone in the rocks? Where is her home?"

"She says her father's village is two days riding from here."

"Tell Farium I wish to speak with him. He'll send a guard to take her to her father's home."

"She doesn't remember the name of her village," said the old man. "It could be anywhere in the desert."

"We cannot leave her here." I said. "She'll die of hunger and cold."

"Ask Damri Samar what to do with the child." He gathered his leads and kicked his camel forward.

"Bring her to me." Samar had a caravan to watch over, he would not want the problem of a lost child. I would find a way to take her to her home.

The old man muttered under his breath as he turned and rode back to the girl. She backed away when he leaned down to speak to her. He sat up on his camel, pointed to the desert with one hand and at me with other, as if to say, "Choose."

She let go of her goat and held her arms up to the guard. Her animal jumped away through the rocks, his black ears flapping above his head. The girl reached for the upkicking heels of her goat, but the guard pulled her up and onto his camel and brought her to me.

She was a bundle of cold arms and legs falling into my tent. She smelled of dust and goat. I pulled the sheepskin over her legs. "Warm yourself, child." I handed the water bag to her. "I am Bilqis of Saba."

She drank from the bag; little sips at first and then filled her mouth until water dripped from her chin. "My name is Samsi," she whispered. "My father is Da'rum. My mother is Hadra." Tears spilled from her eyes and rolled down her dusty cheeks. "The sayl took them from me yesterday. I was on the other side of the wadi with my goat when the water came. My mother tried to cross the wadi to reach me." She squeezed the water bag as she spoke. "My father grabbed her and they fell under the water. I waited until dark for them to come up again. Then I ran up the hill because I was afraid the water would grab me during the night." Samsi stopped, panting from speaking fast.

I patted her arm. "You must be hungry, I have food for you." I picked up my bag and shook out a handful of dates.

Samsi picked up a date and chewed it, watching as I laid dried meat and cheese on the cushion between us. She ate like a hungry little dog, stuffing food into her mouth until her cheeks were round as a desert mouse caught inside a sack of grain.

I opened my red bag, pulled out my scented comb and waited until she finished chewing. She drank another mouthful of water and wiped her lips with her dirty hand. Her eyes were clear brown, the color of new honey. "My mother would be angry with me for eating so fast," she said.

"Your mother would be proud of you. You were brave to stop the caravan."

Samsi's eyes filled with tears again. "Are my father and mother dead?"

"You said you didn't see them come up from the water, so I think they must be dead."

Samsi nodded and wiped her eyes. "Turn around," I said. "Allow me to comb your hair." Sand pattered into my lap as I unraveled her braids and worked the comb through her tangled hair. She yawned, slumped against me and fell asleep. I held her in my arms, remembering when I was a girl and comforted my younger sister when she woke at night from a bad dream.

"Bilqis, Bilqis," Tylos's voice was loud outside my tent. I rolled the sleeping girl onto a cushion, covered her with the sheepskin and opened the curtain.

"The guards say you found a girl in the desert." Tylos held her curtain closed around her neck. Her face was the color of burnt wood against the rough linen, her hair was silver wire in the sun.

"Shh, Tylos, she's sleeping." I leaned out of my tent so I would not wake the girl. "Her father and mother drowned in the sayl yesterday. She slept alone in the mountain all night."

"Where is her village?" asked Tylos. "She should be with her people."

"She doesn't know where it is."

"What will Samar say when he hears you've picked up a stray child?"

"She is my concern, not Samar's. She will die if we don't take her with us."

"Leave her in the next village," said Tylos. "Her family will hear and come for her."

"That's three days ride from here. I will not leave her with strangers."

"She's with strangers now."

"She is safe with me," I said. "We will return her to her family when we travel back from Jerusalem."

"She's another mouth to feed, Bilqis."

"We'll talk of this later," I said and closed my curtain.

I called Samsi guest friend when we stopped at midday and placed her next to me at the cookfire. Tylos sat on the other side of me, looking at the desert while she ate, ignoring the girl. Timora handed Samsi a bowl of bread soaked in butter and honey, bowing to her as an honored guest.

We ate without speaking until Samar stepped over the boundary stone between our camps. "So, this is the child you picked up in the mountains." He stood over us. His voice was loud in our silence. "We don't have enough food for strays, Bilqis."

"Her name is Samsi and she is my guest." Samsi looked up at Samar and then down at the bowl in her hands.

Samar rubbed his beard, considering my words. "We reach the village of Adhah in three days. You will leave her there."

I stood and faced Samar. "I won't leave her with strangers. She will join my tent for the journey."

He waved his hand as if my words were not important. "Then keep her, feed her. She belongs to you." He walked away from my cookfire toward his camp.

I sat down and spoke to Tylos. "Samsi will sleep with us and I wish Timora to move from the supply tent to our tent." Timora looked up from cleaning her bowls. Her hands did not stop moving.

"There's not enough room," said Tylos.

I raised my voice to cover hers. "Samsi is my guest and I would protect Timora. She says men are bolder about entering the tents of female slaves at night. We'll sleep together."

Timora gathered the food bags and nodded at Samsi to join her. The two girls walked toward the pack camels. Timora pulled the bags away when Samsi tried to take them from her hands.

"Bilqis," Tylos said, "let the guards watch the supply tent. We'll be crowded with the girls sleeping in our tent."

"My guards are busy watching my goods and my camels. We'll keep a closed tent, Tylos. We will be safe."

A voice that sounded like Hazza's woke me. For a moment I thought I was in my house in Myrb, with Darmalay's mother shouting that I was idle and a bad wife to her son. The voice quieted by the time I opened the curtain and stepped outside. Timora knelt before the cookfire, mixing dough in her wooden bowl.

"Where is Samsi?" I asked.

Timora wiped her forehead with the back of her hand and pointed toward the supply tent where Tylos stood, glaring at Samsi. The girl stared down at the sand with her hands behind her back. "Raise your head, girl," said Tylos. "Tell me why you refuse to eat with us."

Samsi's hands fell to her sides, but she would not look up.

"Ungrateful girl," Tylos said as I approached. "We should have left you in the desert!"

"Tylos!" I placed my hand on her shoulder. "Every tent hears you this morning. What is your quarrel?"

"She will not eat with us." Tylos walked away from my hand, toward the cookfire. "The little stray refuses your hospitality."

"What is wrong, child?" I asked. Samsi shook her head until her braids swung around her chin. "Samsi, I ask you again, what is your quarrel? Why do you refuse to eat with us?"

Samsi took a deep breath. Her eyes were dark brown in the shadow of the tent. "I have been your guest friend for three days," she said. "My father said a guest who stays longer is a bad friend." She looked down again. "I do not wish to be a bad friend." Her voice was quiet. "My father would be angry if I do not work for you."

"You have worked with Timora every day since you joined us."

Samsi shook her head. "I haven't worked. Timora says I am your guest and she will not let me lead the camel and she pushes my hand away when I try to carry her food bags."

"Eat with us this morning," I said. "I will decide what you will do to help our tent."

She took my hand and placed it against her cheek. I held her small warm hand and we walked to the cookfire. Timora was setting a platter of fresh bread, butter, and honey near Tylos's rug.

I glanced at Samar's camp as we approached my fire. A male slave was sweeping sand from Samar's tent. His cookfire was cold. I wondered where Samar ate his morning bread.

"Tylos," I said. "Samsi is no longer my guest. She belongs to our tent now and she will help Timora."

"Let her gather dung," said Tylos as she reached for a piece of bread.

"She's too young to walk behind the caravan by herself," I said.

"Khe gathers dung, let her walk with him."

"That is wise." I turned to Samsi. "Khe is the son of my chief guard. He will protect you."

"I know Khe," she said. "He gave me a feather." She opened her small waistbag and pulled out a black and white striped feather. She stroked the end until it curled around her finger. "He says there are many feathers in the desert."

"That's from a hoopoe bird." I touched the feather. "I saw hoopoes when I traveled on caravan with my father. I thought they were pretty."

"We called them stink birds in my village," said Tylos. "They nest in shit."

"They nest in trees," I said.

Samsi sniffed the feather. "This doesn't stink. I think it's pretty." She looked shyly at me. "I'll find more hoopoe feathers for you."

"Bilqis." Tylos tapped my arm to gain my attention. "We have traveled for many days and the wives of the Myrb merchants still wait for welcome to your fire."

"How many are on the caravan?"

"Fifteen merchants from Myrb travel with the caravan. Six of them brought their wives."

"Go this morning and invite the women from Myrb to feast with me tonight," I said. "Today we stop at the village of Adhah. Timora will go to the market and buy fresh fruit and meat."

"They'll be happy to feast with you." Tylos rubbed her belly. "Every woman will invite me to eat at her fire this morning. I will be stuffed with bread when I return."

"Samsi," I said, when Tylos had gone. "Help Timora pack up camp. You'll go with her to the market when we stop at midday."

Samsi ran around the cookfire to Timora, dropping to her knees in a spray of sand next to the older girl.

"Finish eating your bread," I said.

"I'm not hungry. I wish to help Timora." Samsi picked up a food bag and tied it closed.

I finished my meal, scrubbed my hands with sand, and walked into the tent. I sat behind the front curtain, braiding my hair and listening to Samsi talk while she helped Timora gather the food bags.

"Tylos is a mean old goat," she said. Her voice sounded happy. "She told Bilqis to leave me in the desert. Bilqis is beautiful. She said I was brave to sleep alone in the mountain. I don't like Tylos. She spits when she yells."

"Tylos is companion to Bilqis." Timora's voice was so gentle that I had to lean through the curtain to hear her words. "You must honor Tylos and show respect to her on our journey."

"Where are we going?"

"We travel to Jerusalem to meet King Solomon. He is a wise king. He lives in a great palace built of gold and precious stones."

"I want to see his palace. I want to meet the king!"

Timora laughed, "Damri Samar and Bilqis alone will meet King Solomon. Tylos will attend Bilqis and you and I will stay in the tent."

I stepped from the tent and told Samsi I wished to speak with her. Timora stood with the food bags in her hands. "I will fetch Khe to take down the tents," she said.

I turned to Samsi. "I heard you talking about our journey to Jerusalem. Do not worry, child, we'll find your village when we return to Myrb."

"I don't want to leave you," she said. "I want to stay in the tent and help Timora."

"You belong with your family and they want you back."

"I don't want to go back to my village. My mother and father won't be there and my aunts will marry me to an old man with bad breath. That is what happened to my friend. She was my age and she had to marry an old man."

"We will talk of this later," I said. "Help Timora pack the tent."

Women's laughter fluted through the darkness like the sound of birds nesting for the night.

"I leave you, Bilqis," Tylos said. "I'm tired and my head aches." The tent curtain closed behind her as four women stepped into the light of my fire. Tylos said that two of the wives were pregnant and desired to rest after a long day of traveling.

I gave each woman a kiss of welcome. They smelled of incense and rose water and had dusted their hair with so much gold that the air sparkled when they turned their heads. A man's laughter and then Ma'zur walked into the firelight, leading a young woman by the hand. She looked about fifteen years, my age when Darmalay took me to wife. She wore a silver headband over her unbound hair and bracelets of braided gold around her slender wrists.

"My wife, Yazil," said the merchant. "I wished to bring her to you, Bilqis. She is precious to me as you are precious to our chieftain, Darmalay of Saba."

He looked around my camp, at the rugs laid by the fire, the platters of food, and at Samsi pouring wine from a large jar. "A fine meal," he said. He pushed Yazil toward me, like a father with a shy child.

"Your wife is welcome," I said.

Ma'zur smiled and backed out of the light. I waited until I saw him walk toward Samar's tent before I kissed his wife's soft cheek. "You are young to be on the caravan," I said.

"My husband would not leave me at home." Yazil's eyes were dark brown under thick eyebrows. Her full lips were red as if she had rubbed them with pomegranate juice.

We sat on rugs around the cookfire. Timora and Samsi had prepared platters of fresh seared goat meat, white cheese, dates, and rounds of anise bread. Samsi carried wine around the circle. I smiled when she handed a cup to me. Her hair was combed and braided and she wore a dark blue tunic that Timora had sewn for her when they returned from the market. Samsi looked cared for, no longer the frightened child we picked up three days ago.

"I regret I did not ask you to feast with me before this night," I said, lifting my cup to the women.

"We all have been busy settling into the caravan," said Shadru, the wife of a merchant in salt and honey. She looked older than the other women.

"I haven't settled, I've bounced like a ball for days," said another woman, a wine merchant's wife named Wa'dab. "My old camel seeks out the hardest rocks."

"Mine stumbles over every rock. Sometimes I fear I will fly out of my tent." Usa was thin and wore a light blue tunic. She held up her wine cup for Samsi to refill. "I wish I had stayed at home."

Shadru laughed. "I ride with my husband's caravan when he visits villages and the big market in Myrb, but I've never traveled so far. Sometimes I miss my home."

"I came because my husband needs me," said Wa'dab. "He does not take a step without me telling him where to set his feet." The women around the circle laughed. I thought Yahmed must be a weak man to be commanded by a wife who talked about him as if he were a child.

"We have another hard day of travel tomorrow and the day after," I said. "Damri Samar believes there are bandits in the pass beyond this village. The journey to the oasis will be easier after we leave the pass."

"Samar brings us that news, too." Wa'dab held bread stuffed with meat in one hand and a cup of wine in the other. "My husband isn't worried, he says our guards are stronger than the starving dogs who hide in the mountains."

"My husband thinks the same," said Usa.

"What does Ma'zur say?" I asked Yazil.

"He's not afraid." She pushed back her silver headband. "He says I must stay in my riding tent and not look out until we have ridden through the pass."

"I am not afraid of any man," said Wa'dab. "I carry a knife for any fool who tries to enter my tent when my husband is feasting at another cookfire."

"Do men try to come into your tent?" I said. "I thought only slave women were being approached."

"No man but my husband comes near me." She lowered her voice and the other women stopped chewing to listen.

"But I have heard that more than one woman on the caravan will carry a bastard on the journey home. My husband calls it desert fever. He says it happens on every caravan; men sneak out the front of their wives' tents while their wives open the back curtain to other men."

"Samar travels alone," Usa said.

"I wonder who he will choose to be his bedmate on the journey," Wa'dab said. She and Usa smiled at each other as if they shared a secret.

I tossed a dried root on the fire. There was a curl of smoke and orange flames flared around the edge of the wood. "Damri Samar joins my cookfire sometimes," I said. "But I do not know who shares his bed."

"Samar must be lonely in his tent after he leaves your cookfire." Wa'dab smiled at Usa again.

"Samar is not the only man on the caravan who travels with an empty tent," Shadru said. She turned from Wa'dab to me. "Have you heard of Andwa Oasis, Bilqis? The guards say it is a great oasis with water enough for bathing."

"I dream of a cool bath," said Yazil. She yawned, stretching her arms over her head.

"Are you tired, Yazil?" I asked.

"I'm always tired. I sleep so much during the day that I feel as though I'm dreaming when I'm awake."

"I feel the same," I said. "Sometimes I think I'm dreaming all day."

Yazil yawned again making the other women yawn. I laughed and stood while the other women helped each other stand.

"We thank you, Bilqis." Wa'dab brushed breadcrumbs from the front of her tunic. "I welcome you next to my cookfire."

The women walked from my camp, talking loudly in the dark. Samsi gathered cups and bowls while Timora carried food bags into the supply tent.

"Are they gone?" Tylos sat up on her mat, blinking, when I lit a candle.

"I thought you were asleep," I said.

"Who could sleep? They sounded like birds at a water hole." She rubbed her bare arms. "Wa'dab wonders if you visit Samar at night. I could not tell if she was warning you or wanted to hear of Samar's strength in bed."

"She was like a young girl, trying to find out if I liked him. But Samar is my husband's friend. He protects me. He would not try to enter my tent."

Tylos yawned. Her yawn ended in a bark of laughter. She pointed at Samsi and Timora's sleeping mats, laid side by side near the front curtain. "He would have a hard time finding you among so many women."

"Bilqis," Timora parted the curtain. "Damri Samar wishes to speak with you."

He stood in front of my cookfire, warming his hands. "The women were pleased with your hospitality," he said. "I heard them talking about your fine meal when they walked past my camp."

"They are welcome to my fire. We talked of the bandits waiting for us in the mountains."

"Don't fear, Bilqis, you won't be their first choice. Farium says they'll want the pack camels. They won't take captives."

"I rode on caravan with my father when I was a girl. He taught me to use a knife."

Samar's smile was quick. "I fear for the bandits if you fight as well as you speak." He placed his hand on my arm. "But don't worry about tomorrow, you'll be well-protected." He dropped his hand. "Sleep now. We leave early, well before dawn."

I watched as he stepped over the boundary stone to his camp. I thought of the women at my fire tonight, wanting to know who would be his bedmate.

Samar opened the curtain to his tent. He stopped in the opening and looked back at me. I wondered if he thought me beautiful in the firelight.

He entered his tent. I stayed by the fire, stroking my arm that was warm from his touch.

~ Eight ~

We traveled by starlight until the village of Adhah was left far behind. Our riding tents were closed against the night air. The camel bells had been wrapped in wool and swung silently under the riding tents. The only sounds were the low voices of the camel men and the padding of the camels' feet on the sand.

Samar was riding beside me when I opened my curtains at first light. He wore a brown tunic, the color of the guards. He nodded to me and pointed with his dagger at the pass in front of the caravan. The lead camels were entering the opening, a wide path bounded on either side by huge boulders.

"Are the bandits ahead?" I whispered.

Samar leaned toward me. "Yes, Farium thinks they're hiding in the middle of the pass."

He smelled of wood smoke and I thought how warm he would feel in my arms and how surprised he would be if I pulled him down into my tent. I wondered if he would hold me close or push me away. I sat back against my cushions. My thoughts of embracing Samar troubled me. I was a married woman and he was my husband's good friend.

We rode in silence as we entered the pass. Sunlight turned the sand white as milk. Small birds hopped about in bushes and lizards hurried in and out of the dark cracks in the rocks, flicking their tails as we rode past.

Samar left me to ride up the caravan. A woman riding in front of me poked her head through her curtain when he rode past. "Samar," she called. "Have you seen anything?"

He frowned at her and put his finger to his lips. She laughed and I could hear laughter from the woman traveling with her. I thought of the women at my cookfire, eager to know who would share Samar's bed.

Khe held the leads to my beast and Timora walked with Samsi, pulling Tylos's camel. The girls did not laugh and sing this morning, but turned their heads from side to side, looking for bandits. I pulled a small cutting knife from my red bag. I wished I had a bigger knife. My father had given me a boy's dagger when I first joined his small caravan carrying honey and palm wine from our village to the markets in Myrb.

"Keep your blade close, my Bilqis," he said. "Most of the people we meet will be friends, but there are men who will try to rob us."

We met many friends on our journeys; men who invited us to their cookfires and praised me as a good daughter helping her poor old father. He laughed at their words; he was no older than any of them.

Some of the travelers we met were not our friends. These men rode up close to us, not stopping at a distance to throw sand in the air and show their empty hands. My father kept his hand on his dagger when they approached. "Say nothing," he said, "they will think you are my son." The men usually passed by, shouting good journey while they looked over the big camel my father rode, our pack camel, and the smaller camel under me.

One day two men did not ride past. They stopped in front of my father and asked for water. The humps of their camels were flat from thirst. My father could not refuse; sharing water was law in the desert. The first man's cheeks sucked in as he drank from the waterskin, the other man spilled water from his mouth down the front of his dirty tunic.

"What do you carry?" the first man asked. My father sat tall on his camel and did not answer. I clutched the hilt of my dagger. The dirty man dropped the waterskin on the sand and laughed and farted so loud his camel turned her head to look at him.

"A poor caravan," said the first man. He spit in the sand by the water bag. "Bags of salt pissed on by dogs."

They kicked their camels and rode past us. We watched them until they were out of sight. My father feared they would return, so we rode hard and fast until we reached Myrb. We camped outside the city walls and kept a fire burning until morning light when the guards pushed open the heavy city gates.

A loud cry woke me from my dream. Two men stood up at the top of the pass, shouting as they threw rocks down at the caravan. A large stone hit my camel on the side of her neck. She jerked her head and moaned, a high-pitched sound that said the rock hurt.

Camels around us bellowed as they were struck. The noise grew louder as men ran screaming from the rocks, waving their daggers over their heads. Khe pulled out his dagger and looked up at me. I showed him my knife. He nodded and quickly turned back to the battle in front of us. Dust rose until the air was brown and filled with the sound of men shouting and women screaming. Leads flew upward like tossed snakes over the heads of frightened camels. Khe kept his dagger ready and held tight to my camel as she shifted under me, frightened by the noise of battle.

A man with a short, black beard ran toward the boy. I screamed, "Khe, Khe," as the man stabbed at him with his long blade. Khe jumped to one side and slashed the bearded man. The bandit dropped his knife. He slapped at blood spraying from his throat. Khe thrust his blade deep into the man's eye. The bandit fell on his back. Red blood poured from his mouth and eye.

A camel in front of me dropped to its knees. A woman rolled out of her riding tent. Her unbound hair covered her face, her blue robe was wrapped around her legs. She pushed her hair from her face. I saw the woman was Yazil. She stumbled, trying to stand in her tangled robe. An old man with a short white beard stopped in front of her, tucked his knife in his waistband and grabbed her by her hair. Yazil's mouth opened in a scream. The man laughed and yanked her to his chest.

A young man ran up to Yazil and the bandit. He scooped up a handful of sand and threw it at the old man's face. The bandit let go of Yazil, wiped his eyes and pulled out his blade. Khe ran up behind the old man. He stabbed him in the back. The bandit fell to his knees. The young man kicked him hard in the face. The old man fell on his side, thrashed his legs in the sand and was still.

Khe ran back to me. He grabbed my camel's leads and faced the fighting again, waiting for another attack.

The cries of battle died to moans. I was astonished that violent attack seemed over. Dust settled into the sand and the air cleared. Below me, the young man held his hand out to Yazil. Her lips jerked upward as she tried to smile at him.

A man screamed and I looked to see who was wounded. Ma'zur ran toward Yazil, like a fat dog running after a mouse. "Do not touch my wife," he yelled.

He stepped on the torn edge of Yazil's robe, making her fall, and pushed the younger man away from his wife. Yazil put her hands over her face. The man who had saved her from the bandit wore no beard, just a trace of dark hair over his lips. Ma'zur kicked sand at him. The young man backed away.

"Bilqis!" Farium rode up to me. "Are you hurt?"

"No, your son fought bravely and protected me," I said.

Farium pointed to a slave rolling the body of the white-bearded bandit to the edge of the path. "The thieves were hungry, but we did not lose a pack camel."

"My goods are safe?"

"I counted your camels. They are safe."

"How many bandits were they? The attack was over so fast."

"Ten, maybe more. They look like an army when they run at you." He clicked his tongue and his camel moved away from me. "We have some wounded but they have many dead. Their hunger made them bold. I did not expect them to hide so close to the path."

"Are you safe, Bilqis?" Tylos stood on the ground next to my camel, shading her eyes as she looked up at me. Behind her, Timora and Samsi clung on to the leads to her camel.

"Yes," I said. "Are you hurt?"

"The battle passed by us," said Tylos. "We hid behind my camel and watched the fighting."

Samar appeared, pushing through a knot of men cleaning blood from their daggers with handfuls of sand. He stared at the bloody blade in Khe's hand, then up at me. I dropped the small knife into my bag. "I'm unhurt," I said. "Khe protected me."

"We're stopping to let the camel men retie their bundles," Samar said. "We'll camp in the valley tonight to care for the wounded."

Khe pulled my camel and the caravan moved from the pass and down into the valley. Samsi and Khe gathered dung while Timora built the cookfire. I sat under the awning in front of my tent, sorting through a bag of dried lentils. My hands were still shaking from the fear I felt in the battle.

The front curtain was open and I could see Tylos working inside the tent, packing clothing that she had taken out of the bags and refolded. Tylos was like Timora, her hands were always busy or her thoughts were busy, thinking of tasks for the two girls.

Samsi's waistbag was full when she returned to our camp. "Khe and I picked up enough dung for two days." She poured balls of dried camel dung into a pile next to the cookfire where Timora was working.

"You were gone a long time, my girl." Timora added water to the flour in her mixing bowl and began to stir the dough.

"Khe and I met Amdar," said Samsi. "He's a poet. He saved Yazil from a bandit this morning. Amdar wrote a poem for her. He says she is a woman of honey and he sees the sun in her smile."

"How did you meet Amdar?" asked Timora. She patted a round of dough and laid it on the cookplate.

"We heard someone singing and then Amdar rode his camel around a rock toward us. His camel's name is Tooky. He says she listens to him and does not laugh when he recites his poems."

"Does he have a master on the caravan?" asked Timora.

"No, he sings at cookfires at night to earn his bread. He's traveling to Jerusalem to learn songs from King Solomon's poets."

Samsi pulled a white feather from her waistband and waved it in the air. "Look what I found. Khe and I walked so far from the caravan that all we could hear was the wind."

"Bilqis would not like you to leave the caravan, Samsi. Remember, there are bandits in the desert. "

"I was safe. Khe was with me. He showed me the tracks of Bilqis' camel."

"How does he know her animal?" Timora asked.

My hands slowed as I listened to Samsi. My camel was like other animals, she had four long legs and feet covered with fur to shed sand.

"She has an old cut on her back foot," said the girl. "If you look hard at her footmark you can see the line of the cut."

The smell of baking bread traveled toward me. My stomach growled. Tylos dropped the tunics she was sorting. "I'm hungry," she said. "I'll pack these after we eat."

Samsi served dates and warm bread seasoned with anise. The bread settled my stomach after the fear and excitement of battle. I drank a cup of mint tea with a drop of golden honey melting in the bottom of the cup. "Timora takes good care of us," I said to Tylos. "Samar says her food delights the appetite but does not overpower the senses."

Beside the fire, Samsi talked to Timora. I heard her say, "He sleeps behind her tent at night. He says he dreams her dreams."

"Who sleeps near a women's tent?" I asked.

"Amdar," said Samsi. She jumped from the cookfire to my rug and sat next to me. "He loves Yazil. He says her breath is as soft as the morning breeze."

"Amdar speaks pleasing words," I said. "But I saw Ma'zur push Yazil aside this morning when Amdar touched his wife. Ma'zur will be angry if he finds another man sleeping close to his wife's tent. Tell your poet to stay away from Yazil."

Two days after the attack we woke to the sound of slaves wailing a death on the caravan. Tylos lit a candle and I sat up, yawning in the bright light and wondering who had died.

"My mother cried like that when my brother died." Samsi knelt at the foot of my sleeping mat and began folding my sheepskin.

"How old was your brother?" I pulled a clean tunic over my head, sucking my breath as the cold linen slid over my breasts.

"He had three moons," said Samsi. "He cried and cried one morning and wouldn't suck. His face was red and his skin was hot. I went outside to help my father water the goats. We heard my mother screaming and we ran toward the house. I was afraid, running toward that sound."

"Do you have other brothers or sisters?" Timora said.

Samsi patted the sheepskin, bouncing her fingers in the fuzzy wool. "He was the only one. My father buried him close to our house. He set four rocks around the grave and said I could not step inside. I stood outside the rocks and looked at my brother's grave. I thought he was sleeping under the sand and one day he would wake up and play with me."

"Why did you live far away from your village?" I said. The wailing stopped. I heard voices as people in camps around us opened their curtains and stepped outside into the morning air.

"We lived in the village with my father's brothers and their wives. My aunts did not like my mother because she was from another village. They were mean to her and called her stranger instead of sister. My aunts wanted to marry me to the chieftain of the village. He was an old man. He liked to stroke my hair when he visited our house. I didn't like it, but I stood still under his hand because my aunts were smiling at him."

She twisted tufts of white wool between her fingers. "I didn't want to marry him. I was happy when my father said I would wait two more years to wed, until I had twelve years. My aunts said the old man wanted me now. I cried and told my mother I would run away if I had to live with him. My father protected me. He told his brothers that our goats needed better pasture. We moved to the valley and lived in a little house that my father built for us. My father said we would stay until I was old enough to wed."

The tent pole at the front opening was struck two times. Tylos sighed as if she had been busy all morning, and pushed open the curtain. She talked with a man, keeping her voice low so it would not carry to the other tents.

She dropped the curtain and turned to me. "The merchant Gandham Ashum died this morning. He was stabbed in the attack. Samar sent a slave to ask you to attend his wife at the burial." She pointed to the folded sheepskins and the unrolled sleeping mats. "You girls pack our tent and stay with the caravan. We'll join you after the burial."

Tylos and I accompanied the merchant's wife and her companion to the burial. Two slaves in clean waistcloths walked in front of the widow, carrying the dead man between them, one at his shoulders, the other holding his legs. The merchant was wrapped in cream-colored linen. There was a red stain on his chest where his wound had opened.

The wife of the dead merchant held a basket of grave goods in her hand. A black silk mourning veil hung down her back. The last time I saw her, she was kneeling beside her husband on the bank of the wadi, weeping with him, as their camel and bundles of silk were carried away by the sayl. She wept today, her face wrinkled with grief over a fistful of black silk.

We walked behind the dead man toward Samar, who waited for us in the desert at the head of a newly dug hole. The slaves stepped into the grave, easing in the wrapped body. They turned the merchant's body face down at the bottom of the grave so his seed would enter the earth.

The wife wiped her nose with her veil and handed the basket to Samar. He reached into the basket and brought out a handful of golden incense and a pinch of white salt. Samar scattered the incense around the merchant's bound head to scent his time underground. He placed the salt near the dead man's hand to pay his way into the next world.

The last item in the basket was a length of crimson silk. The wife swept her hand in the air over the grave and Samar unfurled the silk, pulling it forward until it covered the man's body.

The wife fell to her knees, pulled the black veil from her head and poured a handful of sand over her hair. "My husband, my husband," she cried. "Do not leave me."

Her companion helped her stand and she walked away from the grave, bent over and holding her belly as if she held her grief between her hands. Behind her, the slaves pushed sand over the bright silk, filling the hole until there was a shallow place in the sand to show that a man lay underneath. Samar set a pointed stone at the head of the grave to mark it, brushed dust from his robe and walked with us back to the caravan.

"What will happen to his wife?" I asked Samar.

"She returns to her village." He pointed to a group of camels standing in the path, gazing at the tails of animals waving at the end of the departing caravan. Two men on camels guarded the small herd.

"It is dangerous for her to leave the caravan," I said.

"You take in strays, Bilqis, invite her to join your tent."

"My tent is filled with women, but she may set her camp next to mine if she wishes to stay with the caravan."

"She wants to return to her village," he said. "She is not a merchant. She wants to go home."

Farium sent guards to ride ahead and watch for another attack, but they saw only boys, far out in the desert tending their sheep and goats. We rode past small villages without stopping. Our caravan was too big to enter their narrow gates and drink from their wells. Merchants eager for our trade rode to us from the villages on camels laden with fat waterskins and fresh goat meat.

Samar occasionally came to my fire in the morning, but more often he appeared when we had set up for the night. After a few days, Samsi laid a rug for him and Timora asked me what Samar would like to eat before he sent a slave to tell me he would join us for our evening meal.

One evening while Samsi and Timora were sewing in our tent, Tylos left me alone with Samar to fetch a warmer robe. While Tylos was inside the tent, Samar pulled a dagger in a leather sheath from his waistband and handed it to me. "The knife you carried during the attack is too small. Take this. It belonged to my youngest son. He died a year ago. I kept it to remind me of him."

I unsheathed the dagger, a bronze blade with a hilt of dark blue lapis. The hilt was striped with raised gold bands to keep it from slipping when the hilt was wet with blood or sweat. The blade was heavy in my hand, sturdy enough to cut through bone. I imagined stabbing a bandit with it as Khe had done.

I was honored by Samar's desire to give me his son's dagger, but I hesitated, feeling I should refuse the gift.

"It is for your protection," he said. "Keep it close. We will encounter bandits again before our journey is over and next time they may want more than camels."

I sheathed the dagger. Samar had vowed to protect me with his life; if he thought giving me a better weapon would keep me safe, then I would accept it.

I hid the dagger under my robes as Tylos stepped out of the tent. I didn't want her or any of the women in my tent to know about Samar's gift. I felt I could trust them, but even an idle mention that Samar had given me his son's dagger would provide rich food for talk about my friendship with Samar.

"I am honored," I said. "I will take care of the blade and return it to you when we reach Jerusalem."

Samar kept his eyes on the fire as he replied. "It is yours to keep, Bilqis. This is my gift to you."

I feasted the women from Myrb again when we were a day's ride from the Andwa Oasis. One of the pregnant women, Lila, came and told me that her pregnant sister was unwell and unable to attend my feast.

Wa'dab sat next to Usa. She asked if Samar would join us since he was seen sitting at my fire every night.

I sipped my wine and said, "Damri Samar promised my husband that he would protect me and he visits my fire to honor that vow."

I watched her turn her eyes to Usa, sharing her belief that Samar's visits were more than obligation. I had to be more careful, I thought, and never sit alone at my fire with Samar.

Word might reach Darmalay's ears if Samar visited me without a companion present. When I returned home my husband could turn me out of his house if he believed I had encouraged the attention of another man.

Shadru did not ask about Samar. She smiled at Samsi when the girl served wine to her and waited with respect for me to speak. I thought I would invite Shadru to visit the great house when we were safely home. We shared a long journey and would have much to talk about when we returned to Myrb.

Yazil spoke in her soft voice. "The poet Amdar asked to come to my fire. My companion said he could not, that only my husband could sit with me."

"I have seen the little poet near your tent," Shadru said. "He carries sticks in his hands and pretends he is gathering firewood, but he looks at your tent when the wind moves your curtain."

She laughed. "Ah, I remember when my husband looked at me the way Amdar stares at you."

"The poet is not the only man who looks at her." Wa'dab gulped her wine and waved the empty cup over her head. She pointed a finger at Yazil while Samsi filled her cup. "I worry about you, Yazil," said Wa'dab. "You do not close your tent. Men will talk about you."

"Does your husband know the poet watches you?" I asked.

"I see my husband only at night," said Yazil. "He feasts at other fires and comes to my tent late at night. He wakes me up." She frowned and rubbed her arms. "My companion says I must let him come to my tent, but I do not like it when he stinks of wine."

"We all are the same," said Shadru. "We are long for our husbands when we begin our marriage, but after bearing children and caring for our house, sometimes we are happier talking with our women friends than welcoming our husbands to our beds."

The other women nodded. I didn't know what to say. Darmalay had left my bed before I tired of him.

~ Nine ~

Palm trees waved welcome as we approached the oasis. A pool of water shimmered beyond the trees, promising a cool bath to wash the dust off my skin and the fleas out of my hair.

Samsi led my camel to a cleared area between two tall palms where Timora and Khe were lifting tent poles from a pack camel. Samsi pulled my animal to kneeling. I jumped down and stretched, happy to be out of my riding tent.

"Come with me," I said to the girl. Samsi grabbed my hand as if she were my child and we walked toward the silver line of water, stepping on dried palm leaves that cracked under our feet.

We stopped at the edge of a large pool of green water. Samsi pointed at camels drinking from the muddy edge. A group of camels stood in the shallow water, pissing as they drank. At the far end of the pool, the water was dark green under bushes growing around the rocks.

"You and Khe fetch water from the deep end," I said. "I do not want to drink camel piss."

"There are good wells here," said the girl. "Khe told me to leave this water for the camels."

"Khe is wise." I looked at the deep water. "Ah, I would like to bathe in that water."

"Tell Farium," she said. "He would guard you."

"I would not appear unclothed before the men on the caravan, Samsi. We'll bathe in our tent, away from the eyes of men."

We returned to our tent. The air inside was steamy with the smell of jasmine and cinnamon oil that Tylos had poured into our bath water. Samsi left to pick up dung for our cookfire while I bathed in the scented water. Tylos opened the back curtain to cool the air after I dressed again. She sat next to me, unfolding the white clothing we were to wear that night to Ilumqah's full-moon ceremony.

"Timora finished sewing your tunic last night." She held up the long garment. White pearls formed a full moon on the front of the tunic. Tiny stars worked in silver with rays of clear crystal beads surrounded the moon.

I touched the smooth pearls. "I watched Timora sew this cloth, but she kept it in her lap so I could not see what she was making."

Tylos laid it aside and held up another white garment. "This is what she made for me." She brushed her hand over rows of fine silver thread that flowed like water down the front of the tunic into a deep border along the hem. "I have never worn anything so beautiful."

"Timora's hands are clever," I said. "Her work is as good as a jeweler's."

"She is a good girl," said Tylos. "And she honors our tent. She doesn't stop to talk with the camel men or the guards when she fetches water from the well."

"Samar is pleased with our tent." I gathered my wet hair and dropped it down my back. "He says we keep our proper place and no men talk of four women alone in a tent. I feel as though I'm traveling with Hazza. She used to clap her hands at Darmalay and me when we kissed in the hallway and tell us to save lovemaking for our rooms."

"What did your husband say to his mother?" asked Tylos.

"He laughed and called her beloved mother until she smiled at him. Darmalay would not say a word against her even when she spoke harshly to me."

"Well, Hazza is dead and cannot harm you now." Tylos set her tunic aside and unfolded two more garments. The linen was soft from many washings. Crescent moons were worked in silver beads around the neck of each tunic. She held up the smaller of the two, "This will fit Samsi."

"She'll be happy to wear it," I said. "Timora should teach her to sew. I want her to return to her aunts knowing more than gathering feathers and camel dung."

"She says she wants to be a poet," said Tylos. "Amdar tells her there are many women poets in the big cities who are wealthy and famous."

"She's not from a big city and no one will pay to listen to a village girl," I said.

The air brightened as the curtain was pulled aside and Samsi stepped into the tent. "Timora sent me to ask if we can watch the priests set the sacred stone."

I held up Samsi's tunic. "This is what you'll wear to the ceremony tonight."

"Is that for me? It's so pretty!"

"This is a great honor for you," Tylos said. "It marks you as being from our tent." She folded the garment and laid it on top of the stack of white clothing. "Bilqis wants you to learn to sew before you return to your village. Timora will teach you."

"I don't want to go back to the village. I want to stay with Bilqis." Samsi bit her lips, looking like the lonely child I found at the side of the path.

"You will do as Bilqis commands," said Tylos.

"Watch the priests set the sacred stone," I said to stop their quarrel. "Then return with Timora. You both must bathe before we dress for the ceremony."

"I want to eat now. I'm hungry." Samsi rubbed her belly. "The slaves at the wells say their masters are angry and yell at them."

"Everyone is hungry," said Tylos. "We do not eat until the priest sends meat to us from the sacrifice. But there is another reason why the merchants are unhappy." Samsi and I looked at her. "No man is allowed to, ah…lie with his wife until the ceremony is over. The merchants do little else on this journey besides eat and drink and rut." She laughed. "Their wives will be sore tomorrow."

"Tylos, Samsi is a young girl, she doesn't want to hear of men and women mating."

"I watched the goats rut," said Samsi.

"It's different between people," I said.

"How is it different?" Samsi and Tylos said together.

"It's different because you love your husband and want to be close to him."

"Hmm," said Tylos. She gathered the folded clothing and walked to the back of the tent.

"Join Timora and watch with the other women," I said to Samsi. "Stay away from the men."

She slipped out of the tent. I watched as Tylos carefully draped the white clothing over a large basket. She picked up a bag of blue-dyed leather from the pile of bags and baskets stored next to the back curtain and turned to me.

"Tylos, you are not unhappy to be without a husband?" I asked.

"I had no enjoyment with my husband. I'm no longer able to bear a child. My worth to another man would be that of a slave caring for a master. I would be turned out when I no longer was useful." She looked at me. "My place is with you, Bilqis."

"You always will have a home with me." I patted the rug next to my cushions, inviting her to sit. "I took great pleasure with Darmalay, I miss sleeping with him."

"You cannot take another husband unless Darmalay commands you to leave his house, but many women take other men while their husbands are away." Tylos sat with the blue bag in her lap. "Is there anyone who has caught your eye?" She lowered her voice though we were alone in the tent. "You'll have to be careful. There are women on this caravan, like Wa'dab, who would like to see you dishonored."

"Tylos, I am Darmalay's wife. I would not shame him on this journey."

She shrugged. "Who would see?"

"Who would not?" I said. "I'm careful. I speak with few men and only in the presence of their wives."

"You speak with Samar every day and at night when he eats at your cookfire."

I thought of Samar, his laughter at my cookfire when I said something that amused him. "He talks with many women on the caravan. They open their curtains when he rides past their riding tents to ask him how long before we stop for the night."

"He's a handsome man. Those women desire his company, but he stops longest to talk with you." Tylos looked at the curtain and back at me. "I would help if you wished to visit him at night."

"Tylos, enough! Samar is my husband's close friend." I was shocked that my companion spoke easily of helping me dishonor my husband. I gathered my comb and drying cloth. "I think of him as a brother and that is all."

Tylos laughed. "No brother looks at his sister the way he looks at you." She untied the strings of the bag. "He smiles at your words and you smile at him before he speaks."

I stood for a moment, thinking of her words. Did other people see our smiles? Did they think I shared Samar's bed?

I changed the conversation. "I hope Samsi listens to me and stays with the other women. She is young and does not know that men can be wicked."

"Samsi follows Timora and does not talk to men other than Khe and Amdar."

"When does she talk with the poet?' I asked.

"He walks with them when they gather dung."

"Well, he is harmless, he has eyes only for Yazil."

Tylos pulled a bundle of ivory silk from the bag. "Yazil should be careful. Her slaves tell Timora that she does not pull her curtain closed during the day when she is inside her tent. They say Ma'zur yells at her for smiling at other men."

"Yazil is young and foolish. Her companion should tell her to be careful. We must protect Samsi and Timora. I don't want to find them weeping tomorrow with blood between their legs."

"Timora will watch over Samsi. Ah, here is the jewelry you will wear tonight." She lifted a silver headdress from the silk wrappings. Gold rosettes were fastened around a band of polished silver. Under each rosette hung long ribbons of curled silver that would cover my unbound hair. The headdress was beautiful. I would be beautiful wearing it.

Tylos set it on the rug and pulled two wrist cuffs of hammered silver from the bag and laid them next to the headdress.

Samsi stepped inside the tent, letting the curtain fall closed behind her. "We saw the priests set the rock." She knelt before us and reached for the headdress. "Are you wearing this tonight?"

Tylos slapped her hand. "That is for Bilqis, girl."

"Ow." Samsi rubbed her hand and stuck out her tongue at Tylos, quick as a snake.

"Tell me about the rock," I said.

She turned her back to Tylos and smiled at me. "Timora and I saw two priests carrying a white rock from a white tent." She held her arms open. "The rock was this big. An old priest walked in front of the two priests and we followed them to a pile of rocks in the desert. They set the white rock on top of the other rocks. Timora said that was the altar. The two priests walked around the rock and dropped black stones until they made a circle around the altar. Timora said we could not walk inside the circle, only the priests are allowed to touch the sacred rock. The old priests held his hands up to the sky and closed his eyes. Then his priests waved at us to leave."

"Our head priest waits in his dream until the ceremony," I said.

"I have seen the white tent at the back of the caravan, but not the old man," said Samsi. "Timora says he stays in his tent and comes out when Ilumqah shows his face."

"He carries the sacred rock from the temple in Myrb and talks only with his priests," I said. "Tell Timora to come into the tent and bathe. We have much to do before the ceremony."

As we waited inside the tent for Samar to arrive and escort us to the ceremony, I saw Timora pick up a small goatskin bag, her gift for Ilumqah. Across the front of the bag, two crescent moons worked in silver beads enclosed a full moon of white shells.

"Your work is beautiful," I said. "Tylos and I think you are as skilled as any jeweler in Myrb." I ran my fingers over the shell moon. "Did you sew for Hazza?"

Timora nodded. "I mended her clothing and I made a cushion for her when she was sick. She died before I could give it to her. I don't know what happened to it. Maybe it was burned after she died."

"What did it look like?" I asked.

"It was brown wool with green and gold leaves embroidered around the edge."

"I remember that cushion," I said. "Hazza was buried with it. I placed it under her head when we laid her on the burial shelf."

The girl smiled at me, her round smile that made her face glow. Samsi laid her head against Timora's arm.

Samar arrived, wearing a dark blue robe worked with silver thread around his neck and wrists; the colors of the night sky behind Ilumqah. He stared at me when I stepped through the curtain. He held out his hand and pulled me close to his side. I breathed in the smell of incense he used to scent his beard and thought of Tylos's words, "I would help if you wished to visit his tent at night."

Tylos emerged with Timora and Samsi. Samsi had tucked a white feather, her gift for Ilumqah, inside her waistband. Timora carried the goatskin bag. Samar kept my hand in his as we began to walk toward the altar where the priest waited. I liked the feel of his warm hand but feared the smiles of the women of the caravan if they saw my hand in Samar's.

I pulled away to untangle a silver ribbon from my hair. "Damri Samar," I said, "we are honored that you accompany us to the ceremony."

He did not take my hand again as we walked through the center of the camp, past tents with their curtains closed, and cold cookfires that would stay unlit until Ilumqah showed his face tonight. Men and women waited in front of their tents, joining us as we walked past. Men were dressed in dark blue, the women in silver and white to celebrate the return of our god.

Samar led us from the camps toward the altar in the desert. The robes of the priests were white as morning birds against the dark sky. No one spoke, just a cleared throat here and there. Samsi coughed. I wondered if this was the first public ceremony she had attended. If her parents had honored Ilumqah, there would have been a house altar in Samsi's home; a white stone with an offering of bread or meat placed upon it to welcome the arrival of our moon god.

As we approached the altar, the old head priest opened his eyes and looked at the far edge of the desert where a faint light glowed above the sand. A young priest stood at his side. A silver knife and bowl were placed at one end of the altar. A white clay bowl was set at the other end, next to a burning candle.

Samar stopped in front of the sacred rock. When all had gathered, the old priest held up the candle, lifting the light to guide Ilumqah's return to us.

"I see Yazil." Behind me, Samsi whispered to Timora. "Her husband is fat. Amdar is here, he's watching Yazil."

I looked back through the crowd. Ma'zur was looking around, smiling at his friends. He stopped smiling when he saw Amdar. He looked from the poet to his wife and moved closer to Yazil. I saw her face twist in pain as she pulled away from her husband, rubbing her arm. Ma'zur's face was dark and heavy. He pushed Yazil's shoulder until she faced forward again.

The old priest picked up a handful of golden incense and poured it on coals burning in the clay bowl. White smoke from the incense swirled up with the familiar scent of dried honey. The young priest clapped his hands once, and we moved forward to offer our gifts to the god.

Samar knelt first to lay a small silver bull on the sand. Next to his gift, I placed a gazelle carved from ivory with turquoise eyes. Tylos tucked a tiny alabaster bowl under my gazelle. Timora placed her shell bag on the sand next to the bowl. Samsi dropped her white feather on top of Timora's bag.

People brushed past me to lay their gifts on the sand. Yazil bent over with a bracelet of silver moons in her hand. Ma'zur pushed her aside and carefully set a silver statue of a ram down on the sand. One of the ram's long, curled horns covered Yazil's bracelet, the other horn lay across a silver dagger offered by another merchant. An amethyst eye set in the ram's head stared upward; a neckpiece of jade and ebony covered its chest. It was a splendid piece, worthy of a niche in the temple at Myrb.

Tylos turned to whisper in my ear as Ma'zur and Yazil backed into the crowd. "Ma'zur shows his wealth," she said, "but his wife does not obey him. She says he stinks and she will not sleep with him at night."

"Yazil should take care," I said. "Ma'zur laughs and calls her a child, but he will not forget her insults."

When the last gift was presented, the old priest picked up the silver knife. We moved aside to make a path for a young priest who walked through the crowd leading a white goat at the end of a gilded rope. The goat was a young female. Her long ears and hooves were dusted with gold. A necklace of dried yellow flowers hung around her neck.

The priest led the goat inside the ring of stones. He held her between his legs, gripping her tightly as he pulled back her head, showing her throat. The goat's eyes rolled in her head as the old priest stepped forward, holding up the silver knife and bowl. He stabbed the goat in the throat and pulled the knife across the white fur. The little gold hooves kicked up sand while blood sprayed from her neck. Tears stung my eyes. I heard Samsi weeping.

The old priest held the silver bowl under the deep cut, filling it with blood until the goat stopped kicking. The young priest tied a length of white linen around the wound to keep blood from dripping onto the sand. Her blood was a sacrifice to Ilumqah and belonged to him alone, not the sand under our feet.

The priest picked up her limp body and carried her back through the crowd toward the white tent. After he entered the tent, the old priest placed the bowl on the altar, next to the burning incense. He dipped his fingers in the red blood and sprinkled it on the incense, praying as smoke drifted from the bowl toward the dark sky above us:

"Praise Ilumqah, accept our sacrifice.
Return your light and guide us over the dark sands.
Give us safe journey to Jerusalem.
In the name of Ilumqah, protector of Myrb."

With these words, our god rose round and heavy above the edge of the sand. Moonlight felt hot on my face and arms. I closed my eyes. I felt as if my heart were laid open under Ilumqah's bright gaze. I thought of the long days when I lay awake in my riding tent, listening for Samar's voice, smiling at him when he walked into the light of my cookfire, the warmth of his hand when he took mine tonight.

The old priest clapped his hands. I opened my eyes; the ceremony was over.

No one spoke as we walked away from the rock, carrying the silence that follows Ilumqah's return. The sand was white in moonlight; a brightness that seemed covered with a fine black veil.

Samar bowed to me when we reached my tent. "I wait for you at my feast."

I watched him walk away until Tylos called me to come inside.

~ Ten ~

Tylos held up the tunic of blue-glazed silk I had chosen to wear to Samar's feast. This was the garment I wore on the day my husband asked me to leave our house. She unfolded a veil of gold silk edged with amber beads and laid it next to the tunic. "Samar will not take his eyes off you tonight," she said.

I stepped out of my ceremonial tunic and pulled on the blue silk, smoothing it over my breasts and hips. "There are many women on this caravan who seek to catch his eyes," I said.

"But he looks at you." She draped the veil over my hair, stepped back and smiled at me. "Ah, you are beautiful." She held up a hand mirror. The blue and gold silks were rich against my dark skin; the amber beads glowed in the candlelight. I looked younger; happiness seemed to rest on my lips.

Samsi and Timora were preparing their evening meal when we emerged from the tent. Timora laid a piece of goat meat from the sacrifice to cook on the fire while Samsi poured two cups of wine.

"You girls close the curtain and eat inside," said Tylos. "Do not leave to visit other camps. There are men out tonight who will fall on you like dogs if they catch you outside the tent."

"We'll stay inside," said Samsi. "Timora is teaching me to sew. I'm making a bag for Khe."

"That girl thinks too much of that camel boy," Tylos said as we walked toward Samar's camp.

"She's a child," I said. "He's a brother to her."

Two cookfires burned next to Samar's supply tent. Slaves at one fire filled platters with golden rounds of bread, sliced cheese, ripe figs, and pots of butter and honey. A whole goat was roasting over the other fire, tended by a boy holding a long dipper and pouring a line of oil over the top of the goat. I almost dropped to my knees at the delicious smell of roasting meat.

Rugs and cushions for Samar's guests were laid around a third fire blazing in front of his tent. "Bilqis." Samar walked toward me, holding out his hands. "Help me welcome my guests."

We turned toward a man and woman stepping over Samar's boundary stone. Ma'zur walked in front of Yazil who kept her eyes on her husband. She nodded at me but did not smile while Samar led Ma'zur to a rug at the far end of the fire.

The merchant glanced back at rugs laid near Samar's cushion and tightened his lips. I wondered if he was angry because he had not been given the honored place next to Samar.

"You are lovely tonight, Yazil." I kissed her cheek and stood back. "You're shaking, are you unwell?"

"My husband is angry with me." Her voice was a breath in my ear as we followed the men.

"Why is he angry?" I asked.

"He says I made the little poet fall in love with me. He pinched me at the ceremony and slapped me tonight when I did not dress fast enough." She rubbed her shoulder. "It hurt."

"Calm down, child," I said. "Everyone is anxious tonight, everyone is hungry." I patted her arm. "Your husband will be happy again after he has eaten Samar's good food and drunk a skinful of wine."

We reached Ma'zur and Samar. Ma'zur waved his hand at the pile of cushions placed on the rug at his feet. "I thank you for this excellent seat at your fire," he said. "I will watch from here. A good merchant watches the whole market."

"You are not a merchant tonight," said Samar. "You are my honored guest."

"I am always a merchant." Ma'zur looked at Yazil, pulling his bottom lip as though he was appraising a tray of local jewelry.

Samar and I walked back to the head of the fire where other guests waited to be greeted. "My friend," Samar kissed the cheek of the man in front of us, Yahmed, the wine merchant from Myrb. I kissed the plump cheeks of his wife, Wa'dab.

"I've missed you, Bilqis," she said. "I wanted to ask you to my fire." She fluttered her hand at her husband. "But he's been sick. He's drunk only soup for two days." She leaned toward me and whispered, loud enough for Samar to hear. "He should rest but he would not dishonor his friend by staying away from the feast."

Yahmed's eyes were half closed. He looked like he wanted to be back at his tent, sleeping. Poor little man, I thought, you could not say no to your wife.

Samar pointed to a rug. Wa'dab helped her husband sit down. She pushed cushions behind his back and snapped her fingers at a slave to bring more cushions.

I kissed the scented cheeks of other women while Samar greeted the men. When all had been seated, I sat down next to Samar. He clapped his hands and slaves approached the fire carrying filled wineskins and platters of smoking meat.

The night was filled with color. Gold shone around the necks and wrists of the laughing men and women. Silks of crimson, gold, green, and blue were bright in the firelight. Silver wine cups gleamed in every hand. Everywhere was noise and color and platters heaped with food. We filled our mouths with spiced bread, roasted meat, sweetened cheese, and figs poached in honey.

I felt Samar's eyes on me. Every gesture I made felt graceful, from lifting a cup of wine to my lips to pushing the beaded veil over my shoulder. Samar leaned forward to listen to a story told by the merchant sitting next to me. I gazed at his full lips and the lines that showed around his eyes when he smiled. I turned away before he could see desire in my face.

Ilumqah's light had revealed my longing for Samar. I thought again of Tylos's offer to help me if I wanted to visit Samar's tent. I felt a moment's fear of Darmalay discovering my desire for another man, but Darmalay was far away, enthralled with his new wife, and I was lonely. Who would see if I slipped into Samar's tent in the deepest part of the night? I smoothed my hair. Samar looked at me when I touched my hair and I knew he would welcome me into his tent.

At the far end of the fire, Ma'zur laughed loudly, drawing all eyes to him. He held up his cup and turned it over so we could see it was empty. "More wine," he yelled. He grabbed his neck and coughed as though his throat was filled with dust, "I'm dry, I need more wine."

A slave ran to fill his cup. Ma'zur drank until the cup was empty, belched and reached over to yank one of Yazil's braids. "My wife should watch to make sure my cup is full." She frowned and pulled away from his hand. Ma'zur looked around the fire and laughed. "My wife is yet a child, she does not know how to please her husband."

"She'll learn," yelled a man and I laughed with the others, thinking of my first year with Darmalay, holding him at night with our arms wrapped tight around each other, feeling his heart beat under my lips.

Samar clapped his hands and an old man appeared in the firelight, walking carefully with a finger to his lips like a drunken man who hopes his wife is asleep. Guests around the fire laughed at his arrival. Ma'zur laughed loudest of all. "Here is a good poet," he yelled. "A famous poet, not the trash that hangs around the caravan picking up dung." Yazil glanced at her husband and down at her hands.

The old poet opened his arms and began to recite the first lines of a poem. His voice sounded as though he had swallowed a mouthful of sand as he sang about the virtues of a fast camel and a village of lonely women whose husbands were away hunting.

The poet finished speaking. He held a wineskin above his head and poured wine into his mouth until his eyes bulged. He threw the bag on the sand, wiped his lips, and began reciting another poem.

"Samar," I said, "I didn't know you brought a poet with you."

"He does not belong to me." Samar moved closer until I could feel his breath against my cheek. "Bilqis," he whispered.

I leaned toward him, feeling drowsy from the heat of the fire and the wine.

"Who is that?" Ma'zur's loud voice woke me. The merchant was pointing at Amdar, who stood next to the old poet while the old man shouted the last lines of his poem. The old poet bowed to Amdar and abruptly sat down. He yawned and laid his head in the lap of a merchant's wife. She laughed, pushed him away, and he rolled over on the sand, folded his hands under his head and closed his eyes.

Amdar was dressed in a tunic of faded blue linen, patched at the knee. His hair was loose under a headband of twisted leather. He held a wooden staff in his hand. He laid the staff on the sand, bowed to Samar and opened his arms to embrace the circle. I sipped wine as I listened to Amdar's words. His voice was low and soothing after the raspy shouting of the old poet.

"Listen, O my brothers, listen, O my sisters, O, listen.
I am a poor poet.
I possess a robe of holes upon my back,
I possess a staff to count my steps across the burning sand,
and I possess the memory of my beloved.
She stood in the opening of her black-striped tent
like a gazelle before a river of spring rain.
Her black hair flowed to her waist and her face was the bright moon
pushing aside curtains of night.
I watched beneath a thorn tree while slaves braided her hair with
jasmine and pearls, and there floated to me a fragrance that was
sweeter than incense and crushed mint.
The sun burned down the sky and shadows grew long when slaves
brought bowls of fresh milk to her tent.
Ah, the sight of her brown throat lifted to drink sent arrows through
my heart."

"Careful, little poet," yelled Ma'zur. "You will lose your head if you speak of our wives."

"I speak of every woman," Amdar said. "For every woman is beautiful."

"You speak of our wives." Ma'zur placed his hand on Yazil's shoulder and pushed up from his cushions. She bit her lips and did not move under the weight of his hand.

Amdar smiled across the fire at the merchant. "How would you know your wife's tent, Ma'zur of Myrb? If I had spoken of a tent with brown stripes, a slave's tent, would you have known the woman?"

Ma'zur shook his fist at Amdar. "I'll feed your tongue to the dogs if you do not watch your words."

Samar clapped his hands and the two men looked at him. "This is a celebration, my brothers," he said. "Forget your quarrel tonight."

People around the fire laughed, picked up their empty cups and waved them at the slaves. Ma'zur again leaned his weight on Yazil to sit down. She rubbed her shoulder when he lifted his hand. Amdar picked up his staff, glanced at Yazil and backed out of the firelight.

"The young poet should not cross words with my guests." Samar held up his cup to an approaching slave. "I do not want a fight around my fire tonight."

"Ma'zur is angry with Yazil." I watched as the young woman smiled at her husband and offered him a piece of meat. He knocked the meat from her fingers and crossed his arms over his chest when she reached for his hand.

"He is her husband," Samar said.

Ma'zur spoke to Yazil. She gathered her robes and stood. He turned his back to her and talked with a man sitting next to him, making him laugh. Yazil walked around the circle toward me, her eyes cast down.

I stood when she was close to my rug, ignoring Samar's whispered, "Bilqis, do not interfere."

"Yazil." I held my hand to the girl. Her eyes were wet. "Are you sick?"

"My husband says it is time for me to return to my tent," she whispered. Tears slid down her cheeks. "He says I have brought shame upon him."

I said loudly so the people closest to me would hear. "I regret you are unwell, my child. Let my companion walk you to your tent."

Tylos stood and put her arm around Yazil. "I'll take you home," she said.

"Bilqis." Samar spoke in a low voice when I sat down again. "You must not come between a man and his wife."

"He slaps her and dishonors her in front of your guests."

"He is her husband and she is a child. She has much to learn."

"Is that how you trained your wives?" My whisper was a hiss. "Did you beat them if they did not obey you?"

The eyes he turned on me were hard. "I did not take girls for wives. I married women who knew how to please a man."

He looked away from me and the air between us was cold.

I told Tylos my head ached and we left Samar's feast and walked back to our camp. My head was spinning from the wine. Tylos held my arm so I would not stumble over the dried palm leaves that grabbed my feet. Behind us, Samar's guests were laughing at another song by the old poet.

"Poor Yazil," yawned Tylos. "She was afraid of her husband tonight. Samar should tell Amdar he must not anger Ma'zur by speaking of her."

"Samar thinks Ma'zur is correct in punishing his wife," I said. "I will speak with Amdar."

"This is not your concern, Bilqis, let Ma'zur handle his wife."

Tylos stopped in front of our tent to pull a palm leaf from her foot. "You seemed to enjoy Samar's attentions. I saw him whispering to you before Amdar spoke."

I hung on to a tent pole to keep from falling. "Samar won't defend Yazil," I said. "He's not my friend."

Timora and Samsi were asleep on their mats. Candlelight cast our shadows, jumping against the side of the tent. Tylos yawned and shrugged off her robe. I fell on my mat and held on to it while it tilted from side to side until I fell asleep.

~ Eleven ~

Oh, my head was heavy the next morning. My heart felt sore from the bitter words I had spoken to Samar. The smell of baking bread made my stomach heave. I pulled the sheepskin over my head and went back to sleep.

When I woke, Timora was sitting beside my sleeping mat, sewing a tunic of faded blue linen. A steaming cup of mint tea was placed on the mat next to me.

"Timora, my girl, you are a blessing from the god." I sat up, groaning at the pounding in my head and picked up the fragrant tea. "Where are Samsi and Tylos?"

The girl tugged thread through a patch she was sewing on the tunic. "Samsi and Khe are gathering dung for the fire. Tylos is at the well. She said to let you sleep as long as you wished. Damri Samar announced the caravan will stay at the oasis for three days to rest the camels."

"What are you sewing?" I pointed to the garment in her lap.

"Amdar's tunic. It was torn when Ma'zur's slaves beat him."

"Amdar was beaten? When did this happen?"

"The slaves found him sleeping behind Yazil's tent after the feast last night and beat him." She held up the tunic. There was a spot of darker blue at the neck. "I washed out the blood."

I held my aching head while I sipped the tea. "That little poet will dishonor Yazil if he doesn't leave her alone. Tell Khe to bring Amdar to me after our midday meal."

I woke again when Tylos laid a cool cloth on my forehead. "You do not have a head for wine, Bilqis. You drank too much last night and you didn't eat enough food."

"I drank two cups of wine." I sat up and pressed the cloth against my temples. "Ah, this feels good."

"I counted four cups and Samar's wine was not watered."

"That many?" I wiped my face and neck and drank a mouthful of the cooled mint tea. "Timora said Ma'zur's slaves beat Amdar last night after the feast."

Tylos shook her head. "This morning, she heard women at the well say that Ma'zur has vowed to kill Amdar if he looks at his wife."

"Khe is bringing Amdar to our fire today," I said. "I will tell him to stay away from Yazil."

"You take great care for a masterless poet, Bilqis."

"He is young and in love. Ma'zur is a fool to have him beaten. Yazil will turn her eyes to Amdar when she hears he has suffered for her."

Timora's midday meal of spiced bread and barley soup cleared my head. I rested in the shade of a palm tree, talking with Tylos and watching Samsi and Timora laughing together while they cleaned the tent and hung our sleeping mats and sheepskins over bushes to air in the sun. Slaves talked quietly as they walked past the camps to the wells. I smelled smoke from cookfires, but the rest of the caravan seemed asleep and no one visited us during the long afternoon.

Tylos said she was unwell and laid down inside tent to sleep. Samsi and Timora sat together under the awning outside the closed curtain. Samsi worked green thread around a design of palm leaves that Timora had drawn for her. The older girl was bent over her mending. I saw blue silk in her lap from the tunic I had worn the night before. I remembered stepping on the hem when I stood to leave Samar's feast after our harsh words.

Timora worked quickly, repairing the torn silk with tiny stitches. Her hands were always busy, I rarely saw her at rest. She rose before the night sky paled to make the fire and cook our food. She worked quietly all day, sweeping sand from the tent and putting away our clothing to make our tent a comfortable home. I wondered if she missed Myrb. Other female slaves had found friends in the different camps. They walked to the wells together and flirted with the guards and the male slaves. Timora seemed content to stay in our camp with Samsi as her only friend.

She should be content, I thought. Tylos and I were not demanding, we did not punish her if smoke from the cookfire blew into the tent. I had heard the cries from female slaves in other camps being beaten for spilling a bucket of water or burning the morning bread. I had learned long ago to treat a slave kindly. Before Tylos came to me as my companion, Hazza had given a slave girl to me to keep my room clean and tend my clothing. The girl was clumsy and broke a beautiful clay cup my father had given to me as a wedding gift. I slapped her when I saw the broken cup on the floor, so hard that she wore my handprint on her cheek all morning.

Hazza rushed into my room when she heard the girl crying. Hazza's brown eyes were almost black with anger as she faced me. "You stupid girl. Your slave is with you always. Treat her badly and her eyes will be daggers in your back. Be kind and she will care for you as if you were made of gold."

I had not liked Hazza yelling at me, but I heard the truth in her words and tried to be more patient with the slave.

Timora had folded her mending and was winding thread around her needle when Amdar walked into my camp. One of his eyes was closed under a dark bruise and his bottom lip was swollen and split in the middle. He wore the blue tunic Timora had mended for him.

Samsi jumped up and seized his hand. "Amdar, you're hurt."

He smiled and touched his bottom lip. "I'm well, Samsi. It's a small cut."

"Amdar." I pointed to a rug laid next to me. "Sit with me." I waited until he was seated and said, "Ma'zur had you beaten when he found you sleeping next to his wife's tent. I fear for you, poet, and I fear for Yazil if you continue to notice her." I held up my hand when he started to speak. "Listen to me, you must leave Yazil alone."

He licked his sore lip. "I love Yazil. I have vowed to protect her."

"You do not protect her by speaking of her in your poems and sleeping next to her tent. Ma'zur will beat her if he thinks she is acting the wanton with you."

"Ma'zur is a bag of shit," said Amdar.

"Shit he may be," I said. "But Yazil is his wife."

"I fear for her."

"I'll ask her to eat at my fire tomorrow," I said. "Ma'zur will value his wife if I honor her with attention."

The young poet leaned over, raised my hand to his lips and kissed it. "She is the love of my heart," he whispered. "Keep her safe."

After he walked away from my camp, I thought again of my first year with Darmalay; how I could not swallow even the softest cheese when I felt his gaze upon me, and the nights we made love until morning light. We laughed when we heard the city gates pushed open at dawn. "It is too late to sleep," Darmalay would whisper, and we made love again until a slave coughed outside my curtain, waiting for permission to enter with a jar of fresh water for my room.

The camp came alive when the sun slid behind the mountain and the air grew cooler. I heard laughter around cookfires but I did not invite other women to feast with me. Timora wiped the cups and bowls after our meal. Tylos lay by the fire wrapped in her sheepskin, sipping a cup of feverroot tea and complaining that her head hurt. Samsi sewed beads on the waistbag she was making for Khe.

I looked at the white face of the moon and wondered where Samar feasted tonight. I had seen him during the day, visiting other camps, but he had not approached my boundary stone and did not look at me when he walked past.

Tylos raised her head. "Have you thought of questions for King Solomon? You said you would think of questions to ask him when you met."

I tossed a piece of palm bark on the fire. "I thought of one after we rode through the sayl. I would ask him to tell me when the sky lies upon the earth."

Tylos thought for a moment. "The earth is in the sky during a sandstorm, but the sky does not lie upon the earth." She pulled her sheepskin over her shoulders and yawned. "I don't know the answer."

Samsi waved her hand, "I know, " she said. "It's rainwater. Amdar wrote it in one of his poems. He says the sky joins with the earth when it rains and the rainwater is the gift of his jeweled seed."

"That is not for your ears, my girl," Tylos said. "Your poet should not recite poems like that to you."

"I heard him singing it behind Yazil's tent."

"He should not be singing any of his poems to Ma'zur's wife."

"Well," I said, to stop their quarrel. "If a masterless poet knows the answer it is too easy a question for King Solomon."

"Look at this, Bilqis." Samsi held up a large amber bead. "I cannot thread it."

Firelight swirled bright orange around a crooked line cut through the bead. "It's badly drilled," I said. "See in the middle, where one line stops below the drill mark from the other side? We'll need stronger thread to turn inside the bead."

Timora fetched silver wire and gilded camel hair and I tried to push each through the bead, but each thread bent and stopped when it reached the middle.

"It's hopeless," said Tylos. "Thread will not go through and the bead will break if it is drilled again."

I tossed the bead in my hand, watching it flicker in firelight. "This is a good question for King Solomon. I'll present it to him."

Tylos laughed. "Solomon is a great king, do you think he will listen to a question about women's work?"

"I have heard he enjoys puzzles that make him think," I said. "If four women cannot figure out how to thread a bead, then it is a good question for a wise man."

"Let us think of other questions for the king," said Samsi. She tapped a finger against her lips, humming as she gazed into the fire.

"I know of one." Tylos picked up a dried root from the small pile of wood next to the fire. "My mother taught this to me; which end of this root seeks the dirt and which end reaches for the sky?"

We looked at the piece of wood. The root hairs were rubbed off and both ends were cracked and dry. I wondered how to tell which end was which.

"Tell us, I cannot think of the answer," said Samsi.

"My father was a healer," said Tylos. "He gathered plants from the desert. One day, he brought my mother a dried root like this and told her a beautiful flower was hidden inside. She put one end in a cup of water and when that became soft, she cut away the soft part and put the other end in the water. I looked into the cup every day and watched white hairs growing from the wood in the water. My mother waited until the cup was full of the white hairs and planted that end into the dirt by the courtyard gate. She told me to give it a drink of water every day."

Tylos coughed and drank a mouthful of tea. "A day later, there was a green leaf poking out of the dirt. Then there were more leaves. It grew into a little bush covered with green buds. The buds opened into red flowers that brushed against my legs when I walked through the gate. I would look down to see if my legs were streaked with red."

I leaned over and hugged her thin shoulders, "I will ask King Solomon which end of the root to plant and we will see if the great king is as wise as your mother."

Samsi rolled her needle and thread and the box of beads inside the goatskin bag. "Amdar is clever," she said. "Ask your questions of him. If he cannot guess them, King Solomon will not know the answer."

Tylos yawned loudly. "I hope he is as wise as King Solomon and stays away from Yazil."

Samsi smoothed the leather bag. "Amdar gathered wood near her tent today but he didn't see her. He said the female slave who attends Ma'zur was sweeping out Yazil's tent. He said she was wearing one of Yazil's gold bracelets. Amdar is worried because he cannot find her."

"Enough of Amdar," I said. "I told him to stay away from Yazil. Your poet is to blame if Ma'zur beats his wife." Samsi bent her head at my sharp words. I felt old and tired. "I'll invite Yazil to my fire tomorrow," I said. "We will protect her."

Samsi nodded but would not look at me. She stood with her bag under one arm while Timora gathered her food bags and I watched the girls walk to the supply tent, their heads bent close together.

Tylos tucked strands of silver hair under her headcloth. "Samsi speaks before she thinks. You treat her like a daughter and she disobeys like a spoiled child."

"She is a good girl," I said. "She speaks strongly to protect her friend. But she and Amdar have to learn that their actions hurt Yazil. Visit Yazil's tent in the morning and invite her to join me for the day. We will keep her with us until Ma'zur forgets his anger toward his wife."

Tylos returned from her visit the next morning and told me Yazil's tent was closed. "The slave said her mistress was unwell. Amdar is right, Bilqis, the slave wears a gold bracelet on her wrist."

I sat beside the cold cookfire, shivering inside my wool robe, watching Timora blow on a coal of smoking dung. "Take a bag of herbs to Yazil's tent," I said. "Tell the slave that Bilqis sends a gift to the wife of Ma'zur. Tell her I welcome Yazil to my fire."

Tylos was back before Timora had peeled the first piece of bread from the cookplate. "I didn't see Yazil," she said. "The slave stood before her closed tent and said she was asleep. I spoke loudly when I handed the herbs to her so Ma'zur would hear that Bilqis, wife of Darmalay, sends a gift to Yazil and wishes to see her when she has recovered."

She put her hand to her head. "I feel sick, Bilqis. I'm going to bed."

While Tylos slept, Khe set a large pot of water on the fire to heat. Timora and Samsi brought out a bag of our soiled clothing. They scrubbed at stains on our robes and tunics with handfuls of wet sand and dropped them into the hot water to soak. Samsi lifted each piece of clothing out of the pot with a wooden paddle and piled it in a steaming heap next to the fire. When all of the garments were washed, the girls wrung them out and hung them to dry on ropes they stretched between two palm trees.

Samar walked past my camp at midday. He glanced at me where I sat under the awning, talking with Tylos. I hoped he would stop, but he only nodded when I lifted my hand in greeting and kept walking toward his tent.

"Have you heard more of Yazil?" Tylos said.

I waited until she stopped coughing to answer. "No, I sent Samsi to Ma'zur's camp to ask Yazil to eat with us tonight. A slave told her Yazil still is sick."

"What can you do? You cannot command Ma'zur to show his wife."

"I'll invite Samar to visit Ma'zur's camp with me. Ma'zur will not refuse me entrance to his wife's tent if Samar is with me."

After Tylos went back inside the tent to rest, I sent Timora to ask Samar to come to my fire. I watched as she knocked against the pole holding the front curtain to his tent. He appeared and nodded when she pointed toward my cookfire.

I waited quietly in the shade of a palm tree while he approached. He sat on a rug next to me. "Samar," I said. "I regret my harsh words at your feast. They were not the words of a friend."

He looked at me for a moment. "I think my wine was too strong. Many of my guests woke with aching heads after my feast."

I was grateful that he was willing to forgive my hard words. We sat in silence, watching Timora and Samsi pull dried clothing off the ropes. Timora gestured for Samsi to sit with her under the tent awning. They faced each other and folded the clean clothing. The two girls working in view outside the tent meant no one could say Samar visited me when I was alone.

"I ask you to feast with me tonight," I said to Samar. "And I ask for your help. I'm concerned about Yazil. Her tent has been closed all day. Her slave said Yazil is sick but the slave wears one of Yazil's gold bracelets."

Samar let out a breath. "You sound like my wives, anxious if a child is out of their sight."

"Do your wives worry that you are gone so long?" I asked. "I wonder that you did not bring a companion on this journey."

"My wives are happier at home." He smiled at me as he had before our quarrel. "I feel as though one of my wives is with me now, asking my help in protecting someone who is weak. I'll come to your fire tonight and I'll talk to Ma'zur today and tell him Queen Bilqis wishes to attend his sick wife."

I had forgotten that I was to be called queen when we met King Solomon. I savored the word I would enjoy using it to command Ma'zur to show his wife to me.

Tylos woke after Samar left, drank a bowl of soup and lay down again. I opened the back curtain to let air flow through the tent and told Samsi to watch over the old woman while she slept.

Timora made Samar's favorite dishes when she heard he was joining me. She baked bread with crushed cinnamon kneaded into the dough, goat meat roasted with garlic and rosemary, and a plate of honeyed nut cakes. Samsi unrolled two rugs around the fire.

Tylos woke as I pulled on a tunic and robe of cream-colored wool embroidered with gold thread at the neckline. "Are you attending a feast tonight?" she asked.

I slipped a gold bracelet on my wrist. "I have invited Damri Samar to eat with me. I have not talked with him since his feast. I would be his friend again."

Tylos smiled at my words and then groaned and lay down.

Timora was laying bread and cheese on a platter when I stepped from the tent. "Tylos is awake," I said. "Take soup and bread to her. She'll sleep after she eats. I want you and Samsi to sit near the fire while Samar is here."

She nodded, "Samsi and I will sew."

Samsi looked up as she set a jar of heated wine on one of the rugs. "Tylos gave me two beads for my bag." She opened her waistbag, pulled out the beads and held them to me. A lion and a horse, both carved of bone ivory lay on her palm.

I touched the beads, separating them. "Lions are enemies to horses. Do not sew them close together."

"Have you seen a lion?" Samsi asked.

"I saw one once when I was riding in the desert with my father. The lion was far away and sleeping in the shade of a dune. All I could see was a yellow lump, but I was afraid it would wake up and run across the desert at me. My father told me not to worry. He said lions would attack a man or beast walking alone, but we were safe on our camels."

"Have you ridden a horse?" Samsi said.

"No, I've seen drawings of horses. King Solomon is said to keep large stables of these animals. We will see them in Jerusalem." I turned to Timora. "What are you sewing tonight?"

"Tylos gave me a length of silk to make a robe for you to wear when you enter Jerusalem," she said. While I watched, she shaped the cheese into flowers around the spiced bread, and I noticed again that Timora made beautiful everything she touched.

Ilumqah had risen above the sands when Samar stepped over the black boundary stone to my camp. Timora and Samsi sat before the closed curtain. They looked up when Samar approached and then down at their sewing.

"I welcome you," I said to Samar. He held out his hand to me and we sat down, close to each other on the rugs. I filled his wine cup. We looked at each other until he gently pulled the cup from my hand.

I heard shouts and looked past Samar's tent into Ma'zur's camp. Firelight lit the faces of men and women laughing around the merchant's fire.

"Ma'zur has many friends tonight," Samar said. "I see merchants from Myrb at his feast."

"I do not see his wife by his side. Where is Yazil? Does Ma'zur say she is sick?"

Samar placed his cup on the rug. "He says she is recovering and wishes to keep to her tent until she is well again." He touched the back of my hand. "Your skin is soft."

Tylos called and Samsi jumped up and entered the tent.

"Bilqis," Samar whispered. "Come with me. Come to my tent."

I put my hand on his arm and he pulled me up. He smelled of smoke and incense. "Speak to your women so they will not wait for you."

I walked to the tent. "Samar and I are going to the oasis," I said to Timora. "We wish to view Ilumqah in the water when he moves across the sky. It is good fortune to see his face in the water." I was talking too fast, but Timora only nodded.

"I may be late," I said. "Do not leave a candle burning in the tent for my return."

I followed Samar away from the light of the cookfire, into the shadowed darkness between our camps. We waited in the dark for a moment as a man hurried past my camp, late to Ma'zur's feast. When he was gone, Samar took my hand and we walked to the back of his tent. Samar dropped my hand to untie the curtain. I felt we were alone in the desert. The night wind blew a streamer of sand off a large dune in the distance, skinny caravan dogs sleeping near the camel herds growled at dreamed scents. Moonlight gleamed on the humped backs of sleeping camels as our moon god traveled over the land.

My heart beat faster when Samar pulled back his curtain. I was nervous. I had not been with another man beside my husband. I pushed Darmalay from my mind. He was with Amida, he was not thinking about me.

"Come." Samar took my hand and led me into his tent. The sand was covered with a large red wool rug patterned with black stripes. A candle burned next to his unrolled sleeping mat. A sheepskin was neatly folded at the foot of the mat. I thought of my tent with the garments of four women hanging from pegs or tossed into open baskets at the back of the tent.

"Wait here." Samar walked to his mat and blew out the candle. I could see his dark form in the moonlight. He held out his arms. "Come to me," he whispered.

The feel of his mouth surprised me; his lips were soft, not hard like Darmalay's. He untied my tunic. I put my face against his neck as the silk slid down my body and dropped to the rug at my feet. I shivered. He opened his robe and held me tight against his warm body.

"Bilqis," he moaned, and pulled me down to the mat.

~ Twelve ~

The moon was resting on top of the mountains when Samar and I stepped from the back of his tent. Camps around us were quiet, the smoke of cookfires blown away in the night wind. We walked across the cold sand to the back of my closed tent. Samar kissed me and I held tightly to him until he whispered, "Go inside, my love."

Timora and Samsi were dark forms lying on their mats at the front of the tent. Tylos slept next to the back curtain. I waited inside the curtain for a moment, letting my eyes adjust to the dark. I heard movement. Timora pushed herself up on one elbow and looked at me.

"Go back to sleep," I said. "I'm home."

My mat was unrolled on the other side of the tent, far from Tylos in her sickness. A sheepskin was laid on my mat with a corner pulled back to show the soft wool. I undressed, pulled a sleep tunic over my head and slid under the sheepskin.

I lay awake, too excited to sleep. I touched my lips that were rough from kissing Samar, remembering his hands stroking my face, my breasts, between my legs.

Tylos's groaning woke me the next morning. She walked through the back curtain into the tent holding her belly, followed by Timora carrying a bundle of clothing.

"Oh, my poor Tylos," I said.

Timora dropped the bundle on the ground and helped Tylos lie down on her mat. "Stay with Tylos today," I said. "She needs your strong arm."

Timora sat beside Tylos. "I will care for her as long as she needs me." She pulled a sheepskin over Tylos's shoulder and looked at me. "I will care for all of you in our tent." I knew then that Tylos had lain awake the night before until I returned from Samar's tent, and I knew she would say nothing that would harm our tent or me.

Samsi sat at Timora's place at the cookfire, kneading dough. She smiled when I stepped from the tent. "Timora told me to make bread," she said, proud of her work.

"Make a lot this morning," I said. "Damri Samar will join us."

She looked at me and for a moment I feared she too, knew I had gone to Samar's tent last night. She bit her lips as she added more flour to the bowl. I realized she was nervous about Samar eating her bread

"Add a pinch of anise to the dough," I said. "It will comfort Tylos's belly."

I stood by the cookfire, warming my hands while the bread cooked. I wanted to be alone to dream about my night with Samar, but I could not get away. There was no place for me to hide from the women in my tent.

Samar stepped out of his tent and walked toward my fire. My heart beat faster as I held my hands out in welcome. I could not stop smiling. We sat by the fire as Samsi pulled bread off the cookplate and carefully laid it on the platter. She set the platter of bread and cheese and a jar of heated wine before us.

I told her to take bread and a cup of wine to Tylos. "Come out again," I said to the girl. "I want you to sit with me while Damri Samar visits my camp."

Samar reached for my hand when the curtain closed behind Samsi. As I moved closer to him, he slipped a bracelet of jasper beads on my wrist.

"For you, my love." He caressed my fingers. "Shall I stop, Bilqis?"

"Never," I whispered.

"Come to me tonight." He ran his finger along the back of my hand.

"I will," I murmured.

The sound of Tylos coughing inside the tent made him pull his hand away. He blew out a long breath of air while I moved away from him. "One sees, all know," he said and picked up his wine.

"Ah, Bilqis and Damri Samar." Ma'zur shouted a greeting and stepped over my boundary stone. He walked toward us, smiling, and I wondered why he invited himself to my fire.

"Join us, Ma'zur of Myrb," I said. Samsi stepped through the curtain and hurried to unroll a rug for Ma'zur.

He put his hand on Samsi's shoulder to ease his body onto the rug. He grabbed her hand before she could move away. "You're a good girl," he said. Samsi frowned and wiped her hand on her tunic.

"Ah, a meal with friends," said Ma'zur. "Yes, we all are friends on the caravan, even my wife has a good friend in you, Bilqis."

He accepted a cup of wine from Samsi. She moved away before he could touch her again. "Yazil wanted to join your fire this morning, but I told her woman to let her sleep. She says my wife is sick at first light and hungry in the afternoon." He winked at me. "I think my Yazil is with child."

"A woman bearing her first child is often sick in the morning," I said. "Yazil is welcome to my fire. The company of another woman who has borne a child is comforting to a first time mother."

Ma'zur wiped his lips. "You honor my wife. She will come to you when she feels better."

"I'll visit her at midday if she does not wish to leave her tent." I pointed at Samsi to fill his cup, but Ma'zur waved her away and stood, more quickly than I had seen him move.

"I will tell Yazil to make ready for your visit." He bowed to me and walked from my cookfire.

"He is anxious to return to his wife," I said.

Samar nodded. "Ma'zur will treat her kindly now she is with child."

Samsi began to tie her food bags. "Ask Tylos if she needs anything," I said.

After Samsi left, Samar touched my hand. "I have to leave, my Bilqis."

"Eat with me at midday," I said.

"I'll try to come to you after I visit the other camps. I hear many people are sick."

"Tylos is unwell this morning. She may not be able to ride tomorrow."

Samar glanced at the camps surrounding us. Save for the cook slaves, few people sat around their cookfires. "I want to leave tomorrow morning," he said. "But we'll stay if people cannot travel. Farium has seen this before; the whole caravan sickens as one during the journey."

Tylos's skin was greasy in sleep. Her cheeks were sunken. Her sheepskin was pushed to her waist and her tunic was dark with sweat. Timora laid a cool cloth on her forehead. "She's hot and then cold. She drank bad water somewhere. We're not sick, so the water was from another tent. They must have let it stand uncovered and an evil spirit entered it."

We both made the horned sign against the evil eye. "Samar says many are sick today," I said. "Where is Samsi?"

"I sent her to the well." Timora pointed to a bundle of cloth she had dropped next to the back curtain. "I must wash Tylos's sleeping tunic and we need fresh water for drinking."

"I want Samsi to go with me to visit the Myrb women this morning," I said. "We'll be back soon."

I waited by the fire while Samsi delivered water to Timora and watched two slaves working in Samar's camp. One boy swept the tent, another carried out Samar's sheepskin to air in the sun. I remembered the sheepskin covering us after we had lain together. I gazed at the jasper bracelet on my wrist. The brown and cream-colored beads looked as though they had been formed from the desert around us. Swirls of brown were the soft-sided dunes. Several beads had blue dots that reminded me of the water in the oasis. The largest bead had reddish streak, shaped like the mountains we rode past. I was pleased that Samar had chosen a gift that blended so well with the color of my skin. I could wear the bracelet freely. People on the caravan wore carnelian, lapis, silver, and gold. They would not notice my brown beads.

Samsi said goodbye to Timora and we walked together down the line of camps laid along the common path. Curtains were pulled open at the front and back of tents to air out the smell of sickness. We passed merchants sitting with their wives in front of the women's tents. They waved a greeting but no one sent a slave running to ask us to join them.

"People are not well enough to offer us welcome," I said.

Wa'dab's tent was closed. A slave sweeping out the supply tent stopped and looked at us when we stepped over the boundary stone. "Don't drink the water," I said to Samsi. "It will sicken us if it has been left standing."

"I know," she whispered. "Timora told me before we left."

The slave walked toward us, carrying a handful of dried palm leaves. "Tell your mistress, Bilqis of Myrb visits her," I said.

"Bilqis!" A women's voice shouted my name and Wa'dab pushed through the tent curtain. She hurried toward me with her hands outstretched as though she had waited many days for my visit.

"Let us sit out here, my sister." She pointed to rugs laid at the far end of the cookfire. "My companion is sick. She has not stopped shitting for two days." Wa'dab fanned her nose with her hand. "We keep the back curtain open, but the tent still stinks. Whew!" She clapped her hands and the slave dropped her broom. "Bring food for my guests," she yelled.

We sat around the fire while her slave offered dates and cups of cooled water. "Don't bother visiting the other women from Myrb." Flesh wobbled under her arm when she pointed to a nearby camp. "They are sick, their slaves are sick, only I am well."

"And your husband?" I asked. "He was unwell at Samar's feast."

"He recovered the next day." Wa'dab looked at the cups of water we had not touched. "You are not thirsty?"

"I have appetite only for your good dates," I said.

She smiled, "Come back tonight and I will fill your cup with my husband's best wine. He will join us if you ask Samar to feast with us."

A shock went through me at Samar's name on her lips. "I do not know where Damri Samar eats tonight," I said.

She lifted her eyebrows, "No? But he is your protector. The slaves say he is always at your camp."

"The gossip of slaves is loud but not always truthful," I replied.

She drank from her cup. I stared at her, waiting for her next words. I feared she knew I had lain with Samar.

Wa'dab swallowed a mouthful of water before replying. "They say he still sleeps alone. Ah, no matter, here or there, Samar is welcome wherever he visits."

Samsi touched my arm and pointed to the slave who sat under the awning, weaving the palm leaves into a broom. "Go and learn," I said.

"My slave makes the best brooms in Myrb." Wa'dab held her hand to her heart. "Bilqis, I have heard bad news. Ma'zur visited me before you came. He said his wife ran away with another man after Samar's feast. Ma'zur says he told people she was sick because he is shamed that she ran away."

Wa'dab sat back and slapped her hands together as if she was dusting off dirt. "She was a little harlot, that one. My husband said he could not pass her tent without her opening the curtain to show herself to him."

"Ma'zur told me this morning that his wife was sick because she is with child," I said. "Now he says she ran away? I wonder what story he will tell next. Yazil is still a child. She should be at home, learning to keep house for her husband, not riding on a caravan with many eyes upon her."

"My husband does not seek other women," said Wa'dab. "But he could not help looking when she opened her curtain."

"Yazil is young. She needs the guidance of friends." I stood up before Wa'dab could reply. "I must return to my tent," I said. I was angry at her talk of Yazil, but Darmalay had taught me in the council room that allowing the words of others to anger me was a sign of weakness. Wa'dab was not a friend to me; I would not let her see that her words upset me.

Samsi ran after me. I stopped when we were out of sight of Wa'dab's camp. "That woman's tongue drips poison!" I said. Samsi stared at me. I took a deep breath and said, "Wa'dab is saying what the whole camp will say, that Yazil ran away with another man."

"Maybe Yazil is gone," she said. "Amdar does not know where she is." Samsi ducked her head and spoke softly, worried that I would be angry with her friend.

"What does Amdar say?" I asked.

Samsi slipped her hand into mine and lengthened her steps to my pace. "He says he cannot hear her breath when he listens at the back curtain and there are no footmarks leaving her tent."

"I will find the truth, "I said. "I will ask Samar to go with me today to visit Yazil. Ma'zur will not refuse the leader of the caravan." I pointed toward our camp. "Look, Tylos is awake."

The old woman sat by the fire, waving her cup at us. "There you are, Bilqis," she called. "I wondered if I had to send Khe to track you." Timora sat next to her, mixing a bowl of bread dough. "Timora is cooking early for me. I am so hungry."

I laughed. "I see you feel better."

Samar walked into my camp after we finished eating. I felt my cheeks warm when he appeared. Timora rose and called Samsi to help her gather the food bags for the supply tent. Tylos returned to the tent to sleep.

I filled Samar's cup with cooled wine. "I visited Wa'dab this morning," I said. "She said Ma'zur is telling people that Yazil ran away after your feast, but Amdar says he cannot find her footmarks leaving her tent."

Samar frowned. "I had not heard. I'll send Farium to look for tracks outside the caravan. He knows the marks of every man, woman, and camel. He'll know if Ma'zur's wife left the camp."

"Come with me now and visit Ma'zur," I said. "He will not refuse to let me see Yazil if you're with me."

"We will visit later, after Farium looks for signs that Yazil left the oasis." Samar glanced at the closed curtain to my tent and whispered, "Come to me tonight, my love."

I moved my cushions to the front of the tent after Samar left and lay in the shade of the awnings, listening to sounds in the camps that were as comforting as the sounds of my house in Myrb. Slaves laughed and talked together as they carried buckets of water from the wells near the lake at the heart of the oasis, palm leaves shifted overhead, camels groaned as they settled into the heat of the day. I heard Timora humming as she sewed inside the tent. Samsi walked out of the supply tent with a bucket in her hand and waved goodbye to me as she walked toward the wells. I drew my feet into the shade and closed my eyes.

Samsi's cries woke me. I jerked upright and the girl fell into my arms.

"What's wrong?" I asked. Behind me, Tylos and Timora ran from the tent. .

"Ma'zur grabbed me when I was coming back from the well. He picked me up and rubbed me against his belly."

"Did he harm you?" Tylos knelt next to the girl. Samsi turned her face into my shoulder and would not speak.

"Tell me girl, did he harm you?" Tylos pulled one of Samsi's braids to make her look up.

Samsi jerked away from Tylos's hand. "No. I screamed but he wouldn't let me go. Slaves were watching and they didn't help me."

"How did you get away?" I asked.

"Damri Samar helped me." Her face was smeared with snot and tears, but she smiled when she said his name. "He told Ma'zur to let me go. Ma'zur dropped me on the sand and said Samar could have me."

"What happened then?" I asked.

Samsi shivered, cuddling closer to me. "Samar walked with me until we reached our camp. He told me to go to you."

"Take Samsi inside the tent," I said to Timora. "I will speak with Ma'zur."

Tylos groaned when she stood up. "I'll go with you, Bilqis."

"No, you stay with the girls."

I took Samar's dagger from my red bag and stuck it in my waistband, under my robe. I walked across hot sand toward Ma'zur's camp. I thought of yanking his head back and slitting his fat throat.

Samar stepped from his tent as I passed his camp. I stopped before him. "I thank you for protecting Samsi." I wanted to push him out of the way and find Ma'zur.

"Ma'zur is angry, Bilqis." He kept his voice low.

"I don't care about his anger. He harmed a child from my tent." I wanted to scream the words so all would hear.

Samar looked around to see who was watching us. Behind my tent, Farium and Khe moved among my herd of camels. A group of Farium's men sat in the shade of their camels, guarding bags and baskets piled high on the sand; Darmalay's treasure for King Solomon.

"There is more," said Samar. "Farium reported that no camels or people left the caravan after my feast. Yazil did not run away that night."

I opened my robe slightly to show Samar the dagger in my waistband. "Let me ask Ma'zur what happened to his wife."

"No," said Samar. "Leave this to me. I will ask the merchants of Myrb to sit in council with me tomorrow morning. We'll hear Ma'zur's claim that his wife ran away and we will hear Farium say no camels rode from the oasis."

"And if Ma'zur says he killed Yazil?" I gripped the hilt of the dagger. "What is his punishment?"

"Her family will learn of his crime long before we reach Jerusalem. Ma'zur will pay a blood price when he returns to Myrb."

"A blood price! Her life was worth more than a handful of gold!"

"The price will be decided by Yazil's family. Who knows what value they place on her life?"

"I valued her, more than her worthless husband."

"Bilqis, you do not like Ma'zur because he does not respect his wife. There are many men like him."

"You are not like Ma'zur and neither is Darmalay." My husband's name was a rock dropped between us. I thought of the way Darmalay slowly scratched his beard, his eyes half-closed while he listened to my counsel. I felt tired. It seemed a long time since I had talked with him, a long time since we left Myrb.

"I think of Darmalay." Samar held his hand to me. "He is my brother." He dropped his hand when I did not take it and we stood together without speaking.

"Tylos feels better," I said to end the silence.

"That is good news. People are recovering. We'll leave midday tomorrow if they are well enough to ride." He looked at the palm trees around us. "This oasis feels cursed. Sickness and a missing girl, we are well away from here."

Khe delivered the message before our evening meal that Samar was gathering a council and would not join my fire that night. The boy scratched flea bites on his legs, "He will come to your tent in the morning, after the council," he said.

So I would sleep alone tonight. Another reason to hate Ma'zur.

The merchant feasted what locked like half the caravan at his cookfire. I heard men shouting and laughing while I turned from side to side on my mat. The ground was hard; we had slept on this sand for too many nights.

Tylos kept Timora and Samsi busy the next morning, packing up the tent while I sat behind the front curtain, listening for voices from Samar's camp. I heard nothing until the men left his tent, talking together.

Samar walked toward my camp and I stepped outside the curtain to meet him. "What did Ma'zur say?" I asked.

"He says he beat Yazil after my feast when he found the poet sleeping behind her tent. He says she fell and hit her head against the tent pole and died. His slaves buried her in the desert while the caravan slept."

I sighed heavily, thinking of Yazil dying at Ma'zur's hands. "Why did he lie and say she was sick and then say she ran away?"

"He said he was shamed because men thought his wife was a whore."

"Yazil was not a whore; she was girl who did not know how to behave when she was away from her house."

"Ma'zur and his friends see it differently, Bilqis. He brought men into the council who said Yazil smiled at them when they passed her open tent."

I kept silent. There was nothing to say. The foolish girl had shamed her husband and Ma'zur killed her to protect his honor. He would pay a blood price to her family when we returned from Jerusalem and Yazil's name would disappear.

"Bilqis," Samar nodded at my tent. "Tell your women we're leaving soon. We will ride until we stop at sunset."

"Come to my fire before we pack our tent," I said. "Timora will cook bread for you."

He rubbed his face. "If I can. I have much to do before we leave. Be careful, my love, Ma'zur has friends in the camp who support his anger. Keep your women safe inside your tent."

I held up the dagger Samar had given me. "I wear this always. Let Ma'zur or his friends try to enter my tent. They will find four women inside who cared about Yazil and know how to use a knife."

~ Thirteen ~

Hot winds pushed us out of the oasis at midday. I dozed through the long afternoon and woke to find Samar riding beside me. Overhead the sky was bone-white. "A sandstorm is coming behind us," he said. "Farium is looking for shelter."

I dozed again until I heard someone calling my name. Samar yanked open the curtain and pointed to the supply tent. "Hurry, the storm is upon us."

Behind us, a mountain of brown dust rolled toward the caravan. Khe pulled down my camel. I stepped onto the ground and he ran my beast toward a group of camels kneeling with their backs to the wind, patiently waiting out the storm.

The sides of the supply tent sucked in and out in the wind. Tylos opened the curtain as I ran toward the tent, waving at me to hurry. "Samar told us to let you sleep," she said as I ran inside. "He did not want you to wait outside while we raised the tent."

Light from a single candle burned in the hazy air. Samsi and Timora were laying out a platter of food. Tylos tied the curtain against the wind and we sat together, eating dried meat and cheese and drinking from our waterskins. The water was warm and tasted of goat, but it soothed my throat. Our lips were cracked and our voices sounded harsh in the hot, sanded air.

A blast of wind blew open the front curtain. Timora and Samsi ran to close it against the sandstorm blowing violently outside in the brown darkness.

"Rest now," croaked Tylos when we finished eating. "We can do nothing until the storm passes."

We unrolled our mats, moving slowly in the heavy air. We lay down, covering our faces with a piece of wet linen to keep dust from entering our mouths while we slept. I breathed in cooled air until the cloth dried in the heat, and listened to the wind roaring over the camp. We woke again to wind moaning and shrieking outside and what sounded like bucketfuls of sand being thrown against the sides of the tent.

Timora struck a flame and Samsi laid out bread and cheese. Samsi sat back on her heels. "Is it still night?" she asked. I didn't know if the sun or the cool light of the moon shone outside the storm. The air was filled with dust. I felt as though I was breathing through a heavy wool blanket. We ate without speaking and lay down again, covering our faces and waiting for the sandstorm to pass.

Breaths of cool air woke me. The front and back curtains were tied back. Blue sky, like pieces of Egyptian glass, showed through the openings. I rolled onto my knees, coughing dust. Samsi and Timora's mats were empty. Tylos was asleep. I lifted the sand-covered cloth from her mouth. She mumbled in her sleep but did not wake.

Outside the tent I drank a cup of water and breathed in fresh morning air. Timora was baking bread. My mouth filled with water from the smell. Samsi appeared, carrying a bucket of water. "The caravan is covered with sand." she said. "I saw Samar. He said we dig out today. He told me to make a special bread because he will eat with you at midday." She heard Tylos coughing and ran into the tent.

Timora set a platter before me filled with hot bread and cheese and a bowl of honey. I ate as if I had not eaten in many days.

Tylos walked from the tent, her arm around Samsi's shoulders. "Ah, I ache today, Bilqis. I couldn't sleep, I was afraid I would drown in dust if I slept."

"Samar said people may have died," said Samsi. She held on to Tylos's arm until the older woman was seated on the rug next to me.

"Who is it?" I said.

"He didn't say. I heard him tell Farium to take his guards and dig out tents that collapsed in the sandstorm. Samar said anyone inside the tent would have died under the sand."

"Find Khe when you have finished eating," I said. "Tell him I want to know who died and who is injured. We will help where we can today."

Samar walked into my camp after the morning meal. Tylos and I were sorting bags of dried herbs to brew into soothing eyewash. Skin sagged under Samar's eyes. He looked as though he had not slept since I saw him before the storm.

"What news?" I said. "Samsi says some of the tents have collapsed."

He sat next to me, his knee touching mine. "Two slave tents fell and the tent of a merchant. He is someone you will not grieve over."

I crumbled handfuls of dried honeycup and the yellow root of desert candle into a bowl, waiting for the name of the dead merchant. Tylos stirred the herbs into a pot of hot water.

"Ma'zur's tent is under the sand," he said. "He has not been seen."

"I don't rejoice in his death, Samar." I remembered Darmalay saying he celebrated the death of an enemy when he met him in battle, but not if his enemy died at home.

"We're brewing eyewash," I said. "Timora and Samsi will take it around to the women's camps."

"It's good that you help the women on the caravan." Samar cleared his throat and scrubbed his face with his hands. "We still have a long journey before us. You need every woman to be your friend."

"I have neglected them," I said. My head ached and my eyes felt heavy. Feasting the other women seemed like work I did not want to do. But Samar was right; I was respected because I was Darmalay's wife, but Wa'dab's sly comments about my friendship with Samar could damage my name. I needed friends who would defend me.

Tylos and I waited at the back of the crowd, watching slaves dig into the sand covering Ma'zur's flattened tent. Farium stepped forward when the side of the black and white tent was cleared and cut a long slit in the wool. Slaves held the edges open while two men crawled inside. Sand flew out of the opening and then they reappeared, pulling Ma'zur's by his feet. The merchant was on his back. His head dragged through the sand as he emerged. His robe fell open, showing his fat belly.

"Carry him to my camp." Yahmed's voice was loud enough to be heard by the crowd of people. The slaves carefully lifted the merchant's body. Yahmed closed Ma'zur's robe.

"Yahmad takes good care of his friend," I whispered to Tylos.

She laughed. "And he will take good care of his gold. Ma'zur's family will be fortunate to receive a string of wooden beads from Yahmed when he returns from Jerusalem."

Farium picked up the torn end of a tent rope and pressed it against his hand. He showed the rope to Samar who looked closely at it and nodded. Samar turned to follow Ma'zur's body while Farium talked to Khe. The boy ran to me where I stood at the back of the crowd.

"The rope was cut." Khe was speaking before he stopped in front of me. A man standing next to us turned to listen. "The end is clean, it did not pull apart in the storm," said Khe. "My father told me to find Amdar and bring him before Damri Samar to say if he cut the rope."

"Where is Amdar?" I asked.

"I don't know. He stayed in our tent last night, but left before the storm was over."

The man next to me walked away and I knew the story of the poet cutting the rope would be told around cookfires by midday.

"Did you sleep, Khe?" I said. "You look tired."

"I woke when Amdar left and then I could not sleep because I feared he would be lost in the storm."

"He didn't return this morning?"

"No," said the boy. "I looked for him but I haven't seen him."

Samsi and Timora were back before midday, their empty bags flapping at their waists. "No one is badly hurt," Timora said. "The women were grateful for the eyewash."

"Did you see Amdar?" I asked Samsi.

She shook her head. "Khe told me he's missing. He fears Amdar is dead. He thinks Amdar cut the lines to Ma'zur's tent and got lost in the storm."

We looked around. We had arrived in a sandstorm and did not know what lay under the humps of sand.

"My mother said our dead ones wait for us across the river of stars." Samsi wiped her eyes. "Maybe Amdar will meet Yazil, maybe they are together."

"I hope that too, my Samsi." I brushed her hair from her face. "And I hope Ma'zur does not find them when he crosses the river."

Tylos and I sat under the awning in the late afternoon, watching as Ma'zur was carried across the hot sand to his grave. Samar, Yahmed, and the other merchants from Myrb followed Ma'zur's body. Ma'zur's face was covered with a white cloth and he wore the black and white robes of a merchant. His arms were placed cn his chest. Jewelry on his wrists gleamed in sunlight.

"Well, that gold is safe," said Tylos. "Even Yahmed would not steal from a dead man."

"I didn't know Yahmed was so greedy," I said.

"He grabs for more, but his wife is worse. Their slaves say Wa'dab talks about entering Jerusalem with Samar."

"Before me?" I said. "Does she intend to take my place on the caravan?"

"Wa'dab says her husband now is the wealthiest merchant on the caravan and he will be at Samar's side when he meets King Solomon."

"Tell me no more, Tylos, or I will think Wa'dab cut the lines to Ma'zur's tent. She is welcome to meet with King Solomon, but she will not take my place. Samar and I will ride together into Jerusalem."

"Watch her, Bilqis, be careful around her."

"She's a foolish woman who dreams of being a queen. My gifts to King Solomon are far greater than her husband's jars of wine and Ma'zur's gold."

As we walked back to our tent, I thought of Wa'dab's plan to shove me aside to gain King Solomon's attention. Would the king be fooled? Would he look for me or would any wealthy woman from the south satisfy his interest?

Late that night I lay wrapped in my sheepskin, unable to sleep until I heard Samar's low cough at the back of my tent. The other women did not wake as I tied a robe over my sleep tunic and opened the curtain.

Samar pulled me around the dark corner of my tent and held me, kissing my face. "Your skin is so soft, my love. It is water to me." His lips were dry against my cracked lips but his tongue was wet and delicious in my mouth.

He pushed me against the tent. I put my hands to his chest and held him from me. "I'm afraid someone will see us," I said.

"Who is looking?" he murmured. His breath was hot against my throat.

"Wa'dab's spies," I whispered, shivering as he bit my neck. "She says her husband will stand at your side when you greet Solomon."

"He will stand far behind us when we meet the king." He untied my robe. "Enough talk."

Yahmed gathered Mazur's bags of jewelry and his camels and moved up the caravan until he was riding behind my herd.

Other merchants let him pass; Yahmed's new wealth gave him greater status in the caravan. Wa'dab waved to me as she took her place beside her husband. She wore bracelets of braided gold on each wrist. Yazil's jewelry, said Tylos.

Before we left camp, Samsi laid two brown feathers for Amdar on a small drift of sand. She was quiet while she walked beside Timora, pulling the leads of my camel and barely turning her head when her friend pointed out the thorn trees that were taller in this part of the desert.

We were in a different country; the morning was cooler and warmed slowly instead of the oven blast of hot air that was the Myrb sunrise.

"Bilqis, look!" Tylos said. "A dust spirit."

Out on the desert, far from the caravan, moved a veil of dust. Sand whirled at the bottom. The slender top of the spirit bent like a finger, pointing north toward Jerusalem.

"A good omen," said Tylos.

"Yes," I agreed and lay back against my cushions, relieved for a sign that the journey ahead of us was blessed.

Samar ordered the caravan to ride without stopping to make up the time we lost in the sandstorm. Late at night he finally called a halt and we stumbled from our camels.

Tylos and I built the cookfire while Samsi and Timora put up the small supply tent for our overnight stay. Khe fetched bags of food and water. He handed a half-filled skin to Samsi. "Drink carefully," he said. "We are far from water until we reach the next village."

Timora mixed bread and I tended the fire, dozing in the smoke. We ate our meal, saying little. Timora laid a platter of bread by the fire to keep warm for Samar. He arrived when the fire was low, and sat next to me, our legs touching while he ate his bread and drank a cup of heated wine.

"Farium fears we'll be attacked again," he said when his cup was empty. "The bandits in this land are outside of Solomon's reach and they are bold because they know we are weary of traveling. We will not be safe until we enter Solomon's lands."

"My women have blades," I said. "We will be armed when we ride tomorrow." I laid my hand on his leg. "Will I come to you tonight?"

"Not tonight, my Bilqis. I must visit the other camps to tell the men we ride early tomorrow." He was gone before I could reply. I drew my robe around my shoulders and threw another piece of dung on the fire.

We rose before dawn. Tylos and I sat by the fire while Timora cooked our morning bread. We wore our wool robes while we ate; the mornings were cold until the sun had moved a hand's width above the sand.

"I miss the heat of Myrb," Tylos complained.

"You will be hot enough when the sun rises," I said. "Keep your curtains closed today and stay out of the sun. Khe said our water is low. We may not find good wells for a day or so."

"I wish we had a skinful of Myrb water. This water tastes like camel piss."

"Stop grumbling, Tylos. Think of sleeping in King Solomon's soft beds and eating fresh figs while his slaves rub perfumed oil into your hair."

She sighed, "Ah, that is a good dream."

The caravan was loaded and moving before sunrise. Camels were herded closer together while guards watched the graveled desert for signs of men. Samar and Farium rode at a distance from the caravan, watching for movement around the far-off dunes. In the brightening light, I could see Yahmed had moved his tents and his herds in front of me. Lengths of red and white silk flew from the top of his riding tent and that of his wife.

"Yahmed is bold." I leaned from my tent to talk with Tylos. "I wonder that Samar did not tell him to hide his wealth."

"He spoke to Yahmed," Tylos said. "Khe told me when he fetched my camel. Yahmed laughed and said Samar was worried that King Solomon would think that he, not Samar, was Darmalay's envoy."

"Maybe Wa'dab will get her wish and ride into Jerusalem before me." I pulled my robe tighter against the cold air.

Our camels groaned and jerked up their heads when they stepped onto a flat plain that was covered with sharp rocks. Handlers patted their long necks and whispered to their animals, a chuffing sound that soothed the beasts. I noticed the camel men, like the guards, were watchful for another attack and did not take their eyes off the desert.

Where would it come from, I wondered. Around us was the open desert; mountains and large dunes rose far in the distance. No one could surprise us with another attack.

We rode until midday before Farium held up his hand to call halt. I closed the curtains around my riding tent. My food bag was close to my hand, but I was too hot to feel hungry. Water in my bag was warm as spit and tasted as though it had soaked in goat hair. I swallowed a mouthful, gagging at the taste.

We started again after a short rest, walking over the hard, glinted gravel until the sun slipped behind the mountains and Ilumqah's bright horns showed in the night sky. Again we slept in our small supply tent. Samar ordered the caravan to start moving before sunrise while the day was cool.

Timora made a meal of dried fish and a bowl of spiced barley soup to hide the taste of the rotten water she squeezed from the bottom of the skin. We drank the soup and licked the last drops from the bowls.

"I hope there is a good market at the village." Tylos held up a piece of salted fish. "I dream of fresh meat."

"And water," I said. "We need fresh water."

We mounted our camels while the night was still dark on the sand. Timora handed a small bag of wine to me, and a few dates and a piece of dried fish wrapped in a cloth. My stomach rolled at the smell of the fish.

"Here is water, Bilqis." Timora handed up a waterskin that was cold from being left outside the tent during the night. A few mouthfuls of water sloshed at the bottom of the skin. "I saved it for you," she said.

"Take it back, Timora. Share it with Samsi."

The girl backed away. "Keep it safe with you. We'll ask for water if we are thirsty." She picked up the leads to my camel and began to walk. I could not refuse her gift, but I vowed I would not drink from her skin during the day and I would make the girls drink when the sun was highest.

The gravel plain seemed endless. The heat of the sun dried my eyes when I looked over the desert. We stopped at midday and I gave the waterskin to Samsi. "Share this with Timora," I said. Samsi's face and hair were white with dust; her eyes were dark holes. "Do not let her refuse the water. Tell her I command it."

I drank a mouthful of warm sweet wine and another and was thirsty again. I could not eat the fish; my mouth had not enough water to soften the dried flesh. I ate a date for sweetness and lay back against the silk cushions that were crusted with my dried sweat and waited for my camel to begin walking and bring a breeze, even a hot breeze, into my tent.

We camped that night on rocks I could feel through my mat. Tylos muttered as she turned from side to side, seeking a comfortable spot. The tent was still dark when I heard Timora gather her food bags and step through the curtain to cook our morning meal. I felt as though I had just fallen asleep. We chewed pieces of dried goat meat by the small fire and drank wine heated with honey. I could barely keep my eyes open as Timora and Samsi took down the supply tent, and then Khe was standing in front of me, holding my camel. He helped me step onto her neck. I grasped the sides of the riding tent and fell inside.

Tylos woke me at sunrise, whispering my name. "Where is Samar?" I said. She handed a skin of wine across the space between our tents. "I have not seen him. Khe says he rides with Farium, searching for water."

Samsi and Timora walked below me, bending into the leads of my camel as if they were pulling her across the rocky plain. Khe walked next to them with Tylos's camel. My lips were swollen and my tongue felt like a strip of cracked leather. I wanted to call to them and ask if they had water or wine to drink, but the words would not leave my throat. I pulled off my headcloth and lay back, covering my face against the hot wind.

We walked slowly through the long morning. The sun hung in the sky without moving and the rocks seemed to breathe fire. At midday we stopped and sat under a bush in slivers of shade, eating bread that was hard as fired clay.

Samsi sat next to me. I lifted my hand, wanting to unravel her dusty braids and comb her hair to a shining honey brown, but I dropped my hand, too tired to do more than slide my fingers down her braids. She lay down with her head in my lap and fell asleep while I stroked her hair.

Khe walked over to us, carrying a bowl of camel's milk. The milk was mostly foam, and there was barely enough to cover the bottom of the bowl. I sipped a taste, enough to soften my throat and passed the bowl to Tylos. She drank and passed it to Timora who tipped the bowl to her mouth for the last drops of milk.

"My father says we'll stay here until nightfall," Khe said. "We'll walk through the night and reach the village tomorrow."

"Have we lost camels?" I asked.

"Two belonging to a merchant fell down and would not get up again. Slaves stripped them and packed the goods on the water camels."

"Are my camels safe?" I thought of Darmalay's gifts to King Solomon, dropped on the wayside with the heavy bags of gold and jewels and incense lying open on the path, a glittering feast the carrion birds would circle and leave. Who would pick up the treasure, I wondered. It seemed a problem I looked at from a distance. I no longer cared about the gold plates that weighed as much as sixty men, the many bags of incense, or the precious stones Darmalay had collected for a year to send to King Solomon in Jerusalem. I was content to sit under a bush, smoothing the hair of a sleeping girl.

Khe stood and I heard him say he would look for his father. Tylos shook her head and lay down with her head in a bit of shade. Timora handed the last piece of bread from our morning meal to me. I pushed her hand away. "No," I said. "You eat." Timora held the bread in her hands, unsure what to do with it. I gently shook Samsi awake. Timora broke the bread in two and shared it with Samsi.

"Eat," I said. The two girls bent over their bread, hiding their mouths as they chewed. Samsi rubbed her throat to help her swallow the dry bread. A man's shadow passed over my head and arms. Samar sat beside me, holding a cup of water. My hand trembled when I reached for the cup and he helped guide it to my lips. "Drink, my Bilqis," he said. "There will be more soon. Farium reports we will reach a city tomorrow or the following day."

Tylos sat when I put the cup to my lips. Timora looked away. Samsi licked her lips while I sipped the salty water. I pointed to Tylos and Samar handed the cup to the old woman. She drank a quick mouthful and gave the cup to Timora, who drank and passed the water to Samsi. I could not take my eyes off the cup as it was being passed around. I knew Samar had left when his shadow moved away from me.

We traveled that night over the graveled desert that looked oiled in starlight. Camel men sang to their beasts and I wondered how they found the breath to lift their voices. The sun was gold fire when I opened the curtain in the morning.

My camel walked slowly, pulled by Khe. Timora led Tylos's camel. I looked around for Samsi. Timora pointed to Tylos's tent and I nodded and lay back against the cushions, too tired to sit up. My skin itched. I scratched my neck and thought of the silk merchant who died after the battle. He was lying in his dark grave. No more walking over hard, shining rocks, no more hot wind that dried my eyes and my tongue until it stuck to the inside of my mouth. In the grave, only cool sand would touch my skin.

The sun was overhead when I looked outside again. In the distance rose tall city walls. Khe looked up at me and smiled; my lips cracked when I smiled at him. The walls seemed to grow no bigger until we finally turned from the path toward the city.

As we neared the gates, I saw people standing along the top of the wall, watching the caravan approach. The star guides led the first camels through the arched counting gates. Priests and taxmen sat on benches above us, holding clay tablets and ticking off every camel that walked under the arches, figuring how much gold to charge us to drink from their wells and camp in the pens inside the city walls.

I pulled my curtains closed as my camel passed under the eyes of the villagers and opened the side curtain when we entered an enormous field of graveled sand. Khe led our riding camels around the side of the field, stopping in the shade of a large thorn tree. He ran off to fetch water while Timora and Samsi set the boundary stones around our camp.

Khe returned with a dripping waterskin. Timora dipped out cups of water. I drank without taking a breath, filled my cup and drank again, slower this time. The water was cold and sweet; this village had deep wells.

I sat under the tree with Tylos while Samsi and Khe put up our tent. Timora built a fire and opened her food bags as slaves ran past carrying filled waterskins to the other camps.

Farium and his guards had watered my camels. The beasts were kneeling in a group behind my tent, calmly chewing their feed.

Samar's black tent was raised close to mine. I watched as his two slaves carried his sleeping mat and food bags into his tent. He was so close I could step from the back of my tent into his. But I could not visit him; tents surrounded us, someone would see or hear if I opened my curtain in the night.

Timora pulled off a round of bread and handed it to me. I tore it in two and handed a piece to Tylos. We ate it without butter or honey and it was the best bread I had ever eaten. Samsi returned with another bag of water and we all ate and drank until our bellies were full.

After our meal, Tylos opened her waistbag, counted out two drops of gold and handed them to Timora. "You and Samsi go to the market. Buy sweet wine, taste it, girl, do not let them give you sour, fresh fruit, flour, nuts, and honey." She pulled the bag closed. "Buy carefully, the cost of welcome is high but we will not see a market this size again for many days."

"Buy meat." I yawned in the shade. "I will invite the wives to my fire tonight. It has been too long since we met as friends."

"Do you ask Wa'dab?" said Tylos.

"Yes, she must be invited with the others." Wa'dab talked without thinking when she had drunk enough wine. I wanted to hear of her plan to be the first to enter Jerusalem and greet King Solomon.

~ Fourteen ~

That night we feasted on roasted goat meat, dates stuffed with soft cheese, and spiced nut cakes that Samsi and Timora bought at the market. The women around my fire had dressed in their fine silks. We ate and drank and talked of Jerusalem, so close now, of our families in Myrb and how big the children we left behind would be when we returned.

I briefly thought of Amida and wondered how she was faring with her pregnancy. I was surprised that I no longer felt pain at the thought of her living in my house or welcoming me home with her newborn baby in her arms. My thoughts now were filled with meeting King Solomon. Samar had visited my camp in the late afternoon. He stayed to drink cooled wine with me and we talked about Jerusalem. How would King Solomon hear about us? I asked. Samar said he would send a messenger to the king the day before we reached Jerusalem.

The messenger would bear a large bag of incense for the king to announce the arrival of the Queen of Saba.

"And you?" I asked. "Will your name be linked with mine?"

"Your name will be known before mine. Darmalay planned it so. King Solomon will greet the beautiful and wealthy Bilqis of Saba. You will present me as your advisor."

As we talked, I realized I had not thought of my husband for many days. I would not see Darmalay or my home again for a long time. I might remain in Jerusalem for months, however long King Solomon wished me to stay, and our return home would take another three months.

Wa'dab drank cup after cup of wine and talked louder than the other women around my fire. Her face looked thinner from the hard travel behind us. "My husband says we are safe now." Wine glistened on her chin. "He believes we are close enough to King Solomon's lands that no one dares attack us."

"Damri Samar tells my husband that another attack will come when we are far from this village," said Shadru. She looked ill since I saw her last. Her eyelids were covered with wrinkles and her neck was ringed with lines, as if she had lost flesh.

Wa'dab waved her fingers, brushing away her words. "Our guards say there are no signs of bandits. We are safe."

"Damri Samar said tracks are hard to see in this rocky sand." I spoke mildly, not wanting to argue with the woman.

She lifted her cup to me, "Ah, Bilqis, you would believe your Samar. He eats at your fire day and night. Yahmed says he looks to your camp first when he seeks Samar."

I set my cup on the rug and looked at her. "My husband commanded Damri Samar to accompany me to Jerusalem. We are enjoined to treat with King Solomon for his protection when our caravans approach his lands."

"You will not make a treaty with the king," laughed Wa'dab. She swallowed another mouthful of wine. "Samar, Yahmed, and other wealthy men from the caravan will talk with King Solomon. You will meet his wives who will look at you as a pet; a chieftain's wife from a city in the south."

Shadru spoke, "Bilqis is the wife of the ruler of Myrb. Darmalay sent her with Damri Samar to meet with the king. He did not send her to amuse Solomon's wives."

"Shadru, you ever did defend the helpless." Wa'dab laughed until she started to cough. The woman next to her slapped her on her back.

I looked at Wa'dab, hating her words and her laughing at me. I had traveled a long distance to meet King Solomon. I had survived a bandit attack and a sandstorm. Solomon and his wives would not treat me as a pet.

Wa'dab waved her empty cup at Timora. The girl's necklace swung from her neck as she bent over to pour wine. Wa'dab grabbed the necklace. "Pretty work," she said. "A favor from a man?"

I swallowed my anger and spoke calmly. "A gift from Darmalay's mother," I said. "She thought Timora was worth ten slaves."

"I think many women on this journey have received favors from other men." Wa'dab laughed again and winked at the woman sitting next to her.

I could see that the women at my fire were of two camps. The women nearest Wa'dab looked down at the sand or lifted cups of wine to hide their smiles when Wa'dab spoke of Samar and me. Other women sitting next to Shadru glanced at each other and did not smile.

Wa'dab lifted her empty cup again. I had heard enough of her words. I wanted her to leave my fire. I smiled at the other women. "My friends, I thank you for feasting with me tonight, but it is late and I'm tired. Sleep well for we ride all day tomorrow."

Wa'dab slammed her cup onto the sand. "Who are you to give us orders? My husband is the richest man on the caravan. He'll lead us into Jerusalem." She lifted her chin. She looked fierce and strong in the firelight.

"Say no more, Wa'dab," I said. "Or, you and your husband, whose wealth includes the goods he owes Ma'zur's family, will ride alone into Jerusalem."

"You cannot stop me." Wa'dab waved her hand around the circle. "All of us are disgusted. You do not invite us to your fire, yet you always have room for Samar. Does your husband know he visits you every night? Do you go to his tent? Or does he come to yours while your women visit other men?"

I stared at Wa'dab through the smoke of the cookfire. I did not look away. I would not show her that I worried about the truth in her words.

There was silence for a long moment until Shadru clapped her hands. "Wa'dab, you are as loud on the caravan as you are in Myrb. I have not heard that Samar visits Bilqis when her companions are not with her. I have walked past her camp at night and many times she and her women sit alone at their fire."

She looked at the other women. "We cannot break wind in our tents without our neighbors yelling at us to be quiet. And our slaves talk. Do you think we would not hear if any of us are visited by men other than our husbands?"

The women laughed at Shadru's words, though I noticed a few of them looked down at their hands. "I stand with Bilqis," Shadru said. "I will ride where she bids me ride when we enter Jerusalem."

Wa'dab opened her mouth to speak but closed it when her friends held out their hands to help her stand. They led her from my camp, talking in low voices. Shadru and her friends stayed to kiss my cheek and press their hands to mine.

"Do not listen to Wa'dab," Shadru said. "She has drunk too much wine. Her friends will tell her what she said and she will come to you tomorrow to beg forgiveness."

I kissed her cheek, grateful for her friendship. I wondered if she would still stand with me if she knew that I had lain with Samar.

Timora and Samsi rolled up the rugs after the women left while Tylos and I gathered the cushions "Wa'dab may ask your forgiveness," Tylos said, "but do not think her weak, Bilqis, she is a snake waiting to strike."

"I'll listen for talk at the wells," said Samsi. "I'll help protect our tent."

"I listen and watch always." Timora smiled, and I realized again how rare was her smile.

Samar walked to my fire when sounds of feasting from other cookfires had died down. He sat so close to me that I could smell wine on his breath. Tylos looked around to see that the camp was tidy and sat on the far side of the fire, leaving me alone with Samar.

"Wa'dab boasts to me that she and Yahmed will be first into Jerusalem," I said, holding my hands to the fire.

Samar dug into the hot coals with a stick. "That worries me." He broke the stick into short pieces. "I worry about Yahmed's tongue. Tonight he spoke of women opening their tents to other men and then he asked about your health."

"Wa'dab said the same this evening," I said. "Shadru told her my women attend me when you visit my fire."

Samar threw the wood into the fire. "We must be careful."

"And when we're home again?" I whispered. "Will we be careful or will we stand before my husband and tell him we fell in love on the caravan?"

Samar rubbed his beard and said quietly. "I am deeply sorry that I broke trust with Darmalay." He looked at me. "But Ilumqah knows, I would do it again to be with you." The hem of his robe slid across my leg as he stood. "Sleep now, my love," he said. "We ride early tomorrow."

The rocky plain smoothed out after we left the village. Our camels groaned with pleasure as they stepped off the sharp gravel into soft sand. The path we followed led between a mountain range on one side and low lying hills on the other. As the sun rose, we watched both sides of the path, looking for the flash of a dagger or the flutter of a robe. Green bushes moved in the wind that swept around the foot of the hills and mountains, but no men rode out of their dark shadows that day.

Wa'dab sent a slave bearing a jar of wine to my riding tent when we stopped at midday to rest the camels. "Throw it out," Tylos said. "She sends a slave to ask your forgiveness."

"Keep it to wash wounds," I said. Wa'dab opened her curtain and waved at me. I held up my hand to acknowledge her peace offering.

Samar called a halt when the moon appeared, a shining blade in the dark sky. After our evening meal, I walked to Shadru's camp, carrying a gift of spice cake. She held her hands to me when I arrived. "Honored friend," she said, "you are welcome to my fire." Her companion was her younger sister, plump and dark-haired. I could see what Shadru looked like before age and sickness took her beauty.

An old slave woman limped over to pour wine and another slave brought bowls filled with sweet grapes and roasted almonds. Shadru put her hand over her cup when the old woman again offered the wineskin. "No more for me," she said. "I drank too much wine last night."

"But not as much as Wa'dab," I said.

"Wa'dab says she regrets her words." Shadru glanced at Wa'dab's camp and spoke quietly. Her sister and I leaned forward to hear her words. "Watch her, Bilqis," she said. "She asks your forgiveness but she continues to sharpen her tongue on you. Her husband gained wealth with Ma'zur's death. Wa'dab wants your place on the caravan."

~ Fifteen ~

Samsi swept the tent the next morning while Tylos and I folded the sheepskins. I heard Timora yell my name and we ran out of the tent to see her standing by the cookfire, pointing at a line of men on camels riding from the high mountains toward the camps.

"We have to hide, Bilqis." Tylos yanked me away from the fire. Samsi and Timora ran after us. We stood pressed together against the side of the tent. Khe and another guard, an old man with a grey beard, ran to my tent and stood in front of us.

Mounted caravan guards raced past our camp, screaming with their daggers upraised as they rode toward the bandits. Camels roared when they met, biting and lunging at each other. I saw raised daggers and then dust boiled up from the stamping feet of the frenzied camels and hid the fighting from our eyes.

A small group of men broke away from the battle and raced toward the caravan, followed by caravan guards. Timora pushed Samsi behind her as two men rode into my camp. The old guard ran forward and seized the leads of one of the camels. The bandit kicked him in the head. The old man fell to his knees.

I saw Timora's knife by the cookfire. I snatched it up, ran to the camel and stabbed the bandit's hairy leg. He yelled and leaned over, slashing at me with his blade.

My cheek burned. I touched the skin and my fingers were red with blood. Khe yanked hard at the bandit's robe and was on him before the man hit the ground. I slapped the camel's rump with my bloody hand. She swung her head around and fled into the desert.

The other rider pulled the leads of his beast, trying to escape Tylos and Timora who were hanging on one of his legs, trying to pull him off his camel. He slapped his leads against his camel's neck until it turned, knocking down the women.

I heard Samsi screaming. She was backed against the tent, crying with her hands over her mouth as she watched Khe pull his dagger from the first bandit's chest. The noise of killing grew. I could not tell which screams were from men and which were from animals.

I tightened my grip on my knife as a man on a brown camel rode through the dust at me. His beast seemed to come slowly, though from her outstretched neck I could see that she was running. I tried to grab Samsi and hide with her inside my tent, but my legs would not move as I watched him come closer.

"Father," Khe yelled.

The man slid off his camel before she stopped moving. I was relieved to see Farium. The guard nodded to his son and looked at me.

"You are safe?" he asked.

"Yes." My voice sounded far away. I wiped the blood trickling from my wound.

Samsi looked up. Her eyes opened wide and she pointed at something behind me. I turned and for a moment I did not understand what I was seeing. Tylos sat on the ground, holding Timora. The girl's hair was messy with blood. Tylos was shaking her. I wanted her to stop because it looked as if the shaking would hurt Timora.

Khe knelt beside Tylos and touched Timora's face. He put his fingers on her eyelids and gently closed her eyes.

"Timora is dead?" I stepped toward Khe, keeping my eyes on Timora lying so still on the sand, watching for her chest to rise with her breath. Samsi clung to me. Her weeping swept through my body. I let go of her and fell to my knees beside Timora. Her forehead was crushed in where the camel had kicked her when it threw her off.

Samsi cried louder. I wanted to cover my ears against Samsi's cries and the screaming from other camps. The battle was over. Now women wept for their dead.

"Carry her into the tent," I said. Khe lifted Timora. Tylos ran before him to hold open the curtain. Samsi and I entered the tent behind Khe as Tylos unrolled Timora's sleeping mat.

Khe laid Timora on the mat. "Fetch water," I said, and he left the tent. Tylos sat beside Timora's body with her bag of herbs in her hand. She started to untie Timora's torn robe, stopped and looked up at me. Her lips quivered as she spoke. "I'll wash her. You and Samsi wait outside."

"No," I said. "I'll stay. She was dear to me, too."

Tylos and I did not speak while we pulled off Timora's robe and untied her tunic. I heard Samsi's quick breath before she ran out of the tent.

Khe coughed at the front curtain to tell us he had returned. He handed a pot of steaming water through the curtain to Tylos.

Samsi appeared as Tylos set the hot water on the mat. The girl knelt beside me and laid Timora's broken necklace on the rug. A wing had broken off one of the bees; the middle bee was gone.

"I searched the sand," she said, her voice anxious. "I couldn't find the missing bee."

"You did well, Samsi, wrap the necklace in a cloth. I'll have it repaired."

"Can I have it?" She held the necklace against her chest.

"No, this necklace was a gift for Timora, she will be buried with it." I made my voice gentle, "Find Khe again and tell him to come to me. Tylos and I will wash Timora."

Samsi walked from the tent, wiping tears from her eyes. When the curtain was closed, Tylos dropped a handful of herbs into the hot water and we sat for a moment while the scent of lavender and desert sage filled the air. This was the first time I had seen Timora lying quietly. Even in sleep she had seemed restless, impatient to rise and blow the cookfire to flame or sweep the tent or fetch water from the well.

Tylos wet two pieces of linen, wrung them out, and handed a piece to me. I washed dirt and dried blood from Timora's forehead, wiping the skin around her terrible wound. "Poor girl," I murmured.

Tylos lifted one of Timora's feet to wash. She scraped her finger along the bottom of the girl's foot. "Her feet are tough as a man's," she said.

Tears came to my eyes because Timora did not laugh and pull her foot from Tylos's hands. "She would never wear sandals," Tylos said. I wiped my eyes and remembered Timora repacking my gift of good leather sandals when she thought I was not looking, to walk barefoot across the sand.

The open weave of the tent pulled in sunlight while we worked. I wrung fresh water into Timora's hair and washed out the blood, combing my fingers through her long hair. Tylos opened a leather bag and pulled out the girl's white tunic from the full-moon ceremony. I held Timora's body, heavier now in death, while Tylos slipped the tunic over her head.

She fastened a girdle of white shells around her waist. I laid the girl on her back again and touched the crystal moons she had worked around the neck of the tunic. "I remember every time Timora smiled," I said. "The sun was in her smile."

Tylos brushed Timora's damp hair over her forehead to hide her wound and we sat back on our heels, waiting for Samsi to return. Tylos glanced at me. "You're bleeding." She dipped the edge of a cloth into the water and handed it to me. The cut on my cheek stung as I wiped away blood.

"You'll carry a mark from this battle," said Tylos.

I heard wailing from other tents, but it sounded far away. "I wonder who else died today," I said.

A shadow darkened the tent opening and Samsi stepped inside. She stood for a moment, looking at Timora. "Timora looks pretty," she whispered.

"Where is Khe?" Tylos said. "He was to come back with you."

"I couldn't find him. I can't find anyone. People are crying and there are dead camels everywhere."

"I must find Samar," I said. "We'll bury Timora before we leave camp tomorrow."

"Where will she be buried?" Tears rolled from Samsi's eyes.

"We will find a good place for her," said Tylos.

Samsi dropped to her knees next to Timora's body. I opened the curtain and left the tent. Outside, the sand was kicked up and dark with blood. Slaves were busy rebuilding cookfires and setting up tent poles that had been knocked down in the battle. There were deep grooves in the sand where the bodies of dead camels and bandits had been dragged into the desert from the caravan, toward the mountains. There the bodies would stay, food for jackals and the carrion birds. Their white bones would be scattered long before we returned along this path.

Sand on the other side of the path had been trampled in the fighting, but no bodies lay on the ground between the camp and the low hills. There would be caves in those hills, I thought. I would bury Timora there. I didn't want her to lie under the sand where men had died.

I saw Khe running from Samar's tent. The boy looked up at my voice. "Where is Samar?" I said.

He pointed to the counselor's black tent. "Damri Samar was wounded, my father is with him."

"How many are dead, how many wounded?" I asked.

"My father doesn't know yet," he said.

"Here, take this and find someone to repair it." I handed him the broken necklace wrapped inside a piece of linen. "Have it done quickly. It belonged to Timora."

Samar lay on his back on his sleeping mat. Farium sat next to him, tucking the ends of a wide cloth he had wrapped around Samar's belly. Samar's eyes were closed and his lips were tight with pain.

I watched his chest rise and fall before I could speak. "Is he badly wounded?" I asked.

"He was stabbed in the belly, but he lives." Farium tied Samar's robe loosely around the bandage. "I'll send my son to sit with him."

"I'll stay until he comes. Timora from my tent was killed. Find a cave in the low mountains to bury her."

I sat beside Samar, holding his hand and stroking his brow until his face relaxed and he fell asleep.

"Khe is looking for a cave to bury your slave." Farium's whisper seemed loud as he entered the tent. "How is Samar?"

"He sleeps." I laid Samar's hand on his chest, away from his bandaged wound. I stepped close to Farium and spoke in a low voice. "He cannot be moved for a day or so. Tell me how many others are wounded, how many were killed."

"Two merchants died with their wives. Many camels were taken."

"Darmalay's treasure for Solomon, was anything stolen?"

"Two camels bearing incense are gone," said Farium. "Your beasts were well guarded. Nothing else was lost."

"Are we safe here for the night?" I said.

I saw Khe in his father's smile. "We killed many bandits," he said. "I do not think there are enough bad men left in this part of the desert to attack us again."

"Tell the caravan we will stay here for two days to heal the wounded and bury our dead." As Farium left, I realized he had not questioned my order for the caravan to stay.

Tylos had covered Timora with a mantle of blue wool when I returned. Khe carried Timora's body through the back curtain and laid her on her sleeping mat in the shade of the tent.

I smelled fresh bread and joined Samsi at the cookfire. Samsi was crying as she laid a round of bread on a platter.

"Tylos told me to make food," she said. "But I don't want to eat, I feel sick."

"We have to eat," I said. "We have more work to do before this day is ended."

I ate bread and drank a cup of heated wine while Tylos stayed inside the tent, burning incense to cleanse it of the smell of death. Samsi wiped the mixing bowl and closed her food bags. We sat together, waiting until Tylos opened the front curtain and beckoned us to come inside.

We entered the tent, breathing the heavy scent of incense. Samsi glanced at the side of the tent where she slept next to Timora. "You will sleep with me tonight," I said. "Unroll your mat next to mine."

Samsi tended the cookfire while Tylos and I walked to Samar's tent. Tylos pulled off the soiled bandages that stuck to his wound and I washed the red, puffy skin and sprinkled powdered lavender into the wound. After we wrapped him in clean bandages, I sat with him, holding his hand. Samar's breath was even and his wound did not stink. I hoped he would heal quickly.

Khe entered the tent carrying a bowl of fresh water. "I will give Samar water to drink when he wakes up," he said. "My father will watch over him tonight."

Samsi slept close to me through the long night. Tylos snored at the back of the tent while Khe sat outside, guarding Timora's body against jackals and wolves that would come in the night, drawn by the smell of the dead.

~ Sixteen ~

At first light, while cookfires were being lit in the camps, we walked toward a cave in the hills. Two of Farium's guards rode beside us, watching for bandits in the desert. Khe carried Timora's body, wrapped in the blue mantle. Samsi walked next to Khe, holding the flowers she had gathered in the desert; twigs of desert star and a stalk of sweetflower, a tiny white bell that smelled of grapes.

I glanced at Samar's closed tent as we passed his camp. Farium was inside, tending Samar. He had come to my tent before we left to bury Timora, to tell me that Samar had wakened during the night. He was hot with fever and had drunk a cup of water before going back to sleep. Tylos called it a healing sleep. I worried about Samar's fever.

We stepped through a dark opening into the cave. Inside, light fell through a large crack at the top. The floor was soft with sand and scattered with a few small bones from mice.

There were no footmarks from men or beasts. Timora would sleep in peace.

Tylos unrolled Timora's sleeping mat in the center of the cave. Khe laid her body on the mat, facing up to receive the blessing of Ilumqah's light as he passed overhead in the night. I untied my waistbag and pulled out Timora's necklace. A jeweler on the caravan had repaired it by removing the broken bee and moving the remaining bee to the center of the necklace. Samsi had searched the sand again looking for the missing third bee but had not found it.

I draped the necklace over the mantle, at Timora's throat. Tylos placed a piece of incense in the sand next to her covered head and tucked a bag of white salt under Timora's hand. Samsi laid her flowers on Timora's breast. We stood together after we were finished and looked at her draped body lying in the center of the lighted cave.

Tylos followed Khe out of the cave. Samsi walked behind Tylos, stopping once to look back at Timora. I waited until Samsi was gone and closed my eyes. "Hazza," I prayed. "Protect Timora. Welcome her as your daughter when she crosses the river of stars."

I walked out, leaving Timora alone in her quiet room.

Outside the cave, Khe rolled a large rock against the dark hole, sealing it against the desert beasts.

Our camp felt empty without Timora sitting in front of the cookfire. Tylos and Samsi fetched water from the pack camel while I stood inside our tent. It seemed too big for the three of us. I remembered Timora's shy smile when I praised her good food. I wished I had seen her smile more often.

After Tylos and Samsi returned, I gathered a bag of herbs and walked to Samar's camp. His tent was filled with smoke from incense that did not mask the stink of his wound. I drew the edge of my headcloth over my mouth, handed the bag to Farium, and sat next to the Samar. His eyes were closed and his breath came slow. His fingers were soft and limp when I picked up his hand.

"He cannot be moved," said Farium. He gripped the bag, crushing the herbs. "His wound is worse. He'll die if he is moved."

"How long before he can travel?" I asked.

"Two, maybe three days." Farium dropped the bag next to me on the rug. "Khe will bring water."

He walked out of the tent. The opening darkened again and Yahmed entered. He looked surprised to see me sitting next to Samar, holding his hand. "You are alone?" he said. "Where is the guard?"

Khe entered the tent behind Yahmed, carrying a pot of hot water. He said to Yahmed, "My father sent me to tend Damri Samar."

Khe knelt beside Samar. He shook the crushed herbs into the water and untied the stained bandage. The skin around the wound was black and the smell of decay made me want to vomit. Khe dipped a fresh cloth in the water and began to wash Samar's wound. Yahmed and I left the tent.

Yahmed turned to face me when we stepped outside. He was a skinny old man, tough as chewed bone from years of sitting in the hot marketplace while his jars of wine cooled in the shade. "We leave tomorrow," he said. "We are running out of water." He looked over my shoulder and said, "Ah, here is Farium."

He waved at the guard to join us. "I have decided we will travel tomorrow," he said to Farium "We need to find water. I will leave men behind to protect Samar and anyone who cannot travel."

"My tent stays with Damri Samar," I said when Farium did not answer Yahmed. "He is brother to my husband. We will stay until he is well enough to travel."

"I worry about Samar." Yahmed scratched his ragged beard. "But we need water and Farium says there are deep wells in the next village." The guard nodded at his words. Yahmed reached out to pat my shoulder. "I will leave men to protect you if you wish to stay . I will send water when we reach the village."

I moved away from his hand and folded my arms over my breast so he would not see that my hands were shaking. "Damri Samar is my husband's chief counselor," I said. "My tent will remain here with him." I paused. "As will my camels and my guards."

Farium stepped to my side. "I am sworn to protect Bilqis. My men and I will not leave her."

"Are you ruled by women?" Yahmed shrieked, his voice high as a young boy's.

Farium grasped the hilt of the dagger tucked into his waistband and didn't reply. Yahmed looked from Farium to me. He chewed his lips rapidly for a moment and then smiled and opened his hands as if to show he would be generous. "I'll speak with the other merchants. We will stay to care for Samar." He quickly walked away from us, kicking up sand.

Samsi waited by my rug with a platter of fresh bread and a bowl of lentil soup. "I cannot remember being so hungry," I said as I drank the soup. "Where are Tylos and Timora?"

Samsi looked down at the mention of Timora's name. "I grieve for her," I said. "It will take time for Timora to leave us. I remember my husband asking me where his mother was long after she died."

"My father and mother visit me in my dreams." Samsi picked dried dough off her fingers. "And my baby brother. I tickle him and he laughs."

"Where is Tylos?" I asked again, quietly.

"She's at the well."

"Wake me when she returns." I lay back and closed my eyes. "I want her help tending Samar."

"Is he badly hurt?" she asked.

"Yes, he is very bad, Samsi." I put my arm over my eyes to hide my tears.

"Tylos is a good healer," she said. "She will take care of Damri Samar. He will not die."

I let my arm fall at her kind words and relaxed in the shade while she tied her food bags and carried them into the tent.

The caravan lay quiet in the heat of midday. Voices in other camps sounded far away, dogs and camels slept; only the harsh cries of kites flying overhead broke the silence.

Tylos woke me when the sun was halfway down the sky. We walked together to Samar's camp. The curtains of his tent were tied open to catch the evening breeze. Khe sat inside, watching Samar while he slept. Tylos sniffed the air in the tent and shook her head at the sickening smell of Samar's wound.

I told Khe to go to my fire. "Samsi will feed you," I said. After he left, I asked Tylos to leave me alone with Samar until I called her in.

Samar's face was hot and his lips were open and crusted dry. I dipped a cloth into a cup of fresh water and squeezed a few drops into his mouth. His lips moved slightly at the touch of water.

He opened his eyes. "Bilqis."

"I'm here, my love." I wiped his forehead with the damp cloth. "Yahmed wants the caravan to leave tomorrow," I said. "But I'm not leaving. You cannot be moved."

Samar reached up to touch the wound on my cheek. "You're hurt."

"It's nothing," I said.

He said something I could not hear. I leaned closer. "Do not let Yahmed push you aside," he said.

"I'll stab him with your dagger if he tries to keep me from meeting King Solomon."

He smiled. "Your dagger," he said and closed his eyes.

I whispered his name, but he did not open his eyes. His breathing was slow; his skin was burning hot against my hand.

I called Tylos to come into the tent. She looked at Samar and shook her head. "He's dying, Bilqis."

"I know. I know." I held Samar's hand to my cheek and began to cry. I had wanted to cry since the moment I saw Timora lying on the sand with her head broken and bloody.

I drew a deep breath, kissed Samar's hand and laid it on his chest. "We are not leaving tomorrow," I said. "Not while Samar lives. Yahmed is a fool. He thought to take my goods and leave me behind. He was angry when Farium said the guards would stay to protect me."

"Let Yahmed go," Tylos said. "No one will follow him."

Khe walked into the tent, wiping his mouth. "Watch Samar," I said. "Come to my tent if he worsens, no matter how late."

Tylos and I left his tent and walked back to our camp. The air smelled of smoke. I heard voices and laughter at a few cookfires.

"No one died from those tents," said Tylos.

Khe stood outside my tent when the sky was dark and the cookfires were cold to tell me Samar had stopped breathing. Tylos and I ran after him to the tent.

Samar's face looked calm in the candlelight. His chest did not rise with his breath. I picked up his warm, heavy hand while Tylos held one of Samsi's feathers to his nose. The white feather did not move as we stared at it. Tylos dropped the feather and looked at me. Tears filled my eyes.

"Wait until we leave and then fetch your father," Tylos said to Khe. She pulled me through the curtain. I could not walk straight. I stumbled over the scuffed up sand as though I was drunk with wine. Tylos held me up and led me through the darkness to our camp.

Once inside our tent, I stood near the closed curtain, shaking off Tylos's hand when she tried to make me sit down and rest. I stared at the curtain until I heard the slave women Farium brought to Samar's tent begin to wail. Tylos put her bony arm around my shoulder. Samsi ran to us and hugged my waist. We stood together for a long time, weeping for Timora, weeping for Samar.

My eyes were dry when I stood with Tylos and Samsi at sunrise, watching Farium and two other guards carry Samar's black-robed body out of his tent, toward the sand between the caravan and the hill where Timora lay. Yahmed waited with other men from the caravan until Samar's body appeared, and walked to the head of the burial procession. I followed behind the men with Tylos and Samsi at my side. Wa'dab joined us when we walked past her tent.

Samsi had asked to bring one of her precious black and white hoopoe feathers to place on Samar's grave after the men left. I allowed it because she was still a child. My hands were empty; Samar's wives were the only women who could bring burial gifts to his grave.

Yahmed walked proudly before us, like a high-footed dog. He carried small bags of salt and incense. Another merchant held Samar's sheathed dagger. I waited a few steps away while the men laid Samar face down in his grave so he would seed the earth. One of his guards set a stone marker at the head. Yahmed dropped the bags of salt and incense into the dark hole; the other merchant knelt to place Samar's dagger next to his hand. I recognized the bronze hilt striped with raised gold that looked like the dagger Samar had given to me.

I turned to leave before the guards pushed sand into the grave. Wa'dab followed me. She slipped her hand under my arm.

"You are deeply grieved," she whispered. "I weep for you."

"Yes," I said, "I grieve for my husband's brother."

She gripped my arm harder. "He was your husband's brother and your good friend. He was such a good friend to you, Bilqis. "

I could not speak. I jerked my arm from her hand and walked away.

Farium appeared at my tent a short while later to tell me that Yahmed had called the council to decide who would lead the caravan into Jerusalem. I swayed on my feet, too tired to stand. It seemed as thought I had heard of Yahmed's plans to enter Jerusalem for a long time. "Let them talk," I said. "Leave me now and come back to tell me what they have decided."

"Yahmed will take your place, Bilqis," Tylos warned after Farium left.

"He can have it." I covered my face with my hands. "I'm tired. I want to go home."

Tylos pulled down my hands and looked at me. "We are not turning home. Do not let Yahmed rule you."

I let out a long breath, feeling as though I was breathing out all the fear and sorrow from the past two days. My heart was sore. I blinked slowly; I could not keep my eyes open.

"Sleep now," Tylos said. She unrolled my sleeping mat and unfolded the sheepskin. I lay down on the mat and she drew the soft wool over my shoulders. She sat beside me, stroking my hair. "We've come too far, Bilqis. Going forward is easier than going back." I closed my eyes and drifted into sleep.

Sunlight poured through the back of the tent when I woke. I stretched and then curled tight again under the sheepskin, remembering that Samar was dead.

Tylos stepped through the front curtain with a bowl of water and a cloth in her hands. She sat beside me and wiped my face with cool water. "You were crying in your sleep." She patted the scab that had formed over the wound on my cheek. "This will fall off soon. I'll mix a potion of honey and barley flour to put on the new skin. It will heal faster and you won't be marked when you meet King Solomon." She paused, started to speak and stopped.

"What has happened?" I asked. "Did the council meet?"

She nodded. "Yahmed was made leader. He announced that the caravan would leave in the morning." She dropped the cloth into the bowl. "Wa'dab sent a slave to tell me you are under her husband's protection. Samsi said two of Wa'dab's slaves are sitting outside her tent, embroidering a new robe for her to wear when she meets King Solomon."

I sat up and pushed my damp hair from my face. "She should wait to have new robes made. Jerusalem is many days away. We may die in the next bandit attack or the next sandstorm or we might drink bad water and get sick."

"Or we may arrive safely," said Tylos. "My one fear is that we will enter Jerusalem behind Wa'dab's fat ass."

I laughed and then could not stop laughing. "You must eat," Tylos said. "You didn't sleep well last night and you haven't eaten yet today. Samsi is making barley soup to ease your stomach."

I rubbed my face. I still felt tired, as if I had not slept deeply for a long time. "Timora and Samar are dead," I said. "We have lost much on this journey."

Tylos stood with the bowl in her hand. "We have lost much, my child, but there is much to gain."

Khe arrived to say that Yahmed's slaves were taking down Samar's tent and adding his few camels to Yahmed's herd. Tylos urged me to challenge his ownership but I stopped her hot words. "Samar is dead, Tylos, his belongings are not important to me." My words were true; Samar was dead and his camels and his sleeping mat and his waterskin would not bring him back to me.

"Yahmed thinks you are unprotected, Bilqis. He'll take everything if you do not stop him," said Tylos.

"Let him think I'm weak. He'll leave me alone if I do not challenge him."

~ Seventeen ~

The wind came up at midday, while the caravan rested under the hot sun. I waited until Samsi and Tylos were asleep on their mats, took the sheathed dagger Samar had given me and stepped outside the tent. The camps around me were quiet. At the edge of the caravan, guards sat on the ground next to their kneeling camels, protected from the blowing sand as they watched the mountain for bandits. Black kites circled overhead, drawn by the remains of dead camels that had been dragged out on the sand after the battle.

I walked away from the camp toward Samar's grave. The wind blew harder, swirling sand around my feet. I heard my name. Farium ran to me. "Where are you going?" he asked.

"Damri Samar was our leader. I would stand by his grave again in respect before we leave."

Farium scanned the mountains and desert around us. "I'll come with you. You should not be out here alone."

I shook my head. "I'll be gone a few minutes. Wait for me in the camp."

Farium stood for a moment with his hand on his dagger. He nodded and backed away, keeping his eyes on me.

The wind slowed as I reached the stone marker to Samar's grave. I knelt and dug into the sand where I thought his right hand would be. I unsheathed the dagger that had belonged to his dead son. The blade had turned a dull green in the sheath. I took a handful of sand and rubbed the bronze, scrubbing until the dagger was shining again. I laid it in the hole and covered it with sand. I sat back on my heels, looking at the grave. I had lost my lover, the strong man at my side. I felt helpless and alone without him.

I heard a cough and turned to see if Farium had followed me. A large, yellow-furred animal stood half-hidden under a thorn bush, a stone's throw from the grave. My heart beat fast as the lioness stepped into the sunlight. Her pale fur was dusty with sand, her ribs showed along her side as though the skin had been stretched over her bones. She took another step toward me, limping on her front paw. She stopped and looked at me with her golden eyes. Her mouth dropped open, showing her bottom teeth. One fang was broken to a stub, the other was long and sharp.

The wind changed. I smelled the musky scent of her fur. I kept my eyes on her while I slowly reached down and pushed my fingers into the sand. I felt the hilt of the dagger and pulled it out. The lioness stepped closer, picking up and putting her huge paws down carefully. She paused when I stood up. We stared at each other. She twitched her ear against a sand fly but kept her eyes on me. I saw her back leg shiver and knew she was going to leap at me. I didn't know what to do. I was too far from the caravan for anyone to hear my scream. I was a fool to come out here by myself. I wished Farium were with me. I held the blade tight. I would have to fight if she attacked. The blade trembled in my hand as I thought of her knocking me down and tearing into my flesh. I raised it over my head, ready to stab her if she leapt.

Sunlight blazed off the dagger into her eyes. She shook her head, breaking her gaze. I yelled at her to get away, get away, and waved the dagger back and forth over my head, trying to appear bigger. She laid her ears back and lowered her tail. I kicked sand at her and screamed again. She breathed out a huff of air and slunk lower. I kept kicking and yelling until she slowly turned and limped away from me, leaving deeps prints in the sand. I lowered my hand, keeping the blade pointed at the beast until she walked past the thorn tree and toward a small dune.

I waited until she walked behind the dune, then dropped to my knees, panting in relief. My hand shook as I started to bury the dagger in the sand again. I stopped. Samar had given it to me to keep me safe. It had saved me from the lioness; he would want me to keep it. I heard his voice saying, "Your dagger," to me before he died. I slipped the jasper bracelet off my wrist instead and dropped it into the sand as my gift to him. I stayed on my knees for a moment, giving thanks to Samar for protecting me.

I stood, sheathed the dagger and walked back to the caravan. Farium stood in front of my tent, waiting for me. He lifted his hand as I approached. My women were still asleep when I entered my tent. I opened my red bag and put the dagger inside.

We sat inside our closed tent that night, sewing by candlelight while Yahmed and Wa'dab loudly feasted their friends. "What are you making?" I asked Samsi. She held up a piece of green wool with gold feathers that looked like tiny brushes stitched along the edge of the wool.

"Your sewing is good," I said.

"Timora was a good teacher." She glanced at the side of the tent where her friend used to sit, her head bent over her mending.

"Khe tells me that Wa'dab boasts you will sit at her fire tomorrow night." Tylos glanced at me as she warmed her hands over the candle.

I pulled my robe closer around my shoulders and thought of the dagger in my bag. I had faced a lioness today. Wa'dab would not rule me. "I am not joining her fire or her camp," I said. "We will ride in the middle of the caravan as my husband wished."

A cough outside the front curtain awakened us at dawn. Samsi talked to the man, dropped the curtain and turned to me. "Yahmed sent a slave to say they are coming to take down our tent. He said you will ride with his wife today."

Tylos pulled opened the curtain and called back the slave. Her tongue was sharp as she told him to return after I was awake and had eaten my morning bread.

"Fetch meat and cheese," I said to Samsi. "Do not make a cookfire. Tell Khe to bring my camel before the sun strikes the sand."

"What are you doing?" Tylos asked.

"I hoped Yahmed would ignore me if I stayed out of his sight. But he begins to command me. If I don't stop him now, he'll tell me where to ride and where to sleep and I'll stand far behind him when he greets King Solomon."

Tylos and I had folded our sheepskins and rolled up the sleeping mats when Samsi returned with Farium and Khe, leading my camel. Yahmed appeared as I was closing the curtains to my riding tent. His robe flew open, showing his skinny legs as he ran into my camp. Around us, the noise of the caravan was growing louder as camels were pulled up from their comfortable night's rest.

"Bilqis, my sister." Yahmed held his hand to his chest. "Did my slave not speak clearly this morning? You're under my protection now. You will join my camp."

I held the red bag in my lap. I could feel the hilt of Samar's dagger through the leather. I spoke through the partly closed curtain. "My husband will hear of your generosity, Yahmed. I will not look elsewhere when I need protection."

Yahmed shook his head at me and turned to Farium. "Join her camels with mine until we reach Jerusalem."

Farium looked at me, waiting for me to speak. I opened the curtain and looked down at Yahmed. "My husband, Darmalay of Saba, hired many guards to protect me." I waved my hand at Farium's guards, some of the men were loading Solomon's treasure on my camels, others were watching the desert. The gesture was a long one.

"Darmalay put me in the middle where I am safest. I will obey my husband." I began to close the curtain. "Tell your wife I welcome her to my fire tonight."

Yahmed clenched his teeth in a smile. "My wife will be honored to join your fire."

We reached a village at sunset and camped outside walls that were newly patched with darker rock. Samsi and Tylos raised the supply tent for our stay of one night while Khe fetched water for our tent from the well in the center of the village. It was deep, Khe said, with worn steps cut down the side to reach the muddy water below. The water tasted of iron, but our camels would be happy to drink it.

Samsi made lentil soup spiced with garlic and black pepper to hide the taste of iron. We had eaten our meal and were talking around the cookfire when Wa'dab stepped over my boundary stone. She settled into the cushions next to me and accepted wine from Samsi. I held a cup of heated wine in my hands but didn't drink. My stomach was uneasy and my head ached. Tylos said she feared I was unwell. I was weary from traveling, I said. With Wa'dab sitting at my fire, I did not want to say what was in my heart, that I felt sick with grief for Samar and Timora.

"You don't look well, Bilqis," Wa'dab said. "You cannot be comfortable sleeping in your small tent. Come to my camp, I have made room in my tent for you and your woman. Your girl will sleep with my slaves."

"Samsi is not my slave," I said. "She is my guest friend until I return her to her family."

"Then she is welcome in my tent." Wa'dab swallowed a mouthful of wine and looked up at the stars. "I am eager to see Jerusalem, but I will miss our nights in the desert."

"I feel the same." I said. "The stars are beautiful, they look like silver sparks falling inside a black bowl."

"Bilqis, you speak as a poet." Wa'dab patted my arm. "Save your words to enchant King Solomon and we will return home laden with gold."

I sipped wine and listened to her talk of the famous walls of Jerusalem that were made of gold and amber and precious stones. "The city walls are so bright in the sun that travelers see them shining from a day's ride away. I heard we have to shade our eyes when we approach the city during the day or they will burn from the light."

Wa'dab looked beyond my tent, at my camels kneeling in the dark. "You bring rich gifts for King Solomon. I hope they do not get lost in his rooms that are filled with gold." She tapped my arm and smiled at me. "Come to my tent, my sister," she said. "We will enter Jerusalem together."

"You are as generous as your husband," I said. "But I am comfortable where I am."

Wa'dab's tongue curled in her mouth when she yawned. "I must return to my husband." She placed a hand on my shoulder and stood. "He feasts with the village chieftain tonight. I want to hear what he says about the proper way to greet King Solomon." She waved at me and walked out of the firelight.

"She sounds like my aunts, telling my mother what to do." Samsi tied her food bags, jerking the strings tight. "I do not like her."

Farium appeared at my curtain the next morning before our bread was cooked. "Yahmed moved his camels to the front of the caravan, behind the star guides," he said.

"Yahmed may ride where he chooses," I said. "He is leader of the caravan."

Farium scratched his beard while he listened to my words. "Watch that his slaves do not mix my animals with his herd. Keep Darmalay's treasure for King Solomon close to me."

"Bilqis," Tylos said after I closed the curtain, "even Farium is worried that you allow Yahmed to ride before you."

"Let Yahmed and his wife feel important when we pass the villages. But he will not greet King Solomon with my husband's gifts in his hands." I didn't want to fight with Yahmed and Wa'dab. I wanted to ride quietly and gather my strength. When we were closer to Jerusalem, I intended to follow Samar's advice and send Farium with a large bag of incense to present to King Solomon. The king would hear my name long before I entered his city.

Our waterskins were full, so we rode the next two days without stopping to drink from the wells of passing villages. Their walls were built of clay and their gates were woven palm leaves. "Small walls, small wells," was Farium's only comment.

Wa'dab invited a different woman every day to ride with her. She did not smile or wave at me and no longer invited me to her cookfire at night. She believed I was weak because Samar no longer stood by my side. I was relieved to be left alone.

At the end of the third day, Farium stopped at my fire to tell us of the great city we would enter the next day. "We are four days from Solomon's lands when we reach the city," he said.

We saw high city walls by midday and soon were riding through the counting gate under the gaze of taxmen who tallied our camels. We passed through the gate and entered a walled field. Khe set up the sleeping tent with the help of Samar's slaves, two young boys who had been overlooked by Yahmed and taken in by Farium to serve his guards. We ate our evening meal inside the tent. I was too weary from days of riding to visit other fires.

The next morning, Tylos, Samsi, and I walked to the city's market. We took one Samar's slaves to carry our baskets.

"I think I am in Myrb," Tylos said. The market was crowded with stalls covered with lengths of striped linen.

Merchants called to us, "Beautiful strangers; taste this ripe pomegranate, it is sweet as your smile." Men stood behind bags of green olives, baskets heaped with shredded spices, curled cinnamon bark, and slabs of brownish-white salt. They men winked at Samsi and me, and if older, included Tylos in their smiles.

We filled our baskets with yellow melons, fresh eggs, bulbs of garlic and onions, bags of brown lentils, and sweet, purple figs. A meat merchant picked out a fat goose, smiling at Samsi while he broke the bird's neck. A flutter of wings, a wild squawk and the bird lay still. The slave carried the goose with its head hanging over his shoulder, the yellow beak tapping against the boy's brown back.

Tylos stopped to buy jars of scented oil while Samsi and I walked on, lured by the gleam of gold. A long board laid across the front of one of the stalls displayed shallow boxes filled with polished stones of carnelian, amber, red coral, and bright blue turquoise. The stones were as big as my thumb. They looked like rocks compared to the small beads we used in the south. While I picked out turquoise and carnelian stones, the merchant cleared boxes from the other end of the board and laid out rows of necklaces, earrings, and bracelets. I watched as Samsi's eyes came back to a bracelet of red coral beads separated by tiny gold beads. I pointed to the bracelet and dropped a piece of incense on the board. The merchant shrugged his shoulders. I added a second, smaller piece. He handed the bracelet to me with a bow. I wondered if I had paid too much.

"Give me your hand." I said to Samsi. I fastened the bracelet around her wrist. "You look like the daughter of a chieftain."

The merchant smiled at me. "Your daughter, very pretty."

"Look, Tylos," she said when the old woman joined us. "Bilqis bought this for me. She said I'll look like the daughter of a great chieftain when I ride into Jerusalem with her."

The slave following Tylos carried a basket filled with jars of scented oil. He looked bored and tired. I smelled roasted meat and handed a small chunk of incense to Samsi. "Take the slave and buy food for us," I said. The boy grinned and turned to follow her.

Banners of colorful silks drew Tylos and me to a stall at the end of the row. The merchant stepped from the shade of his awning, bowed to us and flung lengths of brightly colored silk into the air before us. I wrapped a veil of amber silk around my shoulders. The rough skin on my fingers caught on the delicate fabric. My skin was coarse, my hands and arms were burned dark from the sun. I would have to soak in oil for a day before I met King Solomon.

Tylos chose a black veil bordered with silver thread while I picked out pale blue silk for Samsi. The merchant was wrapping the veils when the girl and the slave returned with our food. He handed the bundle to Tylos and pointed to a tree near his stall. "Eat there," he said.

We sat in the shade and ate roasted meat and fresh bread that Samsi said was as good as hers. Tylos showed me the jars of jasmine and rose oil she bought for our baths, while Samsi held out her hand, admiring her bracelet.

Khe arrived at my tent after we returned from the market. He stood tall in front of me, as his father did when Farium spoke to his guards. "My father says Yahmed is invited to feast tonight with the chieftain of the village. The emissary asked Yahmed to direct him to your tent so he could invite you to feast with the wives of the chieftain."

"I am honored," I said.

"There is more," he said. "Yahmed told the emissary you were unwell and offered his wife in your place." Khe laughed and was a boy again. "The emissary said he saw you and your women walking back from the market and you looked well. He said to Yahmed that he would tell his chieftain that Bilqis of Saba would feast with his wives tonight."

Tylos started coughing after we returned from the market. I helped her into the tent. "I'm tired, Bilqis," she complained. "I want my bed. Don't ask me to visit with the chieftain's wives with you. Take one of the wives from Myrb."

"I'll ask Shadru. She seems a friend to me."

"Unlike Wa'dab," Tylos said.

I opened a basket tied with strips of gilded leather and pulled out several boxes I had brought on the journey. Each box was carved out of a precious stone and small enough to fit in the palm of my hand. I had thought to fill the boxes with incense when I presented them as gifts.

Tylos pulled her sheepskin over her shoulders and turned over to sleep. I carried the boxes and a small bag of incense outside the tent.

I sat under the awning with the boxes in my lap, watching Samsi blow on the cookfire. When the dung started to smoke, she sat back on her heels and looked at me. "I miss Timora," she said. "I miss her telling me to fetch water or bring more dung. I miss talking with her during the day and at night when we would sew together."

"I know, child," I said. "She was of our tent and of our hearts."

"I miss my mother and father, too," she said. "They're in my heart always."

I heard Tylos coughing inside the tent. I told Samsi to find the bag of feverroot to make tea for her.

Shadru stepped over my boundary stone as Samsi walked into the tent. Shadru looked tired, but smiled when she saw me. "I've come to ask for herbs for my husband." She heard Tylos coughing. "Harjan suffers from the same sickness. I did not sleep last night from his coughing."

I called through the open curtain to Samsi to make up a bag of feverroot. Shadru sat down next to me on the mat and watched as I dropped a chunk of golden incense inside a box of green jade.

"Are you taking those as gifts to the feast tonight with the wives of the chieftain?" she said. "I heard there are three wives."

"Yes, I hope the wives will be pleased with them." I closed the jade box and picked up one of carnelian and another of purple amethyst.

"Jade is the most precious," said Shadru. "Perhaps you would give that one to the first wife."

"Is that custom in Myrb?" I said. "The chieftains who visited us in the great house brought one wife only. I never had to decide which gift to give the second or third wives."

"Give the more valuable gift to the first wife. As the wife of Darmalay and the highest ranked woman on the caravan, you would present it to her. Your companion will give the boxes to the other wives."

"Tylos is too sick to come with me. I wished you to ask you, but I don't want to take you away from her husband in his illness."

Shadru smiled. "I am honored you wished me to attend you, but my husband is like a child when he's sick, wanting me to care for him"

Samsi appeared with a small bag in her hand and handed it to Shadru. The woman stood with a groan. "I'll be happy when my husband can sleep without coughing. Then I'll sleep too."

I didn't want to ask any of the other wives on the caravan to accompany me to the chieftain's house. After Shadru left, I told Samsi that she would come with me.

Khe led my camel out of the camp at dusk, before our priests opened their tent to begin the full-moon ceremony for

Ilumqah. I did not know if our god was honored in this city, so I concealed the bracelet of white pearls I wore to celebrate Ilumqah's return under my sleeve.

Inside the chieftain's big house we were led to a room with windows of alabaster fretwork facing the direction of moonrise. Candles were lit around the room; the lights wavered in the evening breeze. The first wife, an old woman with white hair stood at the head of the room. The other two wives, both young and pregnant, listened with their heads bowed in respect as she welcomed us to her house. The feeling of calm in the room surprised me. I had thought to meet three women, resentful of each other as Darmalay's mother had been of me and as I had been toward Amida.

I presented the jade box to the first wife while Samsi offered boxes to the second and third wives. The women held them in their hands, admiring the little boxes before opening the lids and breathing deeply of the incense.

"Ah, golden incense, it is precious to us," said the first wife. She reached for my hand, holding it close, as if we were old friends. "I hope you are feeling better," she said.

I touched my belly. "Our water was bad the last few days."

"Perhaps your sickness is a blessing," she said. The other wives patted their round bellies and smiled at me.

"I do not have your good fortune," I said. "I am not with child."

"Will your children be much changed when you return?" asked the first wife.

The old sorrow pierced my heart. "I do not have children. My one child died at his birth a year ago and I have not been blessed with other children."

"You are young." The woman gently squeezed my hand. "You will have many healthy boys." She gestured toward the rug. "Sit, my friend. Tell me, has your journey been hard?"

I smiled at her, liking her kind, wrinkled face. "Our journey was hard sometimes, but not when we travel through lands as beautiful as these."

A slave drew the curtain aside and several young women entered the room carrying platters of food and a jar of wine with five silver cups. The first wife filled a plate with choice pieces of meat and offered it to me. "Please accept the best my poor house can offer."

The second wife placed a few pieces of meat on a plate and gave it to Samsi, welcoming her as my honored companion.

"Samsi is my daughter for this journey," I said. "My companion is resting in our tent. We found Samsi in the desert after her mother and father were lost in a sayl."

The second wife said, "Oh, my poor child." She pulled back the plate and piled more food on it until pieces of meat fell off the plate onto the rug. She patted Samsi's hair when she handed her the plate.

We ate and drank in silence until one of the pregnant wives began to talk of her youngest child who had lost another tooth. We all shook our heads, even Samsi, and murmured that children grew up so fast.

The wives heaped bread and meat on our plates again until we could eat no more. Slaves took away the greasy plates, refilled our wine cups, and laid bowls of ripe grapes and cheese on the rug. One slave placed a small bowl of what looked like sliced pieces of wood next to the grapes. Clear sap oozed out of the wood. The first wife offered the bowl to me. I took a bit of the wood and held it in my hand, waiting until she put a piece of the wood into her mouth and began to chew the end. I bit into the wood and was surprised that the sap was as sweet as honey, though lighter on my tongue.

"Do you like the sweet wood?" she asked. "We buy it in the market."

"Yes," I said. "This is the first time I have tasted it."

We heard running feet and three children ran through the curtain into the room. One of them, a boy of about five years, fell into the lap of the first wife. He grabbed a piece of cheese from the platter and stuffed it in his mouth. The two little girls, dressed in tunics with shoulder ties of blue silk, ran to the second wife, pushing against each other to be first in her lap. One child hid her face in her mother's shoulder, the other girl looked at Samsi and me and at the bowls of sweets. Samsi picked up handful of grapes and held them to the girl. She reached for the fruit, not taking her eyes off Samsi.

The third wife held out her arms. "Where is my boy?" she asked. The old woman patted the shoulder of the child in her lap and he wiped his mouth and walked across the rug toward his mother. He glanced at me when he passed, a swift look that showed his round cheeks and dark brown eyes.

"Come here, my dove." She pulled him to her lap and kissed his hair. He was still for a moment, then wiggled out of her lap and stood up. The woman clapped her hands and then we all clapped as the boy began to hop around the rug. The little girls pushed up from their mother and spun around with their arms held out until they bumped into each other and fell down. They sat up, rubbing their heads, while boy jumped back into his mother's arms. I laughed and felt happy for the first time since the attack that killed Timora and Samar.

"Have you visited Jerusalem?" The first wife turned to me while the children settled into their mothers' laps.

"This is my first time. I take greetings to King Solomon from my husband, Darmalay of Myrb, from the land of Saba."

"You have traveled a long way to greet the king." She leaned over to pour more wine into my cup.

"My husband sent me and his trusted counselor to make treaty with the king and ask his protection when our caravans approach his lands. We bring gold, incense, salt, spices, and wine from the south, and many times our caravans are attacked before they reach Jerusalem."

"I heard the leader of your caravan was killed in a bandit attack."

"Yes, his name was Damri Samar." My heart ached as I remembered Samar's smiling at me when he stepped over my boundary stone at night to join my fire. "Samar was my husband's chief counselor. My husband called him brother." I picked up my wine. "He and many others died in the attack."

"Ah, the thieves are fierce in these lands," she said. "The caravans grow bigger and richer every year and men come from villages far away to raid them."

She gazed at me. "I understand why your husband sent his beautiful young wife to meet the king. You speak well and you are at ease with strangers, but I wonder why you made this long journey. Was it to please your husband?"

I rubbed my arms in the cool night air and thought of the reasons why I had agreed to leave my house. I felt as though I had been a girl when I left Myrb, anxious to be away before Amida bore her child and became the favored wife. But now I knew the true reason I had traveled so far from my home.

"I wished to meet King Solomon," I said. "I thirst for his wisdom. Before my son was born, my husband allowed me to join his council. I sat at my husband's right hand; people listened to me and thought my advice wise."

"And after your child died, did you return to the council room?"

"No, Darmalay said my grief troubled the men who came before him. I hoped to bear another child but I was not blessed. Now my husband has taken a new wife and no longer seeks my bed." I wondered that I could talk so freely with a stranger, but she spoke kindly to me and she too, had to accept her husband's new wives.

She smiled at the little girls who were yawning in their mother's lap. "I made peace with my husband's wives so that we all may live together without quarrel. They bear his children while I sit in council with him. I listen but do not speak when men bring their complaints to him and he listens but does not speak when women bring their problems to me. He and I talk later. That is how I have become more than a wife to him."

"That is my wish, too." My words became true as I spoke them. I might not be able to give my husband a child, but I had learned much about leadership on my journey and would return to him with the gift of Solomon's wisdom, and my own.

I lifted my cup to drink. "Have you met King Solomon?" I asked.

She nodded. "I travel to Jerusalem with my husband when he presents gifts from our village to the king. King Solomon holds council in a great room with gold steps leading up to his throne. He is not tall, but he seems tall even when he is seated, and he listens carefully when others speak."

"He is so wise and famous that I fear my village manners will not please him," I said.

She smiled. "I have heard that King Solomon is eager to meet the young queen from the land of Saba."

"He knows of me?" I said.

She laughed. "News travels swifter than a bird, my friend. We heard of about a caravan led by a queen was coming many days ago."

I smiled, pleased that King Solomon was expecting me. "How shall I greet him?" I asked. "I was told that I am to go on my knees before him."

"Do not go on your knees," she said. "That is for slaves and people who seek his judgment. Lower your eyes when you approach his throne and wait for him to greet you. He respects the words of men and women who speak plainly. When he asks you why you have come before him, tell him what is in your heart. Tell him you journeyed far from your home to learn from him and he will think you worth more than gifts of gold and incense."

The boy woke and climbed from his mother's lap to join the two girls playing a patting hand game with Samsi. He pushed his way between the girls and held up his hands to play.

"He is like his father," said the first wife. "He likes to be in the middle of everything." She turned to me. "You are four days ride from King Solomon's lands. You may be attacked again before you enter his protection."

"After we reach his lands we are another three days to Jerusalem. Does King Solomon's rule extend that far?"

"His law is strong; no one dares steal within his boundaries." She picked up her wine cup and studied the candlelight caught in the silver. "Perhaps the new leader who feasts with my husband tonight will hire guards from this city to protect your caravan until you reach King Solomon's lands."

"If Yahmed does not think of it in all the important things he will discuss tonight," I said, "then I would be in your debt if you would talk of this with your husband. We will hire guards from your city tomorrow to ride with us until we reach King Solomon's lands."

"That is good business," she said. "I invite you now to take your rest with me after you leave Jerusalem and pass through our city again on your return to the south." She put down her cup. "Is the new leader of your caravan a brother to your husband?"

"Yahmed is one of many merchants on the caravan. He is known to my husband, but Darmalay does not call him brother."

"Will he be at your side when you greet King Solomon?"

"I will enter Jerusalem with men my husband calls brother. Yahmed has wealth enough to meet the king on his own."

"You speak wisely," she said. "Your new leader may petition to meet with the king, but I hear King Solomon waits to greet the beautiful queen from the south." She offered a bowl of grapes to me. "My husband will ask of our meeting tonight and I will tell him that we are honored to receive the gift of friendship from Queen Bilqis of Saba."

The fretted windows glowed with light from the rising moon while I listened to her sweet words. From my lips to her husband's ear, the story would travel fast that Queen Bilqis was well and desirous of meeting King Solomon.

I smiled as I ate a grape. Solomon would look at me, not the old wine merchant. Yahmed would choke on my dust when we entered Jerusalem.

~ Eighteen ~

Over the next two days we traveled past villages built close together along the side of the path. "They protect each other," said Farium. I looked at fields of ripe barley waving between the villages and could not see the boundaries between one village and the next. Boys herding sheep and men and women working in the fields stopped to stretch their backs and watch us as we rode past. Wa'dab rode at the front of the caravan with her tent open on all sides. She wore a headcloth of gold silk, heavy gold chains around her neck, and gold bracelets stacked up her arms. She looked like a temple statue made of gold. I wore a plain linen tunic and robes. I looked like a caravan slave next to Wa'dab and her gold.

I leaned over the side of my riding tent to talk with Tylos. "Wa'dab wants the villagers to think she is the queen who travels to meet King Solomon."

"I'll braid gold in your hair tomorrow if you want sheepherders and field slaves to talk of you," Tylos said. "Wa'dab plays the great lady on the caravan, but Solomon will not mistake who is the wife of the most powerful chieftain of Saba when we enter Jerusalem."

Our next camp was outside a village a day's ride from the border of Solomon's lands. Tylos and I sewed together under the awning while Samsi and Khe walked into the village to buy fresh meat and fruit. I looked up when the wife of a merchant approached my camp, carrying a small clay jar. I had seen her often, sitting at Wa'dab's fire.

"I brought a gift for you, Bilqis." She lifted the lid. Inside the jar was a round yellow fruit covered with honey. "This is a lemon," she said. "It is a sour fruit made sweet by the honey. I bought it in the market. "

I accepted her gift and asked her to sit with us. Tylos poured cups of cooled barley water. "We enter King Solomon's lands tomorrow." I offered the cup to my visitor. "We look upon Jerusalem in three days."

"I'll be happy when we are inside the city walls," said the woman. "I do not like sleeping in the desert. Many nights I have heard footsteps outside my curtain. My husband sleeps soundly and hears nothing."

"She hears the wind and thinks men are trying to enter her tent," Tylos said after the women had gone.

"She was eager to bring me a gift," I said.

"She is ambitious for her husband," said Tylos. "She wants him to stand with you when you meet King Solomon."

"She wants my friendship but she calls Wa'dab sister." I watched the woman stop at Wa'dab's camp. She glanced back at me before entering Wa'dab's tent. No, she could not be a friend to both of us.

We rose before dawn and were moving again before sunlight poured across the sand. At midday, Farium pointed to a white rock, tall as a pillar in the distance beyond the fields. "Solomon's lands," he said. The other guards nodded to each other.

I let out a breath and lay back against my cushions. I had not realized how anxious I had been since the bandit attack, when Samar and Timora were killed. We were in King Solomon's lands now. We were safe.

The hired guards stopped at the sight of the pillar and turned their camels back toward their village, four days to the south. A feeling of excitement ran through the caravan after the guards left; camel men sang louder as they pulled their beasts, curtains were tied open and people smiled at me from their riding tents.

"Everyone desires your favor," Tylos said.

We were a day's ride from Jerusalem when we stopped to make our camp behind an outcropping of rocks. Fires glowed in the night as men and women feasted their friends. I rested inside my tent, watching Samsi and Tylos cook our evening meal. I remembered Samar's plan to send Farium with a large bag of incense to give to King Solomon. I shook my head at the thought; according to the chieftain's wife, the king was awaiting my arrival, and I needed Farium and all of his guards to stand with me while Yahmed and Wa'dab schemed to replace me as the leader of the caravan.

Tylos and Samsi entered the tent with a platter of bread and roasted meat. Before Samsi closed the curtain, one of Wa'dab's slaves coughed outside and told Samsi that Wa'dab wished me to eat at her cookfire. I told Samsi to thank Wa'dab, but I was eating at my fire tonight.

"Yahmed invites many men to his fire," said Tylos. "His slaves say he is deciding who will greet King Solomon with him."

"Let him talk," I said. "Solomon wants to meet me and I will choose who will be at my side when I greet the king."

I was reaching for a piece of bread when I heard a man outside the tent, shouting my name.

"What now?" grumbled Tylos. She started to open the curtain when Yahmed pushed through it. He stopped, swaying back and forth in the middle of the tent. His eyes seemed to twist in his head. Tylos grabbed a camel stick and moved around the man, out of his reach, to stand next to me. Yahmed jerked his eyes toward Samsi when she ran past him, through the front curtain and out of the tent.

Tylos raised her stick. "Get out," she hissed. "Leave us."

"Whore," Yahmed yelled. He was so drunk that it sounded as though his tongue had been cut, but I knew what he said. Every woman knew that word. Our mothers taught us to fear it. I was afraid for a moment that Yahmed knew of my love for Samar. I did not back away, I would not let him see my fear. Yahmed was a little man made of borrowed goods. I felt I could swat at him and he would run out of the tent, afraid of me.

Farium pushed through the front curtain and put his hand on Yahmed's shoulder. "Come," he said, "you do not belong here." Yahmed tried to shake off his hand, but the guard gripped his shoulder and would not let go. Yahmed stopped struggling under Farium's hand. He looked like a tired old man.

"Yahmed," I said. "Leave my tent now and I will invite you to my cookfire in the morning."

He blinked his eyes at my words and wiped his nose on his sleeve.

"I wish your advice about my greeting when I meet King Solomon," I said.

He licked his lips. Tylos moved closer to me. "I will be happy to advise you," he said. He belched loudly as Farium pulled him from the tent.

Samsi poked her head through the back curtain. "Is he gone? Farium told me to stay outside until Yahmed left."

"Run after Farium," I said, "Tell him I wish to speak with him after he delivers Yahmed to his tent."

The next morning, Yahmed was all smiles and springing step when he walked around the rocks to my camp. He stopped at the sight of three men sitting around my fire, merchants my husband called brother. I sat under the awning a few feet away from the men. Tylos sat at my right and Samsi sat behind me. One of Samar's young slaves served the men.

Harjan, the salt merchant and Shadru's husband, laughed when he saw Yahmed standing by the rocks. "Are you still asleep, my friend?"

He pointed to the empty rug beside him at the fire. Yahmed walked to the rug, tugging his beard as if he would pull out a fistful of grey hairs. He sat next to Harjan and glanced around the circle at Darmalay's friends, dipping their bread in honey while they talked of meeting King Solomon.

"I heard Bilqis has questions for the king," Harjan said. The men turned to look at me.

"Yes," I said, "but they are a woman's questions."

Harjan laughed. "If they are like the questions my wife asks me, King Solomon will need all his wisdom to answer them."

Yahmed laughed with the other men, but quickly dropped his smile. I knew he worried over what they discussed while he lingered in his tent, perfuming his beard before walking to my fire.

"We are a day's journey from Jerusalem," said Harjan. He turned to Yahmed. "We talked this morning of traveling until midday and stopping to camp at a village close to the city."

"I am head of council." Yahmed held up his cup for more wine. "I will decide when we leave."

"I am on the council as are my brother merchants." Harjan opened his hands to include the other two men. "We are three of the five members, and I speak for us when I say we wish to stop at the village to prepare for our entrance into Jerusalem."

"You speak for her," Yahmed pointed to me. "I do not allow a woman to tell me when to stay and when to leave." He gulped a mouthful of wine and wiped his lips. "Come to my tent," he said to the men. "I have decided who will enter Jerusalem with me and carry the greetings of the caravan to King Solomon."

The men looked at each other but did not answer Yahmed.

I picked up my wine cup and held it to Samsi to fill from a small skin she held in her lap. "I ride first into Jerusalem," I said. "I will present the gifts and the greeting of my husband to the king."

Yahmed stared at me as if he could not believe my words. "A woman does not ride before me. You will ride behind me, with my wife."

I put down my cup. "My husband sent me with Damri Samar to meet with King Solomon. Darmalay did not speak of you." From the edge of my eye, I saw Farium and several of his guards waiting outside my boundary stone.

"You and Samar," sneered Yahmed. "Your good friend Samar is dead and I am head of council. I think you will keep to your tent when I meet with Solomon." He smiled, proud of his threat and dropped his empty cup on the rug.

I held up my hand before Harjan or the other men could speak. "Hear me, Yahmed." My voice was calm and I spoke as if I had nothing to fear. "You may ask to meet with the king, but he has heard my name, not yours. He waits to meet with me."

"Your name is on the lips of every man who walks past your camp." He looked around the circle of men. "She called me into her tent last night."

Harjan slapped Yahmed on the back. "Do not let wine rule your tongue, my friend. You were drunk last night. I saw Farium help you to your camp after you staggered into Bilqis's tent, mistaking it for your own. Say no more about the wife of our chieftain or you will enter Jerusalem long after Bilqis has greeted King Solomon. Now come, it is past time to leave if we are to reach the village at midday."

Yahmed looked around the circle, at the men nodding at Harjan's words. He stood with the other men. I did not look at him as he walked past me and out of my camp.

I let out a long breath after they were gone. Samsi smiled at me as if she enjoyed the battle of words. Tylos hugged me. "You spoke well, my girl," she said.

I stopped outside the tent, watching as Yahmed ducked inside his wife's tent. He seeks her counsel, I thought.

We had rolled our sleeping mats and were folding the sheepskins when Samsi called through the curtain, "Wa'dab is coming."

"Make her welcome," I said. "Offer her a cup of wine."

Wa'dab stood before my tent with her arms crossed over her breasts, shaking her head at Samsi's offer of wine.

"What is it?" I asked. "What do you want?"

"My husband and his many friends have decided the caravan will ride through the day without stopping. We'll reach the gates of Jerusalem before nightfall."

I said, "The other three merchants on the council agreed to stop at midday and enter Jerusalem tomorrow."

She shrugged. "They can ride at their own pace. Come with us now, Bilqis, or we leave you behind."

"Go if you wish, Wa'dab. Ride to Jerusalem without me. But you will not take my goods, or my guards, or my name."

She looked at me, her eyes flicking from my hair to my feet. I had dressed carefully for the meeting with the merchants, but I felt like an unwashed village girl under her hard gaze.

"Keep your camels," she said. "We have gold enough to persuade the king. Keep your name. It will be nothing to King Solomon. My husband's name will be on the treaty, not yours."

I clenched my fists as she walked from my camp. I wanted to leap at her and smash her head into the sand, but I could not let the rest of the caravan see that I was upset by her words. I remembered Darmalay's advice when I first sat on his council. "Do not let small words anger you," he had said. Few merchants remained friendly to me. If they thought I was easily angered, they might regard Yahmed as the stronger leader and follow him.

Yahmed was waiting for Wa'dab when she reached her tent. He nodded when she spoke to him and then ran from her camp.

"He gathers his friends," Tylos said.

"Will Yahmed take many people with him when he leaves?" asked Samsi.

"I don't know how many will follow him," I said. "Find Khe and tell him to move my camel to the head of the caravan after Yahmed is gone."

I turned to Tylos after the girl left. "Come inside and help me dress. I will look the queen when my enemies leave."

I knotted the shoulder straps of my blue silk tunic while Tylos tied a girdle of gold and lapis beads around my waist. Her hands shook when she draped a veil of gold silk on my head. I knew she was distressed about Yahmed's threat to leave the caravan and take as many people who would follow him to Jerusalem. I stood quietly while she smoothed the veil over my hair, listening to camels groaning as they were loaded and pulled up to standing, dogs barking, and men talking as they gathered in Yahmed's camp. Wa'dab's voice and the voices of her friends were loud as they found reasons to walk past my camp, laughing and talking of meeting King Solomon.

Samsi ran into the tent after I was dressed. She was red-faced and breathless. "Most of the tents are coming down," she said. "Only a few are standing."

Tylos pulled open the curtain. "It looks as though the whole camp is leaving, Bilqis. You must stop Yahmed. Send Farium and his guards to keep them from leaving."

I wrung my hands for a moment while my women looked at me. What would Samar have done if the caravan had rebelled against his leadership? Would he have sent his guards against his own people? I didn't want a battle on the caravan. I didn't want their blood on my hands.

I took a deep breath. "I will not force them to stay with me. Let them leave. I'll ride into Jerusalem alone if I have to, with my treasure and my guards."

Tylos dropped the curtain and hurried toward me. "Ride alone, what are you thinking Bilqis. You go nowhere without me."

"Or me," Samsi said. "Or Khe," she added.

"Stand with me now," I said. "I will watch men leave and know who is loyal to me and who follows Yahmed."

I took Samar's sheathed dagger from my red bag and tucked it into the beaded girdle. The touch of the hilt under my hand was comforting, as though Samar was standing beside me. I thought Tylos would disapprove and say that Farium and his guards would protect me, but she nodded her head in agreement and opened the curtain.

We stepped into the sunlight. An enormous herd of pack and riding camels were moving away from the camp, on the path toward Jerusalem. Yahmed and his wife rode at the front of the long line. Wa'dab's curtains were rolled up. She was dressed again in gold, gleaming like a temple statue in the sunlight.

The three merchants who had met at my cookfire, men Darmalay called brother, stood in front of their tents, watching their friends ride past. Behind my tent, I could see Farium and his guards, lined up in front of my herd with their hands on their daggers, ready to fight if any of the traitors foolishly decided to turn thief.

I looked around at the cookfires still smoking in the empty camps. I felt humiliated that so many men had left me and joined Yahmed. At the far edge of the trampled sand stood the closed white tent of the priests. I smiled at the tent, grateful that the priests had decided to stay with me. Our small caravan still was blessed.

Shadru joined her husband as the three merchants turned their backs on the retreating camels and walked toward my tent. Harjan stopped before me. "Yahmed runs to meet King Solomon," he said. "But the king is wise, he will not mistake Yahmed for a great chieftain."

"Or Wa'dab for Bilqis," Shadru said. She smiled at me, but I could see that she too, was worried at being left behind.

Khe approached, leading my camel. I stood with my hand on Samar's dagger and looked at the faces of the people before me. I had known little of them in Myrb, other than to exchange polite smiles at a feast. Now I saw the faces of my brothers and sisters.

"Our hands are still full, my friends," I said. "We have our camels, our guards, and the fortune in incense and gold that Darmalay is sending to King Solomon." I pointed to the cloud of dust hanging in the air behind Yahmed's caravan. "Our old companions will arrive in Jerusalem late in the day, hot and covered with dirt. We will travel at an easier pace and stop at midday to bathe and rest. We'll enter Jerusalem tomorrow at sunrise, when the day is cool."

Men and women looked at each other. Harjan spoke. "We ride with you, Bilqis." He turned to the others. "Who would argue with a woman armed with a dagger?"

I laughed with them. Khe helped me mount my camel. I sat inside the riding tent while Guards and slaves took down the tents and loaded the camels for our journey. Khe led my beast to stand at the front of the caravan. Before me the path was stamped to hard clay from the feet of camels bearing loads for the cities in the north and returning laden with goods for the markets in the south. The wide path seemed to pull me forward, toward Jerusalem and King Solomon. In the distance, the tops of the mountains were covered with a layer of dark purple that looked as though it had been dusted with powdered amethyst. The sides of the mountains were wrinkled and gleamed golden in the sunlight.

I breathed in the fresh air and lifted my face to the sun, wishing I had moved to the front long ago. Khe up smiled at me, happy to be out of the noisy, dirty center of the caravan.

~ Nineteen ~

We walked far behind Yahmed's caravan to let the air clear of dust. The remaining three merchants and their wives rode behind me, followed by the priests in their white riding tents. The curtains to the tents were closed, but once when I looked back, I saw a man lean out to hand a water bag to the white-haired priest riding in the tent next to him.

We reached a small village when the sun had passed overhead and made camp in the desert outside their rock walls. Harjan and Shadru raised their tents close to mine. I invited them and the other merchants and their wives to join my fire for our evening meal.

We feasted as the sun slid down the sky. Our shadows grew long on the sand as we sat around the fire, old friends eating and drinking golden wine from Myrb.

"Have you traded in Jerusalem?" I asked the merchants.

One of the men nodded. "I traveled to Jerusalem two years ago." He glanced at the other merchants. "Finding a place to sell in the market may be difficult. Many of the merchants have traded in Jerusalem for a long time and never leave their stalls. We come and go. Sometimes there is little space left for us."

Harjan spoke. "We have names of merchants who trade in goods from the south. We'll sell through them."

"How long will you stay in Jerusalem?" I asked.

Harjan shrugged his shoulders. "We'll buy new merchandise for the markets in the south and join a caravan traveling back to Myrb."

I started to speak and stopped. I didn't want to undertake the journey home on a caravan with strangers, but I didn't want to ask my friends to wait for me. I didn't know how long I would remain in Jerusalem; all depended on my welcome from King Solomon. I might stay a week, a month, however long the king desired my company.

Shadru laid her hand on her husband's arm. He looked at her and then at me. "You are wife of our chieftain, Bilqis," he said. "We will stay as long as you wish to enjoy King Solomon's hospitality."

I smiled at him. "I will not hold you to a long promise."

Harjan gestured at the merchants seated around the fire. "We are curious about how you will present your gifts to King Solomon," he said.

I put down my wine cup. I had not thought about it. "I've watched chieftains offer gifts to Darmalay. It seems a simple ceremony." In Myrb, slaves would kneel before my husband, holding up jars of wine and boxes of rare spices while their masters praised the sweetness of the wine, the enticing taste of the new spice. After the offerings were taken to the kitchen, the merchant would be welcomed as a guest. But I was offering much more; I had not thought about the way to present it to the king.

"It will not be a modest ceremony," Harjan said. "The amount of gold and incense you bring to King Solomon is greater wealth than any of us have seen. It will require many men to carry it into the throne room."

"Shall I hire men from Jerusalem?"

Harjan glanced at the other merchants. "I would ask you to give us the honor of arranging the presentation. The poets will sing about the gifts you bring to the king."

I nodded in agreement. "Leave the gold for last. It is the most valuable."

Harjan shook his head. "Your gold will be admired, but it is incense that the king will prize. It's rare and hard to obtain. King's Solomon's priests burn it every morning and evening in a great temple when they offer sacrifices to their god. I remember the air smelled of roasting meat."

"Your advice is sound," I said. "It shall be as you wish."

"I have not seen the gold you carry, " Harjan said. "How is it cast?"

"In large discs. Darmalay said each was a talent. He showed me one before we left. " I picked up a round plate that

Samsi used to serve dates. "It was as big as this and it so heavy that it took two men to hold it up."

"How many did Darmalay send to King Solomon?" Harjan asked.

"One hundred and twenty talents."

The merchants looked at each other. "We'll need a lot of men to display that much gold," Harjan said. "

Shadru laughed. "Knowing my husband, Bilqis, he and his brothers will show Darmalay's treasure in a way that no one who sees it will ever forget."

Khe had ridden into the village while we ate, returning with a goatskin filled with water for my bath. After my friends left, Samsi dipped out a bucket of cool water and set another bucket of water to heat on the fire.

Tylos and I worked inside the tent, selecting my clothing for the morning ride into Jerusalem and my first meeting with King Solomon. Tylos laid out a tunic of green silk. "You were wise to gain the consent of your friends to wait for you in Jerusalem," she said. "I do not want to travel back to Myrb with strangers. The journey will be more comfortable in the company of friends."

She added, "I hope Wa'dab and Yahmed and the merchants who deserted you return to Myrb on a different caravan."

"I would not welcome Wa'dab to my fire if she did ride home with us," I said. "I am content with you and Samsi as my companions."

"You must return Samsi to her people," Tylos said.

"I have told her we will take her back to her aunts," I said. "She belongs to them. Samsi is unhappy that she must return home. She said she'll run away if her aunts try to force her into a marriage."

"Who knows how long you'll be Solomon's guest?" Tylos said. "Samsi may be too old for them to marry off by the time you return to Myrb."

I laughed. "I'm not staying that long."

As Tylos pulled out another silk tunic, we heard Khe calling, "Bilqis, Bilqis, come look."

Beyond the village, a column of white dust hung in the darkening sky. "My father says three men in chariots ride toward us," said Khe. "He thinks they are sent by King Solomon."

"They come to see you, Bilqis. Take the water off the fire," Tylos said to Khe. "We'll bathe later."

Khe removed the pot of water while Samsi, Tylos, and I ran inside the tent. Samsi and I stuffed our clothing back into bags. Tylos unrolled a small rug and set upon it a jar of wine and four silver cups. I lit two candles, placing them on either side of the wine. Samsi laid blue and crimson wool cushions around the rug for the men to lean against. "Put one there." I pointed an arm's distance from the other cushions.

I looked around the tent, at the soft cushions that invited rest, the tall jar of wine, and the cups shining in candlelight. Tylos stood behind me, next to Samsi. We listened to the sound of men's voices approaching our tent.

Farium entered first, leading three men. Two men wore dark wool robes over their tunics with sheathed bronze daggers tucked into waist sashes of green silk. Their dark hair was pulled back and tied with leather strings. A third man, shorter than the others, wore his black hair loose to his shoulders. The hilt of his dagger was covered with red and green jewels. He carried a large silver box in his hands. After the men entered, Farium stepped to one side, quietly watching while they greeted me.

The tallest of the three men bowed to me. "I greet you, Bilqis of Saba, in the name of King Solomon who sends you a small gift in welcome."

The longhaired man with the beautiful dagger handed the box to the tall emissary. The silver lid flashed in the candlelight when he opened the box. The tall man pulled out a bundle of white silk and handed it to Tylos.

She unfolded the silk and held up a necklace of amber beads caught in the middle with a large pendant of a hoopoe bird. The body and the crest of the bird were made of gold. The wings were ebony, striped with inlaid ivory. The long bill was curved amber.

"A hoopoe came to King Solomon in a dream," said the tall emissary. "The bird told him a beautiful queen journeyed to meet him from a great kingdom in the south."

"King Solomon has honored me with this gift," I said. "The hoopoe is a welcome sight to travelers in the desert." I pointed to the cushions around the rug. "I invite you to take your ease with palm wine from Myrb."

I sat apart from the men on the cushions. Samsi sat behind me while Tylos served wine to the men. The longhaired emissary held his cup to the candlelight. I smelled jasmine oil in his hair and wondered why he wore his hair loose, like a boy.

"A large caravan entered the city before we left," he said. "The leaders requested an audience with King Solomon. The king asked if they were part of the caravan that traveled with the woman from the south. They said they had left your caravan early to greet the king. King Solomon said he would wait until the true leader arrived, the queen that his dream had foretold."

He sipped his wine. "King Solomon is curious to know why they rode to Jerusalem before you."

"They were impatient to reach the city ," I replied.

"And you, Bilqis of Saba, are you not anxious to meet the king?"

"I would not offend King Solomon by greeting him covered with dust from my journey. We will enter Jerusalem tomorrow morning, when the day is fresh." I gestured to Tylos to pour more wine. "I hope the king will think I am worth the wait."

The man smiled. "He has heard of your purpose in traveling to meet him." The two other emissaries nodded at his words and drank their wine.

"I ask King Solomon in the name of my husband, Darmalay of Saba, for his protection when our caravans approach his lands."

"What will you offer in return?" he asked.

"I will speak of that with the king."

He laughed at my bold words. "King Solomon wonders why Darmalay of Saba sent his young wife to ask for help."

"My husband sent me and his chief counselor, Damri Samar, to greet King Solomon. Samar was killed in a bandit attack before we entered your lands. I wished to finish the journey and present the gifts my husband sent to the king."

I hesitated. "I have a desire of my own. I wish to ask questions of King Solomon."

"What would you ask the king?" he said. The other emissaries looked at me as if they were interested in my answer, so I did not say again that I would speak of it only with the king.

I considered for a moment. My questions about the badly drilled amber bead and Tylos's bare root seemed the questions of a child. I thought back to the beginning of my journey, when Darmalay had asked me to travel to Jerusalem. I remembered his plans to push out the walls to make room for the merchants pouring into Myrb. I had an opportunity to talk to a powerful king about the problems facing my city. Darmalay would welcome his knowledge and wisdom when I returned to Myrb.

I said, "I would ask King Solomon about kingship."

The emissary choked on a mouthful of wine. "What does a woman wish to know about kingship?"

I was growing impatient with his questions and his laughter, but I breathed slowly and stayed calm. I did not want him to report to King Solomon that I was a foolish woman who spoke of matters she did not understand.

"The caravan trade grows bigger every season," I said. "Every day more and more foreign merchants enter Myrb, until our streets are crowded with people speaking strange tongues. King Solomon is famed for his wisdom. I would ask him how to guide my city in peace as it grows."

The men were silent for a moment. The longhaired emissary smiled. "The king will be honored to speak with you."

The men put down their wine cups and stood. The tall man bowed to me. "King Solomon awaits your arrival, Queen Bilqis." The other men bowed and Farium led them from the tent.

We listened to their voices fading away. Tylos gathered the cups and the empty jar of wine. "Help Khe bring in water and the bathing basin," she said to Samsi.

The curtain parted and Shadru walked in, excited as a girl. "My friend," she said, "we are anxious to hear about your visit with the king's messengers."

"King Solomon welcomes us tomorrow," I said. "He sent a gift to honor my arrival." I held up the necklace. The gold and black bird turned slowly in the candlelight.

"It is beautiful." Shadru touched the amber beads. "I will tell my husband that the king sends his greetings."

Samsi and Khe carried the basin and buckets of water into the tent. After Khe left, I unknotted my tunic and stepped into the basin. Tylos poured rose oil into the hot water and mixed it with a bucket of cool water. She poured warm water over my head. I thought of the next morning's ride. Before the sun was high tomorrow, I would enter Jerusalem and meet the famous King Solomon.

"I wonder where we will sleep tomorrow night." I lifted my head and wiped oil from my face. "I wonder if the king will welcome me into his palace."

"He sent his greetings to you as a queen," said Tylos. "He will receive you as an honored guest; you will be housed in luxury." She handed a drying cloth to me. "I hope he does not give you new companions and send us away."

"I need you and Samsi at my side. No one, not even the king will send you from me."

Samsi bathed last. Tylos knelt beside the basin and poured warm water over her head. "Your hair is long enough to wear in one braid," Tylos said.

"Like Timora." Samsi smiled at me, her face gleaming with oiled water.

I nodded. I still expected to see Timora sitting by the cookfire, baking our morning bread. I thought for a moment about Samar. The longhaired man would not have laughed at me if he had been sitting at my side. But if Samar had been with me, the emissaries would have spoken with him. I might not have had the opportunity to talk about my questions for King Solomon.

At the back of the tent, I laid out the garments I would wear to meet Solomon: a tunic of cream-colored wool, a girdle of gold and carnelian beads, and a robe of jade silk. Scrolled around the wrists and hem of the silk robe were flowers and vines worked in gold thread and red and gold beads, Timora's work. Tylos held up the necklace from King Solomon. I nodded and she laid it on my robe.

Khe carried the water and basin out of the tent while Samsi unrolled our sleeping mats. We undressed and lay down to sleep. Tylos blew out the candles. I hugged myself under my sheepskin, smelling rose oil on my skin and hair. Samsi giggled when Tylos began to snore and then the tent was quiet and we slept.

~ Twenty ~

That night I dreamt I was a bird, flying over a great city. Below me, narrow roads curved like streambeds around flat-roofed houses and open courtyards. I flew into a window high in a tower of white stone. Inside the tower, far below, people knelt before a man sitting on a gold throne. He looked up at me and I saw he wore a tall gold crown. He smiled and held out his hand. I flew down through the dark air. My claws tightened as they sank into the rich cloth covering his arm.

"Get up, Bilqis." I woke to see Tylos kneeling on her mat, lighting a candle. "Get up," she said again. "Today you greet the king."

My heart beat fast at the thought of meeting the man in my dream, the king I had journeyed so far to see. Tylos left the tent. I untied my sleep tunic and pushed it to my waist, shivering in the cold air until she returned, carrying a bowl of water. I dipped a cloth in the warm, lavender scented water and wiped my face, arms, and breasts.

"Sit in front of me." Tylos patted the rug and I sat with my back to her, feeling sleepy again as she pulled a comb through my hair. She opened a small bag. "Today you wear gold, " she said as she shook out a handful of shining discs. "You will show your wealth."

Samsi entered the tent carrying a bowl of camel's milk and a platter of bread. She laid the food on the rug and sat in front of me, watching Tylos tie gold to the ends of the row of braids she had fashioned around my head. I ate a piece of the warm bread, filling my mouth with butter and honey while Tylos knotted the last drop of gold in my hair.

"You wore your hair like that on day you found me," Samsi said.

"That seems a long time ago." I remembered the morning I first saw Samsi, standing alone on the side of the path after her father and mother had drowned in the sayl. She had thrown up handfuls of sand to catch my attention. After three days she had ceased being a guest in my tent. Along with Tylos, she was my trusted companion.

Tylos pointed her comb at Samsi. "Your turn." The girl sat in my place. Tylos quickly twisted Samsi's hair into one braid and wove a strand of silver and turquoise beads through the plaited hair.

Tylos would not let me dress myself. "Stand still, Bilqis," she said. She smoothed the wool tunic over my hips. "You will have many slaves in King Solomon's palace. You must get used to people waiting on you."

I held up my arms while Samsi tied the gold and carnelian girdle around my waist. She picked up the hoopoe necklace from King Solomon and held it while Tylos helped me into the jade silk robe. Tylos clasped the necklace around my neck. She and Samsi stepped back and looked at me.

"You are beautiful. You look like a queen." Words tumbled, one over another out of Samsi's mouth. "King Solomon will tell his poets to sing about you." She looked up at me. "Will you wear your dagger as you did when Yahmed left? Can I wear a dagger, too?"

I shook my head. I had thought of wearing the bronze dagger Samar had given me as a sign of strength when I met King Solomon. But the king had sent a gift of friendship. Wearing a blade to our first meeting might be considered an offense, as though I feared for my safety in his company.

"Stop chattering about daggers, my girl, and light the incense," Tylos said. "Bilqis will sweeten her garments before she meets the king. And fetch another bowl of hot water."

Tylos slapped my hand when I reached up to push a strand of hair from my eyes. "Don't fuss, Bilqis, keep your hands quiet."

She brushed the hair from my face. "You must act like a queen," she said. "Everyone will be watching you."

I blew out a breath of air. "I'm afraid I'll say something foolish when I meet King Solomon."

"You impressed his emissaries; they will have told the king that you are a young woman who speaks wisely."

"I've changed since I left Myrb, Tylos, I no longer feel as if I'm waiting for something to happen." I touched the hoopoe necklace. "Now King Solomon waits for me."

"Don't make him wait too long." Tylos pushed me toward the bowl of smoking incense, more concerned about my smelling sweet for King Solomon than hearing me talk about how I had altered. I was learning to command, but to her I would always be the girl she had found in the garden, hiding from Hazza.

I stood over the incense, perfuming my clothing with fragrant smoke while Tylos pulled out Samsi's white tunic she had worn to Ilumqah's full-moon ceremony. Samsi returned with a bowl of water. Tylos dropped dried mint leaves into the warm water, stirred the leaves with her finger and handed the bowl to me. I rinsed my mouth with water that cooled my tongue.

Tylos took a sip of the warm mint water. "Ow," she said and held her hand to her cheek. "I have a sore tooth."

"Chew a clove," I said. "It will ease the pain."

Tylos fetched her bag of herbs. She pulled out a small dark clove and placed it in her mouth, next to the sore tooth. "It hurts too much to chew," she said. "I'll let it soften until the pain is gone."

Samsi stepped into the tunic. The garment stopped above the girl's knee, too short for a young woman to wear. "Dress her in one of mine," I said.

Tylos unpacked a tunic of blue wool and slipped it over Samsi's head. The hem dropped past her ankles to the rug. Tylos sat down in front of Samsi and sewed up the hem with long stitches.

When she was finished, I opened my red bag and brought out a chain of fine, linked gold. In the middle of the chain hung the broken bee that the jeweler had repaired after Timora was buried. I handed it to Samsi. "From Timora," I said. Tears filled her eyes as she fastened the necklace around her neck. She looked down and touched the gold bee and I thought of Timora's shy smile.

I looked around for my sandals. The leather was scuffed and faded from long wear. Tylos kicked them away. "You are not wearing old shoes today." Tylos dug into a bag and brought out a new pair of sandals made of blue-dyed leather.

"I forgot about these." I held the sandals in my hand. The ankle straps sparkled with gold beads, the unworn soles were smooth as waxed leather. I dropped the sandals on the rug and stepped into them. Tylos knelt and tied the straps tight around my ankles.

We heard a cough outside the tent as Tylos was draping a veil of gold silk over my hair. "Khe is here," she said. "The camels are ready."

I stepped into light from the torch Khe had lit. The sky was dark overhead with a streak of crimson along the edge of the sand. During the night, Khe had replaced the faded blue wool over the top of my riding tent with a new red covering that Tylos had packed for my entrance into Jerusalem. The wool was covered with gold stars embroidered within black and gold-threaded squares. A new riding blanket made of white wool showed under my riding tent. Rows of long red tassels, wrapped with gold thread, hung from the bottom of the blanket, halfway to the ground. The gold embroidery flickered in the torchlight.

Riding tents in other camps had new coverings in green and blue wool, worked with swirls of silver thread. I studied the long line of camels. We looked wealthy. The pack camels were heavily loaded with bags of goods. All of our beasts had fat humps and looked well fed.

Merchants and their wives talked loudly as they climbed into riding tents. Slaves tied the last bundles to the pack camels while guards rode up and down the caravan, shouting at each other. We all were excited about entering Jerusalem.

Khe helped me into my riding tent. I unfolded a sheepskin over my legs and pushed open the curtains. In front of me, Farium rode with another guard. Tylos's camel was to my right. Samsi rode a pack camel on my left. I turned to look at the many camels bearing my gifts to King Solomon. The king was famous for his wealth. I hoped I had brought enough gold and incense to turn his attention to me.

The sky brightened to light blue as we rode toward the city. The road became crowded with people walking toward Jerusalem. An old woman leading a donkey laden with baskets of purple grapes moved to one side to let us pass. Two boys with woven cages tied to their backs walked along the edge of the road. The cages were filled with little birds that fluttered their wings and clutched the bars of the cage with tiny black claws as we rode past and into a twisting passage of rocks. Cool shadows and bright sunlight slid over my tent as we rounded bend after bend until I thought the rocks would never end. We finally walked around a large group of rocks that opened into a wide, steep-sided wadi.

I looked up as my camel stepped from the rocks, and stared. There, on a long sloping hill high above the wadi stood an enormous city. "Jerusalem," I whispered.

The city covered the hill and was surrounded by tall stone walls. At the topmost part of the hill, I saw two large white buildings. Rows of windows were cut into the front of the tallest building. Was that King Solomon's famous palace? Was he looking out of a window, watching the caravan approach?

"That is Jerusalem?" Tylos's voice was shrill. "Where are the golden walls? Where are the gates made of gold?"

"We have come to meet King Solomon," I said. "He wisely guards his wealth inside the walls." My voice was calm, but I too, was disappointed that the walls of Jerusalem were built of rock and not gold and precious stones that would blind us in the rising light of the sun.

Tylos had not finished complaining. "We heard the king lives in a big palace covered with gold. Does he live in a house of stone? Is he a chieftain no greater than Darmalay?"

"His kingdom is greater," I said. "His laws are stronger. We have traveled for three days without fear since we entered his lands."

Tylos waved her hand in irritation at my words. I wondered if I believed what I was saying. If the stories about the golden walls were false, were the stories that I had heard about Solomon's wisdom also untrue? Would he take pleasure in talking with me as his emissary had said or would he abandon me to the company of his Egyptian wife until he remembered my presence and ordered me to quit his house.

I sat up and arranged my veil. King Solomon would not ignore me. His emissaries had welcomed me as a queen, not the wife of a village chieftain. The king would speak with me.

The path along the bottom of the wadi turned and swung upward, toward a set of gates built into the thick stone wall. Along the side of the wall a long row of merchants who had arrived after the city gates closed for the night were kicking sand on their cookfires and leading their pack camels toward the gates.

As we climbed up the side of the wadi, the gates opened and two men on horses rode through. One man held up his hand to stop the first of the merchants from approaching, the other gestured at the caravan to come forward. Khe pulled my camel toward the gates. Both men bowed their heads to me as I came near. They were wearing green silk sashes under their robes. I thought they were the two emissaries who had visited me in my tent.

"Welcome, Bilqis of Saba," said one. "King Solomon awaits your arrival."

They turned their beasts and rode before me. Khe followed. I sat forward, my heart beating fast as I passed through the gates and entered the fabled city of Jerusalem.

Flat-roofed stone and clay houses sprawled down the hill. As in Myrb, straw mats were laid along the edge of the roofs to dry fruits and grains. Small cloth tents set in the middle provided the people of the house with a shaded place to enjoy the breezes that blew through the valley. I smelled bread baking and heard voices inside a nearby house. I felt a moment's longing for my home. Jerusalem was a bigger city than Myrb, but the clay houses, the smell of cooked food, and the early morning sounds were the same.

We rode uphill, stopping before a massive structure of stepped rocks. A large house loomed at the top. Samsi's mouth hung open as she looked up. Tylos exclaimed that it must be the palace of the king. Farium rode up beside me and said the house had belonged to King David, King Solomon's father.

The street continued around the steps, leading to a closed gate set in the tall stone wall that separated the upper and lower upper cities. I was unsure if we were to continue upward and through the gate. One of the emissaries signaled Farium. My guard rode over and talked with him. I watched as Farium directed the caravan onto a street leading down into the lower part of the city. The riding tents of the merchants appeared, followed by the white tents of the priests. When the first of the pack camels walked through the gates, Farium waved at his men to go with the caravan and rode back to me. He leaned close and said the priests and merchants would be housed close to the marketplace. He glanced at the caravan moving away behind us. His guards, he said, would watch over my camels in the pens at the lower edge of the city.

The emissaries clicked their tongues at their camels and we started riding toward the closed gate. After we passed the stepped stones, two men opened the gate, allowing us to pass through. We entered another city of houses. The street ran upward, ending at the white buildings at the top of the hill. Farium said Solomon had built the newer city after he became king.

He pointed to the first white building. "That is the hall of pillars where people wait to appear before the king. Behind it is the throne room where King Solomon sits in judgment. Next to it is another building where the king stores his shields of beaten gold."

"Where is the king's palace?" I asked.

"It is the taller building behind the hall of pillars."

As we moved up the street, men and women came to their doorways or looked out of windows to watch our passing. I looked neither right nor left, but kept my eyes the pillared building. A group of men waited on the front steps of the hall. A figure moved and I saw the flash of gold.

Heat from the rising sun warmed my cheek as we grew nearer. I caught my breath when I saw that the man standing in front of the group was wearing a gold crown.

"King Solomon," Farium whispered.

The king smiled and I recognized him as the longhaired emissary who had asked so many questions. He touched his neck to show he saw I was wearing the hoopoe necklace. I nodded slowly, wondering if I should be offended that he had deceived me by pretending to be a messenger from the king. I remembered his smile when he said King Solomon would delight in speaking with me. I decided to accept his friendly greeting and bowed my head.

When I looked up, King Solomon had stepped forward. He opened his arms wide, as if offering me the whole of Jerusalem.

"Welcome, Bilqis of Saba," he proclaimed. "Welcome, oh queen of the south."

~ Twenty-One ~

King Solomon strode down the stone steps and stood before me, waiting for Khe to pull my camel to kneeling. The king wore a robe of fine red wool over a white tunic worked along the hem with gold thread. He held out his hand to help me step off the camel's back. His hand was warm and strong and he smelled strongly of incense. In the sunlight he looked older than he had in my tent, where candlelight had softened the wrinkles on his forehead and around his eyes.

He dropped my hand and held out his arm. I put my hand on it while Tylos and Samsi dismounted. I heard Farium tell Khe to take our camels to the pens and return to the palace.

I walked with King Solomon up the steps, followed by my companions and Farium. I slipped in my new sandals on one of the steps and clutched the king's arm to keep from falling. He slowed while I regained my balance. I took a breath and kept walking with my hand light on his arm. The men waiting at the top of the stairs bowed their heads briefly to me and followed as King Solomon led me into the hall. The hall was long and filled from end to end with rows of immensely tall wooden pillars. I had never seen so much wood in one place. I tried not to stare at the pillars or up at the high, shadowed ceiling. I did not want the king to think I was a village girl who never seen such splendor.

"The hall smells of incense," I said.

"The pillars are made of cedar wood," said the king. "It perfumes the air."

I knew the wood; we stored our clothing in chests made of it. The fragrant cedar made our robes and tunics smell sweet and kept away insects that would devour the wool. We stopped walking at the approach of an old woman leading a group of five girls. They halted in front of us and bowed deeply to the king.

"I have arranged rooms for you in my palace." King Solomon pointed to the old woman. "This is my servant, Sarah. She and her girls will tend to you."

The woman bowed slightly to me. Her eyes slid over me as she straightened, from my new sandals to the hoopoe pendant around my neck. I felt as though I were on the caravan again and being examined by Wa'dab.

"I am honored by your kindness," I said to the king. "I ask you to further the honor and allow me to present gifts my husband, Darmalay, chieftain of Saba has sent to you."

The king smiled. "I will receive your gifts tonight, before the feast to welcome you to my city. Until then, I leave you in

Sarah's care." He placed his hand on mine for a moment and left me to walk down the hall with his advisors.

Sarah beckoned us to follow her. She opened a small wooden door that led into another long hall paneled from floor to ceiling with reddish brown cedar wood. Narrow windows placed high on one wall glowed with sunlight, lighting up pale streaks in the wood. The walls we passed were carved with grasses and tall trees down the length of the hall. Samsi looked back several times at the girls walking behind us. I realized she might be lonely for friends her age.

Farium caught up with us as we walked through another door and out on a large court of cut stone. Long buildings connected with passageways of open latticework surrounded the court. King Solomon's white palace was in front of us. We moved across the stone court, up a short flight of steps, and through an open door.

Sarah led us down another hall and up two stone stairways. "I'm lost," Samsi whispered as we entered another long hallway. The cedar walls were etched with a fields of flowers that opened from bud to blossom as we walked down the hall.

Sarah stopped at the end and opened a door. "The king had these rooms prepared for you."

I stepped into a spacious room that was paneled halfway up the wall with cedar. Whitewashed stone brightened the wall above the paneling. A sheer curtain hung in a doorway to our left. Wool covered cushions circled a low table in the middle of the room. Across the room, a latticework door opened onto a stone terrace, bright with sunlight.

"This is the sitting room," Sarah said.

Sarah's girls waited in the doorway, watching me. Farium stood behind them. I told the guard to fetch our bags and turned to Sarah.

"I am honored that King Solomon has provided your girls to attend me." I said. "I brought my own women and do not need so many."

"The king will be disappointed if you do not keep some of them."

"Choose two to stay," I said. "I will ask for others if I require more assistance."

Sarah darted over to the door, grabbed the arms of two girls and brought them forward. She told the others to return to their family quarters.

"These are my granddaughters, Miriam and Rachel." She pushed the girls toward me. "They will serve you well."

The girls bowed their heads to me. Both wore pale blue headcloths over their dark hair. The older sister, Rachel, stood a head taller than Miriam, who looked Samsi's height and age.

"Come," Sarah said. "I'll show you where you will sleep." We followed her through the curtain into another room walled with the sweet smelling wood. Grasses and flowers carved in the wood were bent over, as if blown by a breeze.

A large bed filled the back of the room. It was beautifully made with a blanket of fine-spun blue wool and a row of pillows covered in ivory silk. Two sleeping niches were built into the walls on either side of the doorway. The beds were furnished with wool blankets and linen covered pillows.

Samsi jumped into the bigger bed. I shook my head. "That one is for Tylos."

Samsi sighed and moved to the smaller niche.

A table with a bronze basin and a pile of washing cloths was placed near Samsi's bed. Above the table, shelves were attached to the wall for us to place our clothing.

I nodded my approval at the clean and comfortable room. I was tired from the long morning and my feet hurt from my new sandals. I wanted to lie down on the soft looking bed and sleep.

We walked back to the sitting room, through the latticework door and onto the terrace. A seating area of wool cushions had been arranged against the side wall of the terrace that provided shade from the morning sun. On the opposite end, I saw a shallow wooden tub set behind a fretted screen. Sarah said the tub was for bathing.

We stood at the terrace wall, looking over the pillared building we had walked through, past the old king's palace with its stepped wall, the dirt streets and close built houses in the lower city, and down to the camel pens located at the far end. The whole of Jerusalem was surrounded by stone walls and built high on a hill with deep valleys on either side. I thought it would be easy to defend the city against attack.

Sarah pointed to a smaller building below us to the right. "That is the harem. The king's wives and his concubines live there."

"I have heard of his Egyptian wife." I wondered if I would meet her at the feast.

Sarah nodded. "She is the first wife."

"Is she called queen?" I asked.

"No, she is not Jewish. She cannot be queen."

"Does the king have many children?"

"A son to carry his name, and two daughters, now grown and married."

I was surprised that King Solomon had so few children from his many wives and concubines.

"The king called you his servant," I said. "Is that different from a slave?"

"Yes. I sold my services to the king. My husband died a year ago, leaving me with his debts. In five years the debts will be paid and I will be free again."

I looked back at the sleeping room. "Are your granddaughters also servants to the king?"

"They are in my charge and live and work with me in the palace. My girls will leave when my service is completed or they may leave before if they marry."

The sun was heating up the terrace. We went inside as Farium and several of his guards appeared at the open door with our bags from the caravan. Sarah gestured at them to place the bags on the floor in front of the curtain to the sleeping room.

I took Farium aside as the women carried our bags into the room. "I want you with me tonight at the presentation and the feast," I said. I didn't fear for my safety inside the king's palace, but I had come to rely on Farium and wanted him close on this first night. He said he would return with Khe to escort me to the festivities. He left, closing the door behind him.

Samsi stood by her bed, laying out her clothing. Tylos and Sarah were watching as the two girls unpacked my bags. They shook out tunics and robes, folded them and laid them on the shelves. I looked at each item of clothing, trying to decide what to wear to the presentation. Tylos took my blue jewelry bag from Miriam and placed it on the highest shelf.

When the bags were empty, the girls stored them in a corner and looked around for something else to do.

There was a knock on the door. Sarah hurried into the sitting room and returned, followed by a servant carrying a large wooden chest. He set the chest on the floor by the bed and bowed out of the room.

Sarah said King Solomon had sent a gift to welcome me to his home. We came closer as she opened the chest. I saw the gleam of silk clothing and square ivory box. Sarah took out the box and offered it to me. I slowly drew out two gold bracelets studded with tiny red rubies. I turned the pretty bracelets in my hand for a moment and then gave them to Tylos to show the other women. Next was a necklace of amethyst stones fashioned into clusters of shining purple grapes. The girls exclaimed at its beauty as Tylos laid it on the bed beside the gold and ruby bracelets. The last items in the box were a pair of hammered gold earrings hung with drops of golden amber.

I handed the empty box to Tylos and looked at the lovely jewelry displayed on my bed. King Solomon had also given me the hoopoe necklace. I worried that his gifts were too lavish from a man who was not my husband.

Sarah told the girls to take the clothing out of the chest. One by one, they laid out silk tunics in purple, pale yellow, deep blue, ivory, and dark green. Each garment was worked along the hem with gold and silver thread showing blooming flowers or birds in flight.

Rachel and Miriam ran their fingers over the shining silks and the elaborate threadwork, saying a few words that I hadn't heard before. Receiving foreign merchants in Darmalay's house had taught me to listen carefully to unknown words until I understood their meaning. I knew the girls were admiring my gifts.

"King Solomon is attentive to his honored guests." Sarah glanced at me as she replaced the jewelry in the ivory box. I wondered if she had guessed I was concerned about the king's generosity and was trying to put my mind at ease.

She set the box on the shelf next to my blue jewelry bag and told her granddaughters to push the empty chest against the wall. "Rachel and Miriam will tend to your new garments and then return to their family in the palace," she said. "Unless you command otherwise, they will arrive early every morning to bring food and fresh water. They will clean your rooms while you and your women take your meal on the terrace."

I left Samsi with the two girls and walked into the sitting room with Tylos and Sarah. "Tell me about the ceremony," I said to Sarah. "Our customs at home may be different from those in King Solomon's court."

She nodded. "I will take you to the throne room this evening. King Solomon will be waiting on his throne. There will be many people in the room who were invited to the presentation. You will enter first. Your women and I will follow you to the steps leading to the throne. You will bow to King Solomon and wait at the steps while your gifts are offered to the king and taken to the treasury room. After the presentation is over, the king will escort you to the feast."

My part seemed small; I would merely watch while Harjan presented Darmalay's treasure. My heart beat faster as I thought of standing before the crowd, with all eyes upon me as my husband's gifts of gold, incense, and precious stones were offered to the king.

Sarah left after repeating she would return before sunset to accompany us to the throne room. Tylos and I stood together for a moment, listening to the three girls chatting in the sleeping room. I asked Tylos if I should accept the beautiful clothing and jewelry from King Solomon.

"He is the king," she said. "To refuse his gifts would be an insult."

I sat down on a cushion, took off my sandals and rubbed my sore feet while Tylos returned to the sleeping room to fetch another clove for her aching tooth.

Rachel and Miriam left at midday as two serving girls appeared at the door. One carried a silver tray of bread, cheese, and honey cakes; the other a jar of wine and three glazed wine cups.

We sat around the low table in the sitting room and fell on the food. I had not realized how hungry I was. Tylos ate slowly, careful not to bite down on her sore tooth. Samsi and I stuffed our mouths, swallowed, and ate more. We finally sat back, our bellies full, after the wine and the last bits of food were gone.

Tylos groaned and got to her feet. "We have to choose your dress for the ceremony."

"I'll wear the purple silk," I said. "And the hoopoe necklace and my silver cuffs."

"Why not the gold bracelets the king sent to you?" Tylos asked.

"I will wear something of my own." I was not the wife of a small village chieftain. I did not want the king to think he gave me everything.

We rested as the room grew warmer from the midday sun. Samsi slept beside me on my bed, Tylos snored in her niche. It felt strange to be lying on a soft bed instead of a thin mat on the sand, to be in a walled city and not out on the open desert.

A knock on the door roused Tylos. I sat up yawning as she came back into the room carrying a pitcher of water. She poured water into the basin on the table and handed a washing cloth to me. Samsi slept while I wiped my face, arms, and neck. The cool water revived me after sleeping in the hot room. Tylos bathed while I woke Samsi.

I put on my new sandals, wincing as the straps rubbed against the tender flesh around my ankles. I stepped into the purple tunic. Tylos fastened the shoulder straps with clasps made of small gold flowers. There was a pucker in the hem where a thread was caught. Tylos took out her sewing knife, intending to cut the thread and re-sew the hem. I told her to stop fussing, that no one would notice.

Samsi covered my hair with gold silk and told me everyone at the presentation would think I was beautiful. My hands started shaking at the thought of appearing before the court of strangers.

Tylos slid the amber silk robe over my shoulders. "Be calm," she said. "All you must do is stand quietly."

~ Twenty-Two ~

Farium, Khe, and Sarah arrived to escort us to the throne room. Daylight was fading from the high windows in the flowered hallway. Two servants carrying thick white candles walked before us, lighting our way along the shadowed hall. We followed Sarah down the staircases, across the stone court, and into a hall leading to the throne room. The sound of upraised voices reached us through the open door of the room.

Farium and Khe entered first and stood aside. I took a deep breath and stepped into the room. A large crowd of people richly dressed in gold jewelry and silk robes stared at me. Guards stood in front of the crowd, keeping a path clear from the door to the steps of the throne.

King Solomon was sitting on a tall gold throne at the top of six white stone steps. Farium had described the throne as being made of ivory, overlaid with gold. Large gold lions stood at each end of each step, facing the room as if protecting the king.

The king looked at me as I entered the room. I heard my name spoken in low voices as I walked toward the steps. The air felt warm and damp from the many bodies pressing close. I moved forward, keeping my eyes on the steps and hoping no one could see that my knees were shaking. I reached the steps and bent my head to the king. He smiled at me when I looked up. My lips felt stiff as I tried to return his smile. I took my place on the first step. Tylos, Samsi, and Farium approached, bowed to the king, and stood on the floor below me. I looked for Khe, puzzled that he was not standing with Farium.

While we waited for Harjan, I glanced around the noisy room. Torches flamed in wall holders, casting a warm light on the high cedar walls. A railed area near the king's left provided seating for a group of women. Two of the women talked to each other behind their raised hands, a third stood with her eyes, on me and came to the railing. She wore a wide collar of red and gold beads strung in a half circle around her neck. A net of gold pearls covered her short black hair. Her eyes were outlined in black lines that extended beyond her eyes to her temples. I thought she might be the king's Egyptian wife.

People in the crowd were talking with each other or looking around to see who else had been invited, impatient for the presentation to begin. I shifted slightly to ease my aching feet. I was wondering how long I would have to stand before the court when Harjan appeared in the open doorway. He wore a robe of dark blue silk and carried a staff of white bone with a gold handle. He walked toward the steps, bowed to the king and to me. Solomon nodded and Harjan walked up to the second step to stand above me.

The king held up his hand and the crowd grew quiet. Harjan cleared his throat and raised his staff. He spoke in a loud voice, as though speaking above the noise of the marketplace, declaring that Darmalay of Saba sent offerings of affection and goodwill to King Solomon of Jerusalem. I thought of my husband waiting in Myrb, hoping his gifts would please the king.

Harjan pointed his staff at the door to the throne room where another merchant waited. The man held up his gold-handled staff and a line of male servants entered the room. They were barefoot and wore tunics of undyed linen. Each man carried a large chest of ebony wood clasped to his chest. I was surprised to see Khe in the line. I looked more closely at the men and recognized other guards and slaves who had traveled with the caravan. The men walked slowly across the cleared area toward the steps. They stopped at the steps and knelt, facing King Solomon.

At Harjan's command, as one they opened the lids. Harjan pointed his staff at the chests and announced that Darmalay of Saba sent King Solomon a treasure of red jasper, black pearls, turquoise, onyx, carnelian, and blue lapis from the southern markets of Saba. I looked at the crowd. Instead of the smiles I expected, I saw many people shrug. They were used to their king being offered riches. I hoped my gold and incense would be better received.

After a moment, Harjan tapped his staff. The servants rose and walked toward an open doorway at the opposite side of the room. A man stood at the treasury door recording the gift of precious stones on small roll of sheepskin.

Harjan struck the step. He raised his staff again, proclaiming that Darmalay of Saba had sent a token of gold to King Solomon.

All eyes shifted toward the door. The room was quiet, not a rustle of silk or a whisper as the crowd waited.

Two servants bearing an ebony pole between them on their shoulders appeared in the doorway. There was a loud gasp, as if the whole room had taken a breath, when the men entered the room. Hanging from the pole were four large gold plates, strung sideways on straps of gilded leather. As the men walked past, the merchant struck one of the plates with the tip of his staff, causing the plate to ring with the clear, chiming sound of pure gold.

The servants started across the floor toward the throne, the gold plates swaying with every step. Another pair came through the door carrying four more gold plates. Again, the merchant tapped a round of gold, making it ring like a bell. The crowd was silent as more pairs of men entered the room, Khe among them. The merchant continued to hit the plates, sending waves of music that seemed to shimmer in the air around the room.

The last pair crossed the floor and joined the men at the foot of the steps. There were six pairs of men standing in five rows before the king. I looked down at the mass of shining gold before me, brighter in the torchlight than the necklaces, bracelets, earrings, and headpieces worn in the crowd. Against my gold, their jewelry looked dull and plain, trinkets for a child.

I looked at Solomon, who was gripping the arms of his throne. He finally nodded at Harjan. At the quick tap of his staff, the servants headed toward the treasury door. The only sound was their bare feet shuffling across the wooden floor.

The room exploded with excited voices. From the smiles throughout the crowd, I could see Darmalay's value as a trading partner had grown. I enjoyed their admiration for a moment and then looked at Harjan, wondering how he would present the incense. He winked at me and lifted his staff. The crowd grew quiet as he slowly pointed to the throne room door.

A man appeared in the doorway holding a wide alabaster bowl piled high with chunks of golden incense. Behind him came another man, carrying a bowl. I remembered Harjan's words that gold would be welcomed, but our incense would be cherished. The people in the crowd stared as man after man came through the door, each bearing a bowl of incense. I saw Khe again with others from the caravan.

The line seemed endless. When the last man finally knelt before the steps, I counted more than a hundred bowls of precious incense held up to the king. Harjan gently tapped the floor with his staff, as if unwilling to disturb the silence in the room. The men rose and walked toward the treasury door. When the door closed, Harjan turned and bowed to the king.

His part was over. He gave me a quick smile as he stepped past me to the floor.

King Solomon stood and extended his hand, gesturing for me to join him. I walked up the steps, feeling stunned. I had expected a speech of acceptance for Darmalay's gifts, but not the honor of standing beside the king at his throne.

In a voice that filled the room, King Solomon said that he was honored by the gifts sent to him from his brother, Darmalay, King of Saba. He bowed to me and said that he gave guest welcome to Darmalay's emissary, his wife, Bilqis, Queen of Saba.

At that, the crowd yelled and clapped their hands, cheering my arrival and my gifts. I bit my lips, feeling nervous that the king had named Darmalay as the King of Saba and me as his queen. I took a breath and smiled at the people below me. I would act the queen now and worry later about the rightness of the title.

King Solomon put out his arm. I took it and walked down the steps with him, past the crowd to the treasury door that opened as we approached. Guards stood at the ends of two heavy stone tables that extended the length of the room. The open chests of precious stones and alabaster bowls of incense were placed on the farthest table. The gold plates had been unstrung and were laid out in overlapping rows on the first table, shining in the torchlight like the scales of a gigantic golden fish.

I smiled at the display. I understood that showing our gifts for public viewing not only honored my husband and me, but also gave notice to chieftains and merchants that more was expected of them if they wished to gain the king's favor.

The room soon filled with people eager to view the treasure again. King Solomon and I left the room and walked down another cedar hall. I was elated with Harjan's magnificent presentation. As if hearing my thoughts, King Solomon said, "All of Jerusalem will talk about your gifts of gold and incense. You have turned our attention to the markets in the south."

"I am pleased." I started to say more and was distracted by the smell of meat cooking. I was hungry. Our midday meal seemed like a long time ago.

Behind us, Samsi was bubbly with excitement and talked without stopping about the beautiful throne room and all the gold, she did not know so much gold existed in all of the world. Tylos shushed her as we walked into the feasting room.

High walls were clad to the ceiling with more of the fragrant cedar. The room was crowded with low tables set on black and red wool rugs that covered the polished stone floor. King Solomon led me to a table with two cushions at the head of the room. I sat down while the king remained standing to greet his guests. Sarah sat with Tylos and Samsi at a nearby table. Farium and Khe waited at the door. The room filled quickly with the handsomely dressed men and women who had attended the presentation. The women sat at their tables, talking with each other while their husbands approached Solomon. They bowed to their king and then to me.

I saw Harjan enter, along with the merchant who had overseen the entrance of the servants. I smiled at Harjan, showing my gratitude for his splendid presentation. I looked for the woman with the gold-netted hair and black lined eyes, but she did not appear. I again wondered if she was Solomon's Egyptian wife. I would ask Sarah.

When every table was full, the king sat down next to me. Servants entered immediately, carrying silver trays with jars of wine and silver cups. The king poured wine for me and for himself. The red wine was sweet and slightly tart. He smiled and asked if I liked it. Lines around his mouth and eyes showed that he smiled easily.

"It is good. It's not as sweet as our wines," I said.

"It is made from pomegranates. The juice is pressed from the flesh of the seeds."

Servants brought in bowls and platters of roasted meat, barley bread, chunks of white goat cheese, shelled fowl eggs, sweet grapes, figs poached in honey, and dark brown raisin cakes. The king gestured for me to begin. I picked up an egg, enjoying the smooth feel of it in my hand. I broke it open and savored the warm, cooked yolk. I had not eaten an egg since I left Myrb.

King Solomon pointed to a small bowl of brown oil with a shred of lemon peel floating in it. Cumin oil, he said, as I dipped the egg into it. The oil flavored the egg with the taste of pepper and the tang of lemon.

The king speared a piece of meat with his dagger. When he had swallowed the meat, he asked if the rooms pleased me.

"They are very comfortable." I touched the neck of my purple tunic. "You honor me with your beautiful gifts."

He looked at me for a moment. His eyes were dark brown, almost black. "They are a small token of what I would give you."

I looked away, unsure if his words were that of friendship or if his regard for me was something more. I quickly said I had admired his city from my terrace.

"Ah, we have much to talk about, Queen Bilqis. I remember that you wished to speak with me about kingship."

"Your advice will be welcome."

"I hope you will be my guest for many days to give us time to meet and talk." He filled my cup again. "My people wonder at the great gifts you gave to me. They think of the south as a land of few villages."

"Many of our villages are small, not unlike the villages I have seen in your country," I said.

He laughed out loud. "You speak well, my queen."

Our fingers touched as we both reached for the bowl of honeyed figs. His fingers lingered on mine before I pulled my hand away.

Behind me, I heard Tylos tell Samsi to sit up and not lay her head upon the table. I put down my wine cup. I suddenly felt too tired to hold it. The long day was beginning to claim me, too.

I said to Solomon that I was ready to return to my rooms. "You are tired," he said. "Rest well, my Bilqis, we will speak again tomorrow."

We walked to the door with my women following. People smiled at me as I moved past their tables. I nodded in return, pleased that they were eager to show their approval of me.

King Solomon stood at the door while Sarah and Farium escorted us down the hall. I could not stop yawning as we walked through the courtyard and into the king's palace. My feet hurt. I was limping when we entered the flowered hall leading to our rooms.

Farium opened the door and stood outside while we entered the room. A candle burned on the low table in the sitting room. The air was cool from the night air flowing in from the terrace. Farium left after telling me to send word when I wanted him again. Sarah followed him, saying she would return in the morning to take me to meet the king.

Tylos carried the candle in the back room. We took off our fine clothing and slipped into sleep tunics. Samsi fell on her bed, Tylos lay down with a groan. I blew out the candle and lay on my bed. I got up again. I was tired, but too filled with emotion to sleep. I walked through the rooms and onto the dark terrace. I leaned over the stone wall and looked up the side of the palace. Light shone from a few of the terraces. I wondered which rooms belonged to Solomon.

I looked at the harem of King Solomon's wives and concubines. Every window I could see was dark. I turned my gaze to the city spread out before me. The streets were quiet; a few scattered windows were yellow with candlelight. I breathed in the cool air. I was glowing with happiness from the success of the presentation. I wanted to shout into the night so that all inside their houses would hear my voice. I had endured a long journey to reach Jerusalem and meet King Solomon. The king had received me warmly and presented me to his people as the Queen of Saba. I was an important guest, the wealthy queen from the south.

Tylos came up behind me, rubbing her eyes. She looked at the city below us for a moment, then turned to me. "During the feast, Sarah said the king talked about you to his advisors after he met you last night in your tent. He said you were beautiful and spoke wisely."

I smiled into the night, waiting to hear more about how I had captivated the king.

"He talked about you so much that his Egyptian wife refused to come to the feast after she saw you at the presentation."

"I do not wish to cause discord between them," I said. "I brought gifts to King Solomon from my husband and he welcomed me as a friend, that is all."

"Sarah said the king's attentions would be more than gifts of silk and jewels. She smiled as she spoke, Bilqis, but I think she was warning you."

"I am meeting him tomorrow," I said. "I reminded him during the feast that he had promised to advise me on how to help Myrb grow peacefully. We are to talk about kingship, not love."

Tylos held my arm. "Be careful. The king has shown that he favors you. There will be many eyes upon you now."

I sighed. "I feel as though I'm back on the caravan with Wa'dab and her friends watching me and listening to my every word."

"Make no mistake," Tylos said. "You are."

~ Twenty-Three ~

I woke at daybreak the next morning. Tylos and Samsi slept while I stood on the terrace and watched the city turn golden in the rising sunlight. My head ached from the cups of wine I had drunk at the feast. A warming breeze brought the heavy smell of roasting meat that turned my stomach. I thought it might be from the morning's burnt sacrifice that Harjan had mentioned.

Samsi and Tylos came into the sitting room as Rachel and Miriam appeared at the door. Miriam placed a pitcher of fresh water in our sleeping room. Rachel carried a tray with our morning meal of bread, cheese, fresh figs, and a jar of wine to the terrace. We sat on the shaded side, eating our meal while the two girls tidied our sleeping room. The light food calmed my stomach. It was pleasant to sit and not be in a hurry to eat, pack our tent and mount our camels for the day.

We finished eating as the girls moved into the sitting room. Samsi stayed behind to help them clean the room and sweep the terrace. Tylos followed me into the back room to help me dress for my meeting with King Solomon. I chose the tunic of ivory silk and a blue silk robe. Samsi came into the room as Tylos was opening the ivory jewelry box.

"Wear the new necklace, the one with the purple grapes," Samsi said.

I shook my head. "I'll wear the hoopoe necklace to my first meeting with the king. I want to remind him that our friendship was foretold to him in a dream."

While I washed my face and arms I told Tylos that the new sandals hurt my feet. "Oil my old ones," I said. "I'll wear them today."

Sarah arrived as Tylos was draping a covering of gold silk over my hair. I told Samsi to stay in our rooms while we were gone and look over the clothing we wore to the feast for stains. Samsi didn't argue, she was happy to remain with Rachel and Miriam.

As Sarah led us down the hall, I asked how deeply I should bow to the king when I saw him.

"Bow slightly as you did last night," she said. "Stand until he gestures for you to sit."

We walked up a long stairway that opened to a large terraced garden at the top of the palace. The terrace was built on a corner facing the morning sun on one side and the land north of Jerusalem on the other. While I waited for the king, I walked to the corner to gaze out over the land. I saw a long white building a short distance from the palace, built on an inner court of white stone. A long rock wall separated the inner court around the temple from another court of white cut stone. The outer court extended the length of the palace building and looked large enough to hold all of Jerusalem.

Smoke wafted from an immense altar in front of the building. I realized I was looking at King Solomon's famous temple.

The temple was lit by the morning sun and shone brilliant white against the brown desert sand. Two bronze columns, each the height of the temple, flanked a white tower at the front of the building. Between the columns were two gold doors. One of the doors was open.

Five small basins on wheeled stands were lined up along the side of the temple building. An enormous basin filled with water stood near the foot of the altar. The basin was supported on the backs of life-sized bronze cattle arranged in a circle. I stared at the huge basin, astonished to see water used so freely in the desert.

As I watched, wind blew the smoke away, revealing the top of the altar that was wide enough for a man to walk upon. Two piles of smoking ash were heaped across the middle of the altar. A third fire burned at the far end of the ash piles. A man dressed in a long tunic and wearing a tall cloth hat, a priest, I thought, was walking down a wide ramp from the altar to the stone court where several priests waited.

I heard the king's voice in the hall. We bowed to him as he entered the room. Tylos and Sarah moved to a table in a shaded corner as King Solomon walked toward me.

"You have seen my temple," he said.

"It is beautiful." I smelled the incense in his beard. I remembered his fingers brushing mine at the feast and Tylos's warning about the king's intentions toward me. I moved away slightly and pointed to the altar. "Why are there three fires on the altar?"

"The largest is for the sacrifices the priests burn every morning and evening. One of the smaller fires produces the coals the priests use to light incense inside the temple, the other is always kept burning as a symbol of my Lord God's eternal presence."

"I've never seen so much water outside of a river. What do you do with it?"

"The priests use the wheeled basins to wash sacrifices and cleanse the alter after they burn offerings to our Lord God."

"And the larger one? It's big enough to bathe fifty men."

"That is the Brazen Sea. Water is drawn from taps around the bottom of the basin for the priests to wash their hands and feet and purify themselves before entering the temple sanctuary."

"How is such a huge basin filled?" I asked.

"The Sea is never allowed to become empty. The water is renewed by a great spring, the Gihon, that runs down from the north."

"Does it bring all of your water?"

"No, there is another spring that brings fresh water into our homes and carries away unclean water outside the city where it's used to fertilize crops."

"We have deep wells in Myrb, but no running springs," I said. "Our waste is dropped into pits in the ground and covered with dirt to keep down the smell."

King Solomon laughed at my words. "I have never before met a beautiful woman who was interested in the workings of a city."

"I told you in my tent that I wished to learn how to help my city grow peacefully." I smiled as I spoke to cover my annoyance that he had laughed at me. He was the king. I did not want to sound sharp tongued in my reply, as though I was scolding him for his remark.

"There is scant peace in the changes that come with prosperity," he said. "More people bring more problems."

"That is why I wish your advice."

Servants entered carrying platters of food and wine. King Solomon and I sat at a table on the far end of the terrace, screened from my women behind a row of potted plants.

As the king poured wine, I asked if I might discuss another reason why I had journeyed to Jerusalem to meet with him. At his nod, I said that my husband, Darmalay of Saba had sent me to make an agreement with him to safeguard our caravans when they entered his lands.

"You do not need a treaty with me," he said. "Every caravan that travels through my lands is under my protection.

Your goods were safe from bandits when you entered my lands."

I ate bread and cheese as I thought about the great treasure Darmalay had sent the king, wondering if his gifts had been for nothing. I remembered speaking with Harjan at my cookfire the night before we entered Jerusalem. The merchant had been worried about securing a place in the market to sell his wares.

I put down my cup and said, "I have one other request."

The king refilled my wine cup. "You are direct for a woman."

I feared I had been too bold. Should I have flattered him first or waited until our next meeting to ask my favors?

"I meant that in praise," he said. "The way to the truth is a straight path. You have traveled far to talk with me. Speak, my queen, I will listen."

I took a breath. "I would ask for a permanent place in the market for the merchants from Myrb to sell their goods. They make a long journey for an uncertain end."

He stroked his beard. "That is reasonable and easily done. Your merchants are known for their excellent wares. I will set aside a place for them." He filled my cup again. "Many of the merchants who witnessed the offering of your gifts of gold and incense have asked me if they might talk to you about the markets in the south. I said they would learn more from speaking with the merchants who traveled on your caravan."

His advice was wise, I knew little about the business of the market, but I felt put aside. "I would know what they say. This is important information for my husband."

He shrugged. "I will arrange it if you wish." He put down his cup and leaned toward me. "Now I will advise you, Bilqis. Your salt and wine and gold from the south do well in our markets, but the one thing we prize above all is your incense. My priests burn quantities of it day and night in the temple, and we use it in our homes. Frankincense and myrrh come from your country only. Bring more incense, that is where your merchants will prosper most."

I nodded. This was valuable advice.

He continued, "I would ask that you bring your harvest to Jerusalem before your caravans travel to markets in other lands."

"I had not thought of taking our caravans farther than Jerusalem."

He raised his eyebrows. "There are markets in Egypt, my queen, that would shake out your bags for every flake of incense and gold."

I considered his words. New markets meant more caravans from Myrb. The wealth it would bring my city would be immense. "Would you help us enter those markets?" I asked.

"In exchange for bringing your incense to Jerusalem? Yes, it would be my honor to help my new brother from Saba." He emptied his cup. "I will come to you again in two days. Tonight at sunset begins the Sabbath. From sunset to sunset is our holy day of rest."

"Why do you have a day of rest?" I asked. "Does all work stop?"

"Yes. We honor the labors of our Lord God who made the world in six days and rested on the seventh. We do not work; we light no ovens, nor put a hand to the plow. We spend the day in peace with our families and think upon the blessings of our Lord."

I wondered if he thought of his foreign wife as his family and if his laws prohibited him from visiting her during his Sabbath.

"My god is of the moon," I said. "Others revere gods of rain, harvest, the sun that warms us. I have not thought of the world being created and governed by one god."

"Our Lord made the earth we live upon," said the king. "He made the moon, the sun, and the stars that bring us light. He filled the sea with water and created the fish that swim in it. He made the clouds that drop the rain, the growing plants, and every living creature that walks or flies or swims.

"Above all," he said. "Our Lord created a man and a woman and from them brought forth the multitude."

I was silent, thinking about his one great god that had created the world and all if its people and animals. "I would like to see a statue of your god."

King Solomon shook his head. "You will not find him in a graven image, it is forbidden."

I hesitated, unsure if I was permitted to ask about his god who could not be seen. Instead, I asked if I would be allowed to visit the temple.

"My priests alone may enter the temple. After the Sabbath is over, I will escort you to the outer court and describe all that is within the house of our Lord."

King Solomon helped me stand. He kept my hand for a moment and then pressed his lips against my palm. He walked with me to Tylos and Sarah and stood watching as we left the terraced room.

I walked back to my rooms, still feeling his lips on my hand. I felt unsettled by his kiss. I wondered if I should heed Sarah's warning. As we walked down to the flowered hall, I thought about his beautiful white temple. I was curious about his god who would not allow an image to be made of him. I wanted to ask King Solomon how he knew his god existed if he could not worship his image.

Samsi and the two girls had been busy while we were gone. The rooms were dusted and swept, my bed had been made with fresh linens. Lighted candles perfumed the air with the warm scent of cinnamon. Before she left with her granddaughters, Sarah told us that our evening meal would be delivered before sunset, along with a basket of cold food for us to eat during the Sabbath.

"We will return with fresh cooked food after our holy day." She added, "You are King Solomon's guest, send for me if you need anything."

As soon as the door closed behind them, Samsi said she had something to show us. She ran into the sleeping room and stood before the wall near my bed. She felt around a carved flower and said Miriam had shown her a secret door. She lifted a petal and pulled. A small door in the cedar panel swung open soundlessly, revealing a dark passageway.

"This is called the king's door." Samsi pointed to a hook sticking out of the inner side of the door. "It can be opened from both sides."

We peered into the dark. I picked up a candle and held it up. A light breeze stirred the flame. The floor and walls were lined with wood and smelled of cedar. The passageway kept going beyond the light of the candle.

"Rachel told me this is a secret door King Solomon uses to visit his favorite women guests."

I was displeased that the king had given me the rooms he saved for every woman who had caught his eye. I was not any woman. Or was I? I had liked being called his beautiful queen. Did he say that to every woman he desired?

Samsi walked to the edge of the candlelight. "I want to see where this leads."

"No," I said and led them back to our room. "I do not want you wandering around the palace alone."

Samsi closed the door. "There's more," she said. She flicked a leaf high on the door, revealing a small hole. I looked through the eyehole down the dark passageway.

"The woman can look through this hole and see who is at her door," Samsi said.

"This gives King Solomon a way to meet with you alone," Tylos said.

I tapped the leaf until it covered the hole again. "I would not open this door to any man who seeks to visit me secretly."

I looked at my women. "And I will not talk with King Solomon alone. One of you will attend me whenever the king or anyone else asks to meet with me."

We rested on cushions in the sitting room as the sun slid down the sky, waiting for our evening meal to be delivered.

"The king was eager to speak with you," Tylos said. "Sarah remarked that he talked with you longer than he has with his other women guests."

"We talked of the temple and his god."

Tylos leaned forward. "He shows you great honor, Bilqis, but be careful, Sarah says his attentions will bring you enemies."

"All of us must act carefully and not encourage dishonorable talk." I looked at Samsi and Tylos. "We will be watched and every word we say will be repeated. Remember that every man or woman, including Sarah and her granddaughters, will be listening."

Tylos put her hand to her jaw. "Ah, my tooth hurts."

"Samsi will grind clove to pack around your tooth for the night," I said.

After they left the room, I touched the palm that the king had kissed. Two days seemed a long time to wait. I could not be alone with him, but I wanted to talk with him, I wanted him to gaze at me with his dark eyes and call me his queen.

~ Twenty-Four ~

We ate meals of cold bread, dates, cheese, and eggs during the long day of the Sabbath. Tylos slept most of the day. In the afternoon, Samsi stood by Tylos's bed and asked if she was sleeping so much because of her sick tooth. I put my hand to the old woman's cheek. She felt warm from the heat in the room. Her breath smelled of cloves, but it was steady. I said she was weary, that this was her day of rest. I woke Tylos at sunset to eat a few dates and a piece of bread and drink a mouthful of wine. She lay back down. I was tired from the past few days and went to bed early.

Sarah and her granddaughters arrived the next morning with food and fresh water. While the girls tidied our rooms, Sarah said she would return at midday to take me to the king. After Rachel and Miriam left, I bathed and dressed in the purple silk and wore the hoopoe necklace. Tylos said her tooth hurt and would remain in our rooms. I told Samsi that she would accompany me.

Sarah led us through the palace to a door that opened onto the busy outer court. We waited inside the doorway until King Solomon arrived. He smiled when he saw me and held out his arm. The court was crowded with people who bowed to him and stared at me as we walked toward the temple. I recognized Rachel and Miriam in their blue headcloths, hurrying through the crowd. Samsi wanted to run after them. I told her they were working and could not stop to talk with her.

White smoke swirled above the altar; the smell of burnt meat was thick in the air. A line of men and women stood by a gate in the stone wall that separated the inner court of the temple from the outer court. Two women at the front held white pigeons under their arms, hugging them close so the birds could not spread their wings. Behind them, a man wearing a red wool robe clutched a rope tied around the neck of a curly haired white lamb. Last in line was an old man dressed in a faded blue robe, holding a round of bread.

King Solomon said the people were waiting for the priests to take their personal offerings to sacrifice as a sign of their devotion to the Lord God. I thought the offerings were based on the ability of the person to give, as were the silver and white gifts we offered to Ilumqah during his full moon ceremony. Samsi had given a white feather, the merchant Ma'zur had presented a large silver ram.

We continued walking along the wall. King Solomon pointed to the stone tower at the front of the temple. "That is the porch with the two bronze columns."

"Are the doors made of gold?" Samsi asked. "May we go inside?"

"The doors are gold," said the king. "We cannot enter the temple. It is closed to all but the priests."

Samsi lost interest in the temple and wandered back to look at the pigeons and the lamb.

I asked the king to describe the temple within. He smiled. "Ah, it is beautiful, a fitting home for our Lord God. I built it of the finest white stone and clad it inside with cedar overlaid with sheets of pure gold."

He pointed to the front of the building. "The gold doors open to the holy sanctuary. Inside are tables of showbread set out as food for our Lord. Ten branched candles, each as tall as a man, provide everlasting light inside the temple. At the far end is the altar of incense. The priests use coals from a separate fire on the altar of sacrifice to light the incense that lifts their prayers to our Lord God."

He moved his hand toward the back of the temple. "Behind the altar is our holiest room. It is there that we placed the golden ark that holds the commandments written by our Lord God."

"Do your priests care for this room, too?" I asked.

"The high priest alone enters the room once a year on our day of atonement. On that day, every Jew prays to our Lord

God for the sins we've committed against him during the year."

I remembered King Solomon talking about the commandments when he told me about his Sabbath. "What are your commandments?" I asked.

"They are the laws that govern our lives. You know two of them; we rest on the Sabbath as our Lord rested after creating the world, and we make no image of our Lord."

He smiled at me. "Now come. Let us return before our shadows grow long. I have arranged a feast for you tonight."

I dressed in the tunic of yellow silk and allowed Samsi to choose the necklace of amethyst grapes and the ruby studded bracelets for me to wear.

The king stood at a table at the head of the feast room, talking to one of his guests. He looked up when I arrived and waved at me to join him. Men and women smiled or nodded at me as I walked past their tables. I wondered if some of the men were merchants that I would meet to talk about the markets in Myrb.

The king nudged his cushion closer to mine as we sat down. He poured wine and said I was the most beautiful woman in the room. I laughed, saying I had heard his harem was filled with comely women.

"I would have no less. But there is none, my queen, as lovely as you."

I glanced around the room, searching for Solomon's Egyptian wife. I did not see her at any of the tables. Sarah had told Tylos that the wife had closed her door to the king, angry because he sought my company and had given me costly gifts. I drank my wine, relieved she wasn't at the feast. I was happy to avoid her.

"I enjoyed learning about your temple," I said. "I would like to know more about your Lord God."

"You will, my queen. I will call for you tomorrow. You may ask me anything."

I ate bread dipped into a savory lentil stew and a piece of honey cake. King Solomon drank another cup of wine but did not touch the food on our table.

I asked if he was unwell. He smiled. "I cannot eat. Your beauty fills me. There is no room for earthly food."

My heart jumped at his sweet words. I also felt caution, wondering if the king flattered me as he would every woman he found attractive or if he truly admired me.

I met King Solomon the next morning in the terraced garden. Tylos and Sarah remained at their table in the corner. I sat with him behind the screen of plants. While he poured wine, I asked him how he was able to rule his country and its many cities.

He sat back with his cup in hand. "I learned from King David, my father, that a king must be the leader of leaders. My father understood that our kingdom was too large for one man to do everything and divided the work of his government among the men he trusted most. I carried on his work. I find out what needs to be done and appoint the ablest men for the tasks."

He described his offices of his government: the priests who performed the temple rituals, a commander of his armies, a secretary who prepared treaties, scribes to record taxes and tributes, and a man to oversee the labor needed to build his cities.

When he finished speaking, I thought of offices that Darmalay could use and others he did not need. He did not require a labor force to build great palaces or a magnificent new temple. He had a leader of the guards that protected the city walls and kept order in the streets. He did not keep an army, for he would not make war on neighboring villages to acquire their land.

What my husband needed, I thought, were officials to levy and collect taxes needed to enlarge and strengthen the city walls, expand the camel pens, and build more houses to accommodate the flood of foreign merchants arriving in Myrb.

I gazed at King Solomon while he filled my cup. I liked that he had answered my questions without dismissing them because I was a woman. I decided to make another request and asked if I might attend his council and listen to his judgments.

He agreed that I could come the next day to his morning council. "Then we will be done with business," he said. "We will talk of poetry."

I sat behind a curtain in his throne room with Tylos at my side as men approached him one at a time, to request justice. Listening, I realized that the issues brought before him, feuds over boundary lines, water rights, and stray cattle were similar to the disputes presented to Darmalay and his council. The king listened carefully to every claim before he ruled. I found myself agreeing with his decisions. He said what I would have said.

After the council, Sarah appeared to take us back to our rooms. As we walked down the flowered hall, I praised King Solomon as a great and wise king. When Sarah left us at our door, I kept talking to Tylos and Samsi, saying I was happy in Jerusalem and that the days were passing too quickly.

Tylos waited until Samsi went into the sleeping room. "You act as though you are in love with the king," she said.

"I admire him and I appreciate his attentions, Tylos. That is all."

She sniffed as though she did not believe me. I didn't believe my own words. My feelings for the king were more than admiration. I thought about him constantly. I longed to be with him.

I walked into the sleeping room and looked at the shelves of silk clothing, wondering what I would wear to our next meeting. Samsi suggested the green silk. I nodded, barely listening as I remembered the king's promise that we would speak of poetry when we met again.

Talk of poetry, I thought, would lead to talk of love.

Sarah appeared as we were eating our morning meal on the terrace. I invited her to sit with us. Samsi offered her bread and wine.

"King Solomon will meet with you this morning," she said as she ate a bite of bread.

I swallowed my wine. I was pleased that the king had asked for me again so quickly. While the women finished their meal, I washed and dressed in the green silk tunic. I wore the hoopoe necklace. It was the first jewelry the king had given to me, and my favorite. I felt it was a sign of friendship between us.

With Tylos and Sarah in attendance, I met the king in the rooftop terrace. Solomon and I sat down at our table. He reached over and gently caressed my cheek, pausing at the scar I bore from the bandit attack. "How did this happen?"

"I was cut during an attack on the caravan."

He laughed softly, "My little warrior."

I smiled at his words, but I felt sad, remembering that Timora and Samar had died from the attack. I shook off my sorrow and waited for him to speak to me of poetry. He sat back with his wine and yawned, saying he had been up late with his advisors. I remembered his request to talk of something other than kingship. I said I had heard he enjoyed riddles and had brought several for him.

He leaned over with his elbows on the table and smiled at me. "Ask your riddles."

I opened my waistbag and pulled out Samsi's large amber bead. "Hold it to the light," I said. "Tell me how to thread this bead."

He laughed when he saw the crooked line. "Have you tried to thread it?"

"Yes, I used gilded camel hair and silver wire, but nothing would go through."

"I need something small," he said. "A spider or an ant. Ah, I have it."

He clapped his hand. A servant standing outside the door hurried to our table. "Fetch a silkworm from the silk merchants in the market," said the king. "The smallest you can find. And bring the leaf they feed upon."

"I have another," I said after the servant left. I showed him Tylos's root. "Which end seeks the earth, which end bears leaves."

He touched each withered end, looking for a root hair or the remains of a leaf. "I would solve this by putting one end in water. If no roots appear, I'd soak the other end." He put down the root. "Do you have other questions?" he asked.

I thought of Samsi's riddle of the sky lying upon the earth. Solomon would say rain or sunlight or moonlight, anything that came from the sky. My questions seemed childish and easily guessed.

The servant returned bearing a bit of a green leaf and a tiny white worm in his hand. King Solomon rubbed the leaf on the back of the beading hole. He laid the bead on the table and held the worm to the front of the drilled opening. The little worm wiggled inside, spinning a wisp of silk thread. The king held the bead to the light and we watched as the worm crept through the bead. It stopped at the bend and pushed forward, easing over the turn. When it emerged from the hole, Solomon pinched off the thread, leaving a thread of delicate silk inside the bead.

I said, "My riddles are too easy, my king. Allow me to ask a question that has puzzled me."

He nodded for me to continue.

I said, "How do you know your god is with you if you cannot see him and are not allowed to worship his image?"

"Men from other lands have asked that question of me. This is my answer. My Lord God created every beast, every grain of wheat, and every drop of rain. He forbids us to worship a carved image of him because he is everywhere and cannot be captured in any one of his creations."

"But how do you know he's there?"

"We know him through his presence. Sometimes he appears and sometimes he speaks to us. My Lord God spoke to me long ago in a dream. He came to me and asked what I desired most."

"What did you say?"

"I asked for wisdom, that I might know between good and evil when I judged my people."

I was surprised. I thought he would have wanted riches and power over his enemies. I pondered his request, and then, as though a door opened in my mind, I understood that the gift his god had given him was an understanding heart that gave him the courage to rule his cities and his vast lands. From this had come his wealth and the love of his people.

The king continued. "I saw him again on the day I dedicated his temple. He appeared when we placed his laws in the Holy of Holies, his sacred room inside the temple. His glory filled the temple with a cloud so radiant that none could look upon it. My Lord was pleased with my work. I heard him say he would dwell in his house forever."

The king's face seemed filled with light as he remembered the presence of his god.

"Is he still there?" I asked.

"Yes, my Bilqis. He is there and everywhere. We may not see or hear him, but his presence is with us always."

I fell silent as I tried to understand a god who could not be seen.

"That is a hard question, my queen. Think on it." He took my hand. "I am needed elsewhere. I will come to you soon. As I promised, we will talk of poetry."

I stayed in my rooms with my women over the next few days. Tylos inspected our clothing and had Samsi repair the slightest pulled thread. Samsi was mending a small rip on my purple tunic when she pricked her finger with the needle. She cried out and threw down the tunic. Tylos told her to take care and not wrinkle the silk.

"I don't want to sew," Samsi said. "I want to go outside." She looked at me. "I want to see Khe. He could take me to the marketplace. Let me go; I'll carry your good wishes to Harjan and Shadru."

I understood her unrest. I wanted to visit my friends in the market. Meeting with the king was a delight to me, but without him, the days spent in our rooms were long.

"I will ask Sarah if we may leave the palace," I said.

"Why do you have to ask her? You're a guest, you can do as you wish."

"I do not know their customs, Samsi. I don't want to do anything that is not allowed."

"Ask the king," she said.

"He's busy. I do not know when I'll see him next."

Samsi sighed loudly and picked up her sewing again.

King Solomon called for me the next afternoon. Sarah and Tylos sat down at their table in the corner while I joined the king behind the row of plants A servant brought bread and wine. After we ate, Solomon put down his cup and said he had written a poem. He gazed at me and in a low voice spoke of a woman from the south. Her neck was a column of dark ivory, her lips were red as pomegranates, her eyes were precious stones polished by the waters of the Gihon spring.

I breathed in the scent of incense as he moved closer. He took the cup from my hand. We looked at each other for a long moment.

"You are beautiful," he whispered. "You are the love of my heart."

My heart was beating so hard I could scarcely breathe. I glanced through the leaves at Tylos and Sarah in their corner, leaning against the wall with their eyes closed.

I picked up a fig from the platter. I pinched the skin and split open the fruit. King Solomon's eyes were on me as I offered him the fig. He bent down and ate it from my hand. His breath was warm on my wrist. I closed my eyes as he moved his lips up the tender skin inside my arm. He kissed my lips, gently at first, then harder. We held the kiss as he pushed me backwards until I was lying down on the cushions. I moaned as he reached under my tunic and slid his warm hand up my thigh. His lips were on my breast when I heard Tylos snorting as she woke up.

Solomon uttered a curse and sat up, catching his breath. I breathed out, feeling disappointed that we had stopped. He kissed my hand, turned it over and bit my palm. I closed my eyes, unable to move.

Tylos and Sarah began talking in low voices. I slowly sat up. The king kissed my neck, whispering he would send them away if the day were younger.

Tylos glanced at me but did not speak during the walk back to our room. She checked Samsi's needlework and then busied herself with shaking out my pillows and straightening the blanket over my newly made bed. I told her to come out to the terrace and walked away. She said it was too hot but followed me through the fretted door.

I crossed my arms over my breast as I faced her. "Speak your mind," I said.

She stared at the city below, then looked at me. "I heard you with the king."

"We kissed, that is all."

"That is all today. King Solomon gets what he wants, my girl. Take heed or you'll return home with his child in your belly."

"Your tongue could cut iron," I said, angry that she was scolding me.

"As long as it cuts through your dreams." Tylos put her hand on my arm. "The king is famous for his pursuit of beautiful women. I have heard that he has bragged to his friends that you soon will yield to him.

That hurt. I didn't like hearing that the king would speak of me so carelessly. I shrugged off Tylos's hand and walked back into the sitting room.

I lay awake in my bed that night, staring at the ceiling. I didn't believe Tylos. King Solomon had welcomed me as a queen and treated me with respect. I knew he desired me as I did him. Sarah was mistaken; the king would do nothing to harm me.

I gazed at the king's door, hoping it would swing open. The night was late when I thought I heard a quick knock. I slid out of my bed and lifted the petal on the wall. The door opened to the empty passageway.

Sarah brought word in the morning that the king was meeting with his advisors during the day and would see me after our evening meal. I paced the sitting room while the girls swept the sleeping room. Tylos asked what worried me. I ignored her and went out on the terrace. I sat down on a cushion, tired from lying awake the night before while I waited for the king.

Tylos woke me at midday. I ate a piece of bread and drank a cup of fig wine, feeling dazed from sleeping in the sun. I rested on my bed during the long afternoon as Tylos and Samsi worked in the sitting room, sewing a new tunic of blue linen for Samsi. Tylos held up the cloth, measuring it against Samsi. The girl was taller; her head was up to Tylos's shoulder.

I got up when a servant brought our evening meal. I ate a few grapes, too nervous about seeing the king to eat more. Tylos and Samsi were still eating when I left the table and returned to our sleeping room. Samsi came in and helped me dress in the light blue tunic and a gold silk veil. I slipped the ruby bracelets on my wrists. Tylos entered the room as Samsi was clasping the amethyst necklace around my neck.

"You look as though you're dressing for a feast," she said.

"These are gifts from the king. I wear them to show him that his generosity pleased me."

Samsi smiled and said King Solomon would think I was beautiful. Tylos pursed her lips as though she doubted that I was wearing the king's jewelry as a courtesy.

~ Twenty-Five ~

I walked toward the king's terrace accompanied by Tylos and Sarah. I breathed slowly, trying to calm my heart. I wanted to run up to the room where Solomon was waiting for me.

A servant was carrying out an empty wine jar as we entered the room. The king stood under a flaming torch at the edge of the terrace, drinking from a large cup. We bowed to him. Sarah and Tylos sat down in their corner. I walked over to the table I shared with the king. Another row of green plants had been added around our table, making a thicker hedge between my women and me. I heard Tylos refuse wine when Sarah offered it and knew she was determined to stay awake and watchful while I met with the king.

King Solomon sat down next to me. He poured wine, slopping red wine over the edge of the cups. I asked him about his meetings. He waved away my questions, saying he was fatigued with the business of his kingdom. He drank his wine in one breath and set the cup down with a bang. He reached for me, knocking the cup from my hand. He grabbed my shoulder, digging his fingers in my flesh and pulled me close. His lips were on mine before I could push him away. He bit my bottom lip, hard. I cried out in pain, frightened by his roughness.

I heard Tylos talking loudly and knew she had heard me scream. Solomon let go of me. I quickly stood and stepped away from him. I straightened my veil. I didn't know what to do. I no longer wanted to be alone with him.

"It's late; I will leave you," I said.

I waited for him to bid me good night. He drank his wine, not looking at me as he gestured for me to leave.

I rushed down the stairway with Tylos and Sarah running to keep up with me. I was angry. The king had used me as though I was a concubine, summoned to tend to his pleasure. Tylos wisely didn't say anything as I walked faster and faster down the hallway to our rooms.

I went directly into the sleeping room, saying I was tired. Samsi was asleep in her niche. I lay down and thought of Tylos saying the king had vowed he would have me in his bed. I believed her now; his behavior tonight had shown a rougher side. My desire for him vanished as I thought of the price I would pay if I had yielded to him. As I would have if anyone had discovered me in Samar's tent. I would not be celebrated as a great queen from the south, I would be mocked as a whore.

I slept badly, waking frequently to stare at the paneled wall, fearing the king would throw open the door and fall upon me.

The next morning, Sarah told me that King Solomon had left early and was traveling north to visit his huge complex of stables and would be gone for ten days or more. I was relieved at first that I would not have to meet him and ate my morning bread with appetite. I soon felt restless, thinking about the long days before us while I waited for his return. I was angry with the king, but I had little to do in Jerusalem while he was gone. He left before he set up a meeting for me with the merchants of Jerusalem to talk about trading in Myrb. No one else in Jerusalem sought my company. Though I met frequently with King Solomon, I did not have the power to sway his judgment nor did I try to persuade him in business matters other than those that involved Myrb. There was no profit in befriending me.

I heard raised voices in the sleeping room. I walked through the curtain to see Samsi arguing with Miriam over who would put fresh sheets on my bed. Tylos snapped at Samsi to hold her tongue. Furious at being chastised, Samsi seized a robe that Rachel was mending and ripped it from her hands.

I was angry at Samsi's bad behavior and told Tylos to send the two girls away. After they left, Tylos shouted at Samsi for her rudeness. Samsi yelled back. I stepped between them and glared at Samsi. "You are ill-mannered," I said. "Rachel and Miriam were sent to us by the king. You insult him when you quarrel with them."

Samsi shrugged and turned from me, heading toward the sitting room. I grabbed her braid and yanked her back. "You will not raise your voice to Tylos," I said. "And you will not walk away when I am speaking to you."

Samsi's lips quivered, her eyes filled with tears as she rubbed her head. I resisted the urge to comfort her. She no longer was a child, she had to learn to control her emotions and show respect for her elders.

Sarah knocked on my door with our midday meal. She asked what her granddaughters had done to be sent away. Tylos took Samsi into the sleeping room while I talked with Sarah. I explained that my young companion had argued with them for no cause. Samsi was restless at having to stay our rooms, I said. I asked if I could take her to visit her friends from the caravan.

Sarah shook her head. "The king alone may approve your request to leave the palace."

"King Solomon offered to invite merchants from Jerusalem to talk with me. He left before he could do so. I would like to arrange a meeting with them."

"King Solomon would not permit men to visit you while he's gone."

"We would meet in a public room. I have my own guards. They will attend me."

"That is not possible, Queen Bilqis. The king would not allow it while he is away."

I breathed out in frustration. The king would be gone for many days. I felt like a prisoner confined his palace

"May I invite my friends to visit?" I said.

She finally nodded. "That would be acceptable."

I asked her to send Farium to me. I had not seen him since the feast after the presentation. Samsi regained her good mood when she saw Farium. She asked about Khe. Farium told us that his son was tending my camels. I asked Farium to find Harjan in the market and invite the merchant and his wife to my rooms the next day for the midday meal. He said he would see him in the market or at the full moon ceremony. I had forgotten that Ilumqah rose that night. I asked Farium where the priests would sacrifice to our god.

"They are not allowed to worship another god openly in Jerusalem," he said. "They will quietly honor Ilumqah in the house where they are lodged."

When Farium was gone, we dressed in silver and white and stood on the terrace, watching Ilumqah rise in the night sky. It was reassuring to see our god in the fullness of his image. I thought of King Solomon's god who would not allow his people to worship his likeness. Not seeing Ilumqah would be a terrible loss. He brought light during the darkness; it was fitting we honored him.

Rachel and Miriam returned in the morning. As I had instructed, Samsi asked their forgiveness for quarreling with them. The two girls swept the terrace while Samsi remained in the sitting room, working silver thread into a scroll pattern on the hem of her new tunic. The girls came in and praised her needlework. I sent Samsi to help Miriam change the linens on my bed. I soon heard them talking together.

The two girls returned at midday with food and wine. Harjan and Shadru arrived soon after. Tylos kept Samsi busy in the sleeping room while I visited with my old friends. Shadru admired the large rooms and the carvings on the walls. We stood on the terrace and looked over Jerusalem.

Shadru pointed to the old city. "The marketplace is close to the gate we entered when we arrived in Jerusalem. Our house is nearby. It's a fine house with a good oven for baking."

We walked inside and sat around the low table where Rachel and Miriam had laid out bread and cheese and a bowl of stewed lentils. Shadru coughed into her hand several times as she ate. She said it was the dust in the air.

Harjan spoke, "I took a boy to work with me in the market and a girl to help my wife. Shadru will not rest while I'm gone but must sweep the house and cook. I fear the girl sits idle.

Shadru smiled at her husband and said the girl had work enough.

"You must take your ease, my friend," I said. "I want to enjoy your company on our journey home."

"I'm anxious to return to my house and my children." She glanced at her husband.

He looked down at his food and I wondered why he hesitated to speak.

"Have you sold well in the market?" I asked

He nodded. "I have a good place. I paid a high price to a wine merchant to set up my stall outside his shop."

I was reminded of Yahmed. "Do you see Yahmed or the other merchants from the caravan?"

"The market is big and crowded. We greet each other in passing and sometimes take a meal at midday."

"You are busy," I said.

"My honey is gone. I have a few slabs of salt left to sell."

I thought I knew why Harjan had been unwilling to speak. "Will you soon be ready to travel back to Myrb?"

He smiled, looking relieved I had asked the question. "Yes, I'm waiting on a shipment of ivory jewelry and Egyptian pottery to take back to Myrb. When it comes, I'll be ready to leave."

I sipped my wine. The merchants on my caravan were starting to look homeward. I had to think of them as I considered how long I would remain in Jerusalem. I was a guest and could not leave while the king was gone. How long did I want to stay after he returned? Could I leave when I wanted or did he have to approve of my departure?

My friends were staring at me, wondering at my silence. I quickly told them of my conversation with the king, that every caravan entering his lands was protected. Harjan nodded, saying he had heard this in the marketplace.

"There is more," I said. "As a sign of the king's friendship with Darmalay, he has promised to set aside a street for the caravans from Myrb to sell their wares."

Harjan smiled, pleased at the king's promise. "That is good news. Jerusalem is a great city for trading. Many times during the year, it overflows with people who come here to observe their holy days and worship their god."

I said the king had told me something that might interest him. Harjan and Shadru leaned forward to hear my words. "King Solomon said our goods from the south are welcomed but the most prized is incense and that merchants who bring nothing but incense will return home as wealthy men."

Harjan thought for a moment. "Ah, that is why many merchants in Jerusalem have asked me and others about the incense trade. They want to know where frankincense and myrrh are grown, how the incense is taken from the tree, and who owns the trees."

"Protect that information," I said. "They may decide to send down their own caravans to buy the harvest."

He scratched his beard. "I don't think we have to worry. The journey back and forth is long and dangerous. It would cost more for them to send their own caravans than it does for them to buy it from us."

~ Twenty-Six ~

A day later, Sarah told me that the merchant Yahmed and his wife wished to visit me. I remembered Wa'dab's unfriendly treatment on the caravan and her husband's efforts to blacken my name. I did not want to see them and had thought little about them while I was a guest in King Solomon's palace. But Yahmed was a wealthy man and Darmalay would welcome him to our house when we returned to Myrb.

I told Sarah I would invite them in two days and sent her to ask Farium to stand guard when they arrived. I was not afraid of Yahmed and his wife, but they had threatened me on the caravan and I wanted them to see that I still commanded the leader of my husband's guards.

I heard Wa'dab's loud voice in the hall before she walked through my door. She kissed my cheeks in greeting and looked around at the sitting room. She nodded briefly at Tylos and

Samsi as she walked past them to peer through the curtain into my sleeping room.

"You live well, too," she said. "We are renting an excellent stone house with a tile floor. I have two servants to cook and clean."

At my invitation, she and Yahmed sat down at the table. Tylos and Samsi retreated into the sleeping room to sew. Wa'dab looked at the bowls of hardcooked eggs, olives in green oil, bread, cheese, small white onions, and two jars of wine.

"My servant cooks the same food," she said. "And we eat meat with every meal."

"You have two servants," I said. "Does this leave you time to work in the market with your husband?"

Wa'dab laughed. "No, I have never been to the market. I send a girl to buy our food."

I filled their cups and asked Yahmed how he fared in the market. Wa'dab spoke before Yahmed could open his mouth. "We have sold everything. Yahmed is buying a new fig wine to take back with us for the southern markets."

She drank her wine. "This is good."

"It is made from pomegranates."

"Buy this wine," Wa'dab said to her husband. "It will sell well in Myrb."

She turned to me. "We have heard of your many meetings with King Solomon. It is said that he does not let a day pass without seeing you." She leaned across the table and touched my hand as I was reaching for my cup. "Take care, Bilqis, King Solomon is known for his love of women."

I sat back and did not reply. On the caravan, I would have become angry and defended myself. Now I merely looked at Wa'dab.

Yahmed wiped his mouth and said all of Jerusalem knew that I was a virtuous woman. He added, "As you were on the caravan."

I knew he was speaking of my friendship with Samar. I raised my cup to my lips to hide my disgust at his sly words, his quick glance at his wife.

Wa'dab said every merchant knew that King Solomon protected the caravans entering his lands. "He gave you nothing that we did not have already."

"I gained something of value," I said. "The king has agreed to give the caravans from Myrb a permanent place in the market."

"That will be useful," Yahmed said. "My profits are less because I had to purchase a good spot to sell my wines." He gulped his wine and continued his story. "I first set up my stall on an empty corner next to a meat shop. The owner hung a skinned sheep in his doorway and stood next to it with his knife in his hand, ready to cut off pieces to sell. Few people came down that street; it was a bad place for his shop and my stall. After a few days, the meat smelled so bad that no one would come near the shop. My wine jars stunk of rotting meat. I had to take them home and set them on the roof until the wind blew the stink away."

Wa'dab interrupted him. "We traded five jars of Myrb wine for a spot that opened up in the food court after another merchant's wine turned sour in the jars."

I filled their cups from the second jar and said the wine was a gift from a merchant who had traveled on the caravan with us from Myrb.

Wa'dab tasted the wine and made a face. "This is not as good as Yahmed's." She turned to her husband. "Do you know the seller?"

"Demir of Myrb," he said. "This is his wine. We didn't see him on the caravan. His wife was sick, he stayed with her."

"King Solomon enjoyed Demir's wine," I said. The king had not drunk the wine, but I wanted to worry Wa'dab; I wanted her to know that Yahmed was not the only wine seller from Myrb.

I asked when they intended to return home.

"We wish to join your caravan." Wa'dab reached for a piece of cheese. "Whenever you are willing to leave King Solomon."

I wanted to slap her hand from my food. I heard the meaning behind her words; she believed I was dallying with the king. She waited for me to say they were welcome to travel with me. I knew they wanted the protection my caravan would provide. I put my cup down and said they would have to leave my rooms soon, before the start of the Sabbath.

"We have heard of this day," Wa'dab said. "They close the market. Yahmed told the officials we were not Jews and asked if we could keep our stall open. He was denied." She stared at me. "You speak as though you observe this Sabbath. Has the king converted you to his god?"

"No, but I am his guest and I respect his customs."

When the door closed behind them, I told Tylos that I would not travel back to Myrb with Wa'dab and her husband.

Tylos shook her head. "If they arrive in Myrb before you, Wa'dab will win glory by being the first to tell of your welcome from King Solomon and the promise he made to accommodate the merchants."

"Or she'll try to poison Darmalay against me by saying I was always with the king."

"You see King Solomon often," Tylos said.

"Never alone and never without a companion. Wa'dab would leave off that part."

The next morning brought a surprise request from Solomon's Egyptian wife to visit her in the harem. Tylos and Sarah accompanied me. I left Samsi in the company of Sarah's granddaughters.

We walked through a cedar hall across the length of the palace and down a passageway of pierced wood that connected the palace with the harem. At the end of the passageway, an enormous man opened a heavy wooden door and admitted us into a large, tall-ceilinged room. The room was empty. Light came through high windows and slanted through smoke from incense burning in holders placed in every corner of the room. The walls were smooth stone and decorated with paintings of winged women with long black hair, palm trees, and tall birds standing in pools of blue water. Low tables and bright colored cushions were arranged in groups around the room. The oiled wood floor was covered with blue and red patterned rugs, fringed with gold thread.

Curtains of undyed linen curtains hung over doorways lining both sides of the main room. I heard women's voices and saw shadows moving behind the curtains. I thought they must be the king's wives and concubines. At the back of the room two doorways were hung with silk curtains, one white, the other red.

I started to ask Sarah how long we would be left standing in the empty room when the white silk was pulled aside and the black-haired woman I had seen at the presentation appeared. She wore a large neckpiece of lapis and white pearls over a tunic of sheer linen that fell in tiny folds from her neck to her ankles. Several women dressed in similarly pleated clothing followed her through the doorway.

The Egyptian wife came to me and kissed my cheek. She smelled of mint and looked older than I had thought. Her mouth drooped at the corners, flesh hung under her chin. I remembered Sarah saying that King Solomon had taken her to wife before he built the temple and his palace. The woman took my hand and led me to a table in the middle of the room. Sarah and Tylos and the attendants sat at a table near us. The wife clapped her hands and a servant brought in two jars of wine. She set the larger jar on Sarah's table and a smaller one before the wife. The servant poured wine for us and left.

The wife and I lifted our cups to each other and drank. She wiped her lips with her fingers and asked if my journey from my home had been long. Her voice was high, that of a girl. I told her it had taken over two moons to travel from my city in the south to Jerusalem.

"I watched your entrance into Jerusalem," she said. "Your curtains were open so that all could see you."

I had been partly hidden in my tent. I hadn't come wantonly into the city as she suggested.

"My curtains were closed," she continued. "My mother would not let me open them in fear I would be seen by a man other than my husband."

"I saw you at the presentation of my gifts. Are you allowed to appear before other men?"

"Yes, when I am in my husband's house."

We drank our wine. My head was starting to pound from the smoking incense. I asked if she enjoyed going to the marketplace. She smiled and said no, every merchant begged to come to her. She waved her hand at the room. "I never leave the harem. Everything I desire is here."

I glanced at the curtained rooms and wanted to ask if she resented sharing her husband with many women. As though she guessed my thoughts, she said, "Many women live here, but I am the king's first wife and his favorite. He comes to me every night. Sometimes he is late if he has stopped first with a guest or a new concubine."

I knew she was attempting to hurt me by suggesting I was one in a long line of King Solomon's women. I no longer cared about the king's affection for me. I had started thinking about returning to my home. I wondered if Darmalay had taken a third wife or a concubine while I was gone. I hadn't liked being cast aside for Amida, what would I do if I came back to a house full of women?? I gazed at the wife. I didn't think I could be satisfied as she was, with a few moments of her husband's attention.

She poured more wine. "You have visited the temple, has the king talked to you about his one god?"

"Yes, I thought there was great wisdom in the words of his god." I looked at her. "Do you worship with the king?"

"No, I offer to the gods of my home. My lord husband permits it, though his priests say by allowing us to worship idols, he breaks covenant with his god."

"Where is your temple?" I asked.

She pointed to the doorway with the red silk curtain. "We honor our gods in that room. My husband has vowed that he soon will build temples in the woods above Jerusalem where we may worship our gods."

"I offer to Ilumqah, god of the moon," I said. "His light led us through the night to Jerusalem; he will lead us back home again."

She set her cup on the table. "When do you return to your home?"

That seemed to be the question everyone wanted me to answer.

"I stay at the king's pleasure."

"He will return soon," she said. "I have heard that he is bringing back a new wife, the daughter of a chieftain." I saw her teeth when she smiled. "Do not be offended if he forgets you are here."

I was irritated at her efforts to upset me and at the same time, worried that she might be right. Would the king ignore me after he returned with his newest wife? I no longer desired him, but I did not want to be treated as an unwelcome guest while I remained in his home.

My eyes were tearing from the smoke and my nose felt stuffed. I wondered when I could take my leave of her. The voices in the rooms grew louder. A curtain moved and two women poked their heads around the edge and stared at me.

The wife put her hand over her empty cup and wished me good speed on my homeward journey.

"We may leave now," Sarah said.

I took a breath of hot air outside the harem door. My head hurt, my throat was sore. The walk back to our rooms seemed long. I lay down on my bed. Samsi bathed my face with cool water while Sarah fetched wine she had steeped in herbs. I drank the wine and slept the rest of the day and through the night.

I felt recovered the next morning and took my morning meal with Tylos and Samsi on the terrace. Sarah arrived with another jar of herbed wine, saying she was anxious for my health. I didn't want the wine but drank a cup to please her.

After our meal, I walked along the terrace, wishing I had asked the king for permission to leave the palace. His first wife was content with living in the harem, but it felt like a cage to me. I missed the freedom I had at home. With Tylos to accompany me, I could leave my house whenever I wished to shop at the marketplace or visit the house of a friend.

~ Twenty-Seven ~

We passed the next few days waiting for the king to return. Samsi embroidered the hem of a dark blue robe that Tylos had sewn for her. I had asked Tylos to make new clothing for Samsi; she had outgrown everything she owned except for the blue tunic I had given her when we entered Jerusalem.

Shadru came again, bringing the young wife of another merchant from the caravan. Her name was Cayla. Her husband, Demir, sold the wine I had served to Wa'dab and Yahmed.

Cayla's belly was round with the child she carried. I greeted her and said I had not met her on our journey to Jerusalem. She rubbed her belly. "I felt sick after we left Myrb and stayed in my tent. My sister attended a feast at your fire."

"I am surprised your husband allowed you to come on the journey when he knew you were with child," I said.

"He is not to blame. I didn't know I was pregnant. I was so excited about traveling on the caravan with my husband that I forgot about my monthly blood."

I counted the months in my mind. "It will be close, but you should be home in Myrb before your time has come."

"Sometimes the path is so rough, I'm afraid riding my camel will bring on the birth."

Shadru laughed. "No more than walking. But don't worry, many women on the caravan have given birth. We will attend you."

Shadru's words reminded me that there would be women on the caravan I had not met on the journey to Jerusalem. I would open my tent to them as we traveled back to Myrb. Their friendship would be welcome during the long days of riding across the desert sand.

"You will receive every comfort," I said. "My woman, Tylos, is skilled with herbs. She will have whatever you need."

Cayla smiled, looking reassured at our words and then drew a sharp breath. Through the thin wool of her tunic, we could see the bulge of the baby's head moving across her belly. "He's eager to come out," she said and pushed the bump away from her ribs so she could breath more easily.

I looked at her, feeling a little envious of her pregnancy. I remembered the feel of my baby moving inside me. He had died at birth and I had not become pregnant again before Darmalay took a new wife and quit my bed. I wondered if I still was barren.

King Solomon returned late one night. I heard shouts and hurried from my bed to the terrace. A line of torches lit men on horseback moving up the street toward the palace. My heart beat fast as I glimpsed a spark of gold on the head of a man riding in front of a covered cart. I watched as the king led the cart toward the harem. His new wife must be in the cart, I thought. My heart was beating faster at the idea of meeting with King Solomon again. I returned to my bed, hoping that tomorrow I would hear from him.

Sarah brought the news in the morning that the king had returned, bringing with him his newest wife. I wondered if Solomon's first wife had put her in the smallest room in the harem or if the king expected the girl to be treated well until his interest turned elsewhere.

I asked Sarah when I could meet with him. She replied that the king was with his advisors and had not said when he would see me.

I waited during the long morning, unable to sit still. I had not forgotten the king's rough behavior toward me, but I wished to see him. I was tired of staying in our rooms. I had few visitors, no one else to talk to other than Tylos and Samsi. I paced the terrace, laid down to rest, and got up again. The bread I ate at midday stuck in my throat. Tylos retreated to the sleeping room with Samsi to refold my clothing.

Sarah returned to my rooms late in the day and said the king would see me. I walked smiling into the sleeping room and told Tylos to lay out the ivory silk tunic, the amber earrings, and the hoopoe necklace.

I bathed while I thought of my meeting with the king. I was eager to hear about his stables and his great herd of horses. I wondered if Darmalay would like a horse to ride instead of a camel.

I waited on the terrace for Sarah to arrive. The setting sun had turned the sky a hazy gold when she knocked on the door. She entered the room and stood before me, holding her two hands together tightly. She said King Solomon had sent word that he would not be seeing me that night.

I stood speechless for a moment. I looked at Sarah, wondering if she would smile, satisfied that the king had treated me as she had warned Tylos he would. She reached for my hand and said quietly, "King Solomon takes new wives to build friendships and trade agreements with other chieftains and kings. His attentions to you have been greater than any other woman he has welcomed as a guest. He will see you soon."

She patted my hand and left. I understood the reason the king had taken another wife, but I felt humiliated and then enraged at the king's disregard for me. I clenched my fists as I thought about Solomon in the harem with his new wife, telling her she was the most beautiful of all women and the love of his heart.

Samsi looked wide-eyed at my anger as I walked past her into the sleeping room. Tylos helped me out of the ivory silk. I unclasped the hoopoe necklace and dropped it on the bed. I wanted to throw it from the terrace into the night.

King Solomon didn't send for me the next day. My heart felt heavy as I wandered about our rooms. I felt there was nothing left for me in Jerusalem, no reason to stay longer. I stood on the terrace and looked over the city walls to the desert beyond. I thought about the long journey home to Myrb.

Two more days passed with no word from Solomon. I smelled clove and knew that Tylos was in pain from her sore tooth, but she didn't complain. She asked if I wanted to invite Shadru to take our midday meal. I shook my head. I was depressed and could not pretend to my friend that I was happy. Samsi worked quietly with Rachel and Miriam and brought her sewing to sit with me whenever I took my rest. She didn't ask why the king did not send for me or grumble about being shut up in our rooms. She bent over her work, leaving me to my thoughts. I found her presence soothing.

Farium came to my rooms on the third morning to tell me that the merchants from Myrb had taken down their stalls and were packing their new goods to load onto the caravan.

"They wait on you," he said.

I felt strengthened by his words. I now had a reason to leave Jerusalem instead of waiting on the king. I asked Sarah to arrange a meeting with Solomon. I wanted to tell him that my merchants were ready to travel back to the south. A day later he agreed to meet me.

I stood before my shelves of clothing, unable to decide what to wear to our meeting. I wanted to dress poorly, to reflect my disdain of the king's behavior. Tylos shook her head when I pulled down my oldest tunic.

"Don't be a goose," she said. She held up the purple silk. "Look your most beautiful. Make him regret that he's stayed away from you."

"You didn't like it before when he admired me," I said.

"I worried that you would be swept away by his attention."

"And now? Are you still worried?"

"No, you have more resolve. You arrived as a queen and are ready to leave as one."

I waited on King Solomon's terrace at midday. The king was late in arriving. He strode past us while we bowed to him, and sat down at our table. I joined him, feeling anxious about telling him I wished to leave his house. His eyes shifted to the door as he took a cup of wine from the servant. I knew he was impatient to get back to his advisors or his new wife.

I took a sip of wine and put down my cup. "My king, I soon must leave Jerusalem. My people have sold their goods in the market and are ready to return to Myrb."

He finally looked at me. His eyes lingered. "My Bilqis, I regret your time with me is over."

I was surprised that he said my name with affection after he had ignored me. "I too, am saddened. I have enjoyed your generous hospitality."

"When do you wish to leave?" he asked.

"The morning after next."

He poured wine for both of us. "That is too soon."

I nodded. I had been angry with him when I arrived for our meeting, but now felt a moment's regret that I was leaving.

"I will hold a feast in your honor tomorrow," he said. "Invite your merchants so I will know them when they come to Jerusalem without you." He added, "Do not forget our agreement, Bilqis. Bring your incense first to Jerusalem."

"My merchants will do so willingly. They are pleased that you promised to set aside a place in the market for them."

"It is done," he said. "I have heard that a caravan from Myrb approaches my lands. When it arrives, the merchants will have a street of their own to set up their stalls."

"I am grateful for your attention to this," I said. "And that you will help my merchants enter the markets in Egypt."

"My friends in the great city of Memphis will welcome your caravans and secure them a place in the market." He drank and put down his cup. "I must leave you. I will meet you tomorrow night at your feast."

I sent word to Farium to tell the merchants the caravan would depart in two days. Samsi jumped around the sitting room, delighted by the news that we were leaving.

"I'll walk with Khe and pull your camel," she said.

I shook my head. "You will ride, my Samsi, my companions do not walk."

She looked at me, her mouth open in surprise. "Why do you call me your companion? You said you were going to take me back to my village."

"I will send Farium to the village closest to where I found you and ask about your people. If you are willing, I will tell them I wish to take you to Myrb to live with me as my companion."

She ran to me, holding me tight. Tylos came out from the sleeping room to ask why Samsi was crying. Her lips twitched upwards in a brief smile when I said Samsi was coming home to live with us.

The following morning passed quickly. Tylos watched over Samsi and the two girls as they packed our clothing. I looked through my jewelry bag and found two bracelets of twisted silver wire. I gave one each to Rachel and Miriam to thank them for their service to us. They slipped the bracelets on their wrists and smiled, pleased with my gift.

Khe and one of Farium's guards came before midday to take our bags down to the camel pens. I told Khe to place my red bag in my riding tent. I was leaving King Solomon's protection. I wanted to keep Samar's dagger close if bandits attacked us on the journey home.

Tylos kept Rachel and Miriam busy bringing up buckets of water to fill our bathing basin. We had washed every morning with the water they brought to our rooms, but this would be our last full bath before the caravan reached a river or an oasis.

I added jasmine oil to the water and stepped into the bath. It felt wonderful to sit in a basin of cool water with the hot sun on my face. I felt calmer, no longer worried about the feast. I had feared that since I was leaving, that King Solomon would place me in the crowd while he sat at the head of the room with his new wife. If he did, I planned to keep up the appearance of friendship with him and talk to the people at my table. Perhaps I would meet some of the merchants from Jerusalem after all.

Tylos bathed next, then Samsi. We sat together, clothed in our sleeping tunics, drying our hair in the sun. Tylos looked around the terrace with a sigh and said she was not looking forward to riding a camel all day. Samsi put her arm around the old woman and said she would give her the cushions from her tent to make her more comfortable.

Tylos combed and oiled my hair and gathered it in a knot high on my head. I dressed in the green silk tunic and slipped on the amethyst necklace and the gold and ruby bracelets. Samsi wore her new blue tunic with the silver scrollwork and her gold bee necklace. Tylos covered Samsi's hair with pale blue silk.

Sarah arrived before sunset with Farium and Khe to escort us to the feast room. Tylos glanced at Khe when he said Samsi looked pretty. I knew Tylos would be keeping an eye on the girl during the journey home. Khe would not be the only man on the caravan to notice that Samsi had grown from a girl into a young woman.

As we approached the feasting room, I felt my heart beating fast. This was my last night in Jerusalem, the last time I would meet with King Solomon. I would leave in the morning and never see him again.

I stopped in the doorway. King Solomon stood at the front of the crowded room, talking with one of his advisors.

There were two cushions at his table. I was pleased the king had not brought his new wife to the feast. People sat at their tables, drinking wine. They looked up when the king shouted my name. He opened his arms, welcoming me as he had on the morning I entered Jerusalem. My silk tunic fluttered against my legs as I walked across the room. I felt as though a gentle hand was pushing me toward the king.

Solomon smiled when I reached him. He looked into my eyes. "Beautiful queen, you have arrived."

He took my hand and helped me to a cushion. He sat next to me with his leg touching mine. I smelled his scent of honey and spice; he had perfumed his beard and clothing with frankincense from Myrb. Harjan and Shadru smiled at me from across the room. Wa'dab and Yahmed were not in the crowd. I didn't see Solomon's Egyptian wife. I had thought she would be pleased I was leaving and attend the feast.

Solomon caressed my wrist as he poured wine. "I have taken great pleasure in your company, my Bilqis. I would have you stay longer."

He turned to the room and lifted his cup. Every man and women in the room hastened to raise their wine. "Our beloved queen, Bilqis, leaves us tomorrow," he said. "We wish her farewell."

I bowed my head in acknowledgement as everyone called safe journey.

Servants carried in platters of food and more jars of wine. We ate and drank. My cup was never empty. I saw Sarah glance at the king as she set a small jar of wine in front of

Tylos and Samsi. When I looked again, Tylos was trying to keep her eyes open, Samsi was leaning against her with her eyes closed. I signaled to Farium to take the women back to our rooms.

The room grew louder as servants brought in more food and drink. I tried to tell the king how much I would miss talking with him. I had to speak slowly; I had drunk too much and could not easily get the words out. Solomon said he could not hear me. He moved closer until his warm body was pressed against mine. I felt trapped. I could not get away from him without falling off my cushion.

Harjan and Shadru had bowed to the king and were leaving the feast when Farium and Khe returned to stand by the door. My head was whirling from the wine and the noise. I put my hand over my empty cup and told the king the hour was late and I would return to my room.

Solomon shook his head. He put his arm around my waist and kissed my neck. "I yearn for you, Bilqis, I want you in my bed." His breath was hot in my ear.

I looked around the room, hoping no one had seen. A few men smiled. A woman dressed in gold silk raised her cup to me. The king reached for his wine, loosening his grip. I twisted away from him and stood up. I quickly bowed and left the table. I heard his laughter as I walked across the room to my guards.

Farium and Khe followed silently as I hurried back to my rooms. A small candle was lit in the sleeping room. Tylos and Samsi were asleep in their beds, both wearing their feast clothing. The floor tilted under my feet as I stepped out of the green silk. I had to sit on the bed to put on my sleep tunic. I blew out the candle and fell into bed.

The room was dim with starlight when I woke to the sound of someone bumping into a wall. I stumbled out of bed and stood listening at the door of the sitting room, wondering who was outside. When I didn't hear the noise again, I started back to my bed. Light flared behind the curtain. I thought Tylos had awakened and lit a candle. I stopped in the doorway, shocked to see King Solomon standing by my bed, swaying back and forth with a candle in his hand. The king's door was open behind him. He was barefoot and dressed in a white silk tunic and robe.

"Come here," he said, slurring the words. I stayed by the curtain. He slumped against the wall and dropped the candle. I hastened to pick it up and set it on the wooden chest. He seized me when I stood and pushed me back onto the bed. He fell on me, grunting. I screamed as he bit my neck, my ear. I raked his face with my fingernails. He growled like a maddened dog, grabbed the neck of my tunic with one hand and ripped it to my waist. He bit my breasts and shoved his hand between my legs. I jammed my knee into his groin, terrified he was going to force me. I wished I had Samar's dagger, I wanted to stab Solomon again and again to get him off of me.

He groaned and suddenly collapsed, knocking the breath from me. He lay on me, unmoving. I tried to heave him off but he was too heavy. I heard Tylos and Samsi shouting my name, then the king was pulled off and I was freed.

I rolled away and stood up, gulping air. Samsi rushed to me and put her arm around my shoulder. She was holding the empty water pitcher. "I hit him to make him stop," she said.

Tylos grabbed my hand and asked if I was injured. I held the neck of my tunic closed, took a deep shuddering breath and shook my head.

We stared at Solomon snoring on my bed. "Should I fetch Farium to help?" Samsi asked.

"No," I said. "I don't want to raise the house. It will be terrible for me if the king is found in my room."

"What do we do?" Tylos said. "He can't stay here."

I looked at the open door. "We'll put him in the passageway. He'll think he fell down before he reached my door. He's drunk. He won't remember anything when he wakes up."

I tilted melted wax from the candle to make it burn brighter and set it on the floor to light the passageway. Tylos and Samsi gathered pillows from the beds and laid them on the floor. They each took one of the king's hands and looked at me. I didn't want to touch Solomon, but they needed my help in moving him.

I held his head, feeling a lump where Samsi had hit him, as they pulled his body off the bed and onto the pillows. Tylos and Samsi picked up his bare feet and we pushed and dragged him on the pillows from the room and down the passageway. We were panting from the effort of moving him when we reached the dark beyond the light of the candle. I told them to stop and looked back at the open door. Solomon was facing my door. If his guards found him before he woke, they would see that he had fallen and hit his head before he reached my room.

The king had stopped snoring and was mumbling in his sleep. We waited, holding our breath, fearful he would wake. When he was snoring again, we carefully rolled him off the pillows to lie on his side on the floor. Tylos arranged his robe to cover his legs.

Samsi asked if he would be cold. Tylos said that worried her, too.

"He's fought in battles," I said. "He's slept rough before. Now leave him, I want to get back to our room."

We carried the pillows back into the sleeping room. "Wait," I said as Tylos started to close the door. I picked up the king's candle. "He brought this."

Tylos lit a candle from the flame and held it up while I took Solomon's candle down the passageway. I blew it out and laid it near his hand to look as though he had dropped it when he fell down in his drunkenness.

I ran back to the room and closed the door. Tylos wanted to push the chest against the door, afraid the king would try to enter my room again. I shook my head. "He's deeply asleep. He won't wake for a while."

"There is something else we must do," I said. "Bring Sarah to me. Tell her I am unwell and ask for another jar of her herbed wine."

"Are you feeling sick?" Samsi asked.

"No, I want her to come here now and see that the king is not in my room. I saw her give you a jar of wine at the feast. I think the wine was drugged so you would be asleep when the king came into our room."

"She said the wine was sent from the king," Tylos said.

"She might have known his plan or was simply giving you what she thought was a gift."

Tylos lit another candle and left to wake Sarah. I lifted the leaf on the king's door and peered through the eyehole. I saw King Solomon's white robe on the floor in the darkness.

"Sarah was bad if she knew the wine drugged," Samsi said as I closed the eyehole.

"She has to obey her king."

Samsi looked at my ripped clothing. "Did the king hurt you?"

"A few scratches, nothing more."

Samsi grasped my hand. "I woke up when I heard you scream. I thought a wild beast had gotten into the room."

I closed my eyes for a moment, remembering the king snarling as he ripped my tunic. "He was a beast at that moment."

I put my hand on her shoulder. "You must never tell anyone about this, not even Khe."

"I won't."

I shook her slightly. "Listen to me. Everyone you meet on the caravan and in Myrb will want to hear about our visit to Jerusalem. You may talk of all of it, but you must hide that the king entered my room tonight or that you hit him. If this is known, it will harm our friendship with the king and bring dishonor to my husband, you, and me."

Samsi took my hand, kissed it and swore she would not say anything.

"Myrb will be your new home," I said. "You must help protect it."

I heard the door to the sitting room open. I jumped into my bed and pulled up the blanket to hide my torn clothing. I moaned as Sarah came into the room carrying a large cup. I thought I saw her glance at the king's door. She bowed and handed the wine to me. She said she hoped I would be well and that she would bring our meal in the morning.

After the door closed behind her, I stood and looked through the eyehole again. I feared I would see King Solomon standing outside the door, his face twisted in anger. The white robe was gone from the passageway. Nothing moved in the darkness.

~ Twenty-Eight ~

I put on a fresh sleeping tunic and told Samsi and Tylos to go to bed. I was too upset to sleep. My throat was sore from screaming, my chest hurt where the king had scratched me when he ripped my tunic.

I walked out onto the terrace and looked over the quiet city and up at the stars in the sky, the same stars that shone over Myrb. I wondered if the king had wakened in the dark and returned to his room or if a guard had found him lying on the floor in the passageway. Tears came suddenly. I wept into the darkness at the memory of the king's savage attack.

I wiped my eyes. I had one more trial before me. The success of our trade in Jerusalem depended on Solomon's goodwill. I would have to smile at the king in the morning and deceive him in believing we parted as good friends. I gave a shaky laugh. I was relieved that I had not stabbed the king. He could have me put to death if I had harmed him.

Torchlights flared at the far end of the city. Farium would be in the pens, overseeing the servants loading the pack camels. I looked at the dark desert beyond the city and thought about the journey before me, the long hot days traveling in my riding tent, the threat of bandits, sandstorms, and maybe the lack of water. I took a deep breath. I had done it before and could do it again, but this time it I would not hide inside my tent. I would invite men and women to gather at my cookfire and share stories about our stay in Jerusalem. I would call them friends and tell them about living in the palace as King Solomon's honored guest. I would tell them the story I wanted them to hear. They would tell it to their friends and families when we returned to Myrb.

I thought of seeing my city again. I would enter the gates in triumph, wearing the hoopoe necklace that marked King Solomon's regard for me. I would bring greetings from the king to Darmalay's council and tell them of his promise to grant our merchants a permanent street in his market and help us seek markets in Egypt. To my husband, I would relate King Solomon's advice about the men he needed to help govern our growing city. Lastly, I would show Darmalay the king's gifts of silk clothing and the ivory box of jewelry. Then I would put them away.

What would I do when I was home again and my travels were over? As first wife I would be expected to rule the harem. It seemed a small role. I knew I would not be content. I smiled into the night. I would allow Amida to manage the harem. She would listen to complaints and settle arguments among other wives and concubines that Darmalay might take.

I remembered the words of the chieftain's wife I had visited on the way to Jerusalem, a first wife who had made a place for herself at her husband's side. I would do the same. I saw myself in splendid new robes, sitting at my husband's right hand as we ruled our growing kingdom together. I would be more than a wife to him; I would be his queen.

"And when the queen of Sheba heard of the fame of Solomon, she came to prove Solomon with hard questions at Jerusalem, with a very great company, and camels that bore spices, and gold in abundance, and precious stones: and when she was come to Solomon, she communed with him of all that was in her heart.

And Solomon told her all her questions: and there was nothing hid from Solomon, which he told her not...

...And she gave the king a hundred and twenty talents of gold, and of spices great abundance, and precious stones: neither was there any such spice as the queen of Sheba gave king Solomon.

And king Solomon gave to the queen of Sheba all her desire, whatsoever she asked, besides that which she had brought unto the king. So she turned, and went away to her own land, she and her servants."

2 Chronicles 9
King James version of the Holy Bible

Acknowledgements

Handfuls of gratitude to Joanna Rose for her excellent editing, Amalia Chitulescu for her stunning cover art, my wonderful readers: William Howell, Douglas Rees, Josie Rees, Rick Kopps, and Julie Neburka. Many additional thanks to William Howell for his eagle eye in spotting typos that slipped through numerous reviews.

Note from Signe Kopps

Thank you for reading Queen of Incense. If you enjoyed it, please take a moment to leave a review on Amazon, Barnes and Noble, or other fine online bookstores.

I welcome contact and comments from readers. You can reach me to leave comments of join my mailing list on my website: signekopps.com.